a magic dark & bright

Jenny Adams Perinovic

a magic dark & bright

The Asylum Saga: Book One

JENNY ADAMS PERINOVIC

Copyright © 2015 by Jenny Adams Perinovic.

This book is a work of fiction. Names, characters, places, and incidents are products of the author's imagination or are used fictitiously. Any resemblance to actual events, locales, or persons, living or dead, is entirely coincidental.

First Edition: April 2015

All rights reserved, including the right to reproduce this book or portions thereof in any form whatsoever.

A Magic Dark and Bright/ by Jenny Adams Perinovic
1. Fiction 2. Horror 3. Romance

Summary: A girl tries to aid the ghost of a woman haunting the woods behind her house and unknowingly unleashes a curse onto her small town.

Cover design by Serena Lawless & Jenny Perinovic
Interior layout by Jenny Perinovic
Editing by Sarah Kettles

ISBN 978-0-9862013-0-1 (paperback)
ISBN 978-0-9862013-1-8 (.Epub ebook)
ISBN 978-0-9862013-2-5 (Kindle ebook)

10 9 8 7 6 5 4 3 2 1

To Eric,
for always

One

A woman haunted the woods behind my house.

I used to watch her from my bedroom window. She glowed silver in the moonlight, a pale wraith in a white dress that curled around her ankles and twisted in an ancient wind that didn't touch the pine trees around her.

My brother, Mark, would tease me about my interest in her. Some days, he called her my obsession. On others, my overactive imagination. "Watch out, Amelia," he'd say, throwing his hand against his chest. "She'll lure you out into the woods and steal your soul."

But that was before. I hadn't seen her in six months, not since the night she'd watched Mark die.

I pressed my palm flat against the screen and waited, like I had almost every night since I'd come home from the hospital. Nothing stirred outside; the line of forest along the edge of our yard stood still, black branches stretched toward the sky. Not even a breeze fluttered the gauzy curtains around my window. The woods were empty.

Everything was empty.

"Come on," I whispered, like I could summon her with my words. The clock in the hallway chimed, its bells echoing through the silent house. Three in the morning.

I sighed and turned from the window—if she hadn't shown up by now, she wouldn't show up at all. Sometimes, on nights like this, when the corners of my brain went fuzzy from exhaustion, I wondered if she had disappeared because of me. If maybe I had wanted to see her too much, and my wanting had scared her away. And then I'd think how absurd that was—scaring away a ghost.

Whatever her reasons, she was gone. They were both gone.

I slid out of bed and made my way down the stairs from my attic bedroom, careful to avoid the third step from the bottom that always groaned underfoot. Mark's bedroom sat directly below mine, right across the hall from my mother's. I turned the knob slowly and pushed open the door, its hinges creaking in protest.

Crap.

I froze, hand still on the knob, and waited for my mom to appear in her doorway. She didn't need to know about my late night habits. I'd told her—and my therapist—that the nightmares had stopped. And they had, technically. As long as I didn't let myself sleep.

I counted to ten. No movement came from behind her door—no rustle of blankets, no shuffle of bare feet across the wooden floor. I let out my breath and pushed the door open the rest of the way.

I kept the lamp switched off and crept across the floor. The silvery-white glow from the full moon gave me enough light to see, and even if it hadn't, I knew my way in the dark.

Mark's bedroom hadn't changed since the accident. His laptop was still open on his desk, next to a doodled-in textbook and his unfinished chemistry homework. A purple University of Scranton hoodie was thrown across the bed, one sleeve turned inside-out. His duffel bag, half-packed full of clean clothes, sat on the floor in the middle of the room, like he'd just gone out for the night and would return in the morning.

I bee-lined for the built-in shelf that held Mark's movies. He had hundreds of DVDS, mostly movies I never would have watched before, sports documentaries and slasher flicks and raunchy comedies, but they made me feel close to him. It was too dark to read the titles, so I ran my fingers over the plastic cases and picked one at random. I tucked the case under my arm and turned to go.

Tires crunched on gravel a moment before headlights cut a wide swath of light down the wall, right over Mark's posters of the Philadelphia Eagles and some red-haired model in a tiny white swimsuit. I frowned. Our street was a dead-end; it was rare enough that someone would drive by during the day.

I crossed to the window beside his bed, the one that overlooked the side of the house. Our driveway was dark, but there was a car pulling into Ms. MacAllister's driveway next door. Her porch light switched on at the same moment the driver parked and killed the engine. Ms. MacAllister stepped out onto the wide, wrap-around porch. She ran a hand over her hair and looked up at the window where I stood. I let out a squeak and ran, heart slamming against my ribs, stopping only to close Mark's door behind me.

By the time I reached my bedroom, I'd managed to get myself back under control. The room behind me had been dark, and wasn't like Ms. MacAllister could have seen me from where she stood. I set the DVD on my bedside table and ran my hands over my face.

Outside, a car door slammed. Voices, one low and deep and one higher, carried across the still night, right through my open window. It would have been so easy to peek outside, to see who was out there, visiting Ms. MacAllister at this hour.

I shouldn't, I told myself as I climbed back into bed, right under the window. *Don't be a creep, Amelia.*

Someone laughed. A very male laugh. My curiosity got the better of me, and I pushed the curtain aside.

A guy, tall and thin, stood next to the car, a bag slung over his shoulder. Ms. MacAllister stood beside him, another bag in her hand. He laughed again and turned toward the car. For whatever reason, I was surprised to see how young he was—maybe only a little bit older than me, with a mop of brown curls and thick, black-framed glasses that glinted in the yellow light.

I stayed there, waiting in the window until the door slammed behind them and the porch light winked out. Exhaustion washed over me, turning my limbs to jelly. I yawned as I reached for the cord for the blinds and cast one last look out to the woods. *Just in case.*

And there she was.

She flickered between the trees, her long white dress twisting in a non-existent breeze, her feet hovering over the ground.

I froze, almost afraid to breathe.

She was *there*.

And if she was there, then maybe, just *maybe*...

Any thought I had in my head evaporated as she left the cover of the woods and floated above the grass along the tree line. She stopped, her entire being flickering like a projection of an old-time newsreel, moonlight dancing across pearl-white skin. She raised her arm and pointed. Pointed straight at the MacAllister House.

I clapped my hands to my mouth, and the blinds crashed down over the window. By the time I had stopped trembling enough that I could lift them again, she was gone.

Two

The ghost was back.

There was a strange guy at Ms. MacAllister's house.

It took almost all morning to wrap my mind around both of these things. When I dragged myself out of bed around nine, I looked to see if the car was still there, just in case I'd dreamed the whole thing.

But there it was, right in the driveway: a vintage Mustang. Fastback, not convertible. I thought that it might have been green at one point, though it was now speckled with rust and the driver's side door was a bright, cherry red.

By the time I made it down to the kitchen, my mom already stood at the stove, cooking. She was dressed in a floral button down and dark jeans, her blond hair curled and styled. I decided to broach the subject of Ms. MacAllister's visitor.

"So," I said as I pulled the orange juice out the fridge, "did you see that car in Ms. MacAllister's driveway?"

Mom poured more batter into the skillet. "I did. I noticed it while I was on my run this morning."

"Is someone visiting her?"

"Her grandson, probably," she answered. "She mentioned a few weeks ago that he was coming to stay with her."

"She has a grandson?" I hadn't ever thought about Ms. MacAllister having children, let alone grandchildren. I hadn't even thought she was old enough to have grandchildren—she looked decades younger than my own grandparents had been before they'd died.

"He's around your age, I think." She set a plate full of pancakes down in front of me at the kitchen island. "Why so curious?"

I cut the pancakes into tiny squares. "She never has visitors. I thought it was weird."

Mom didn't respond right away. She poured herself a cup of coffee and leaned back against the counter. "She doesn't," she said carefully. "I don't think her daughter has been to visit once since she left. Not that I blame her, after what happened. People can be cruel."

I forced a bit of pancake down. "Mark used to say she was a witch."

She lifted her eyebrows. "Your brother said a lot of things," she said. "That doesn't mean they were all true."

I shrugged. As much as Mom pretended otherwise, Mark hadn't been the only one who thought she was a witch. Ms. MacAllister was a playground legend in our tiny town of Asylum, Pennsylvania. She lived alone in that big, creepy house and sold herbs and crystals who knew what else from her tea shop on the waterfront. Mark and I had achieved near hero-status among the kids at school; we'd lived next door to her our entire lives, even *talked* to her, and lived to tell about it.

"Is that why no one likes her?" I asked.

"Plenty of people like her," Mom answered. "I like her."

I'm sure some people liked her besides my mother, but not many. I still remembered when Hannah Green's mother wouldn't let her come over to play when we were in third grade because I lived next door to *that woman*. "You like everyone."

"That's not true. There are plenty of people I don't like. Ms. MacAllister just isn't one of them."

"Mom."

She waved me off and changed the subject. "I'm going to run to work for a few hours today," she said. "You'll be okay here by yourself?"

"But it's Saturday." My voice came out smaller than I'd thought it would.

"And I have a lot of work to do. The Quasquibicentennial Festival isn't going to plan itself."

"Can't you say two hundred and twenty-five like a normal person?" My mother, with her PhD in public history, was the head of the Asylum Historical Society. Actually, she *was* the Asylum Historical Society, the lone staff person among a swarm of blue-haired volunteers. "Why do you have to be such a weirdo?"

"I like Latin. It's a beautiful language."

"Dork."

"Brat."

I stuck my tongue out at her.

"Why don't you call Leah and see what she's up to?"

"She's working a double at the shop." Which was what she would be doing every Saturday for the rest of the summer.

Leah Howards had been my best friend since preschool. We were usually inseparable, but her mother needed help at the coffee shop she owned, and Leah was saving money for a two-month-long trip to Europe after graduation, which meant that we saw much less of each other than I was used to. And after everything that had happened over the last few months, I wouldn't have been surprised if she'd ditched me all together.

I hadn't exactly been fun to be around.

I thought of the ghost in the woods. I didn't want to be home alone after dark, not when she was out there again. Not after that night.

"You'll be home for dinner, right?" I asked. My fingers found the thick, ropy scar that ran down the back of my arm, my permanent reminder that Mark had died and I had not.

Mom's face softened. "I'll be home for dinner," she promised. "We'll do a girls' night."

I didn't point out that in the months since Mark had died and my dad had left, *every* night had been a girls' night. My hand drifted from my scar to the small gold and sapphire ring resting right under my collarbone. Mark had been carrying it in his pocket on the night of the accident. I didn't know where he had gotten it or who it was for, but the minute I'd seen it, I'd claimed it as my own. My piece of him. I'd worn it every day since his funeral.

"Sure," I said instead. "That sounds great."

After she left, I dumped my pancakes down the garbage disposal and made my way back upstairs. I showered, dried my hair, and brushed my teeth. On my way out of the bathroom, my big orange cat, Prime, wrapped himself around my ankles. I leaned down and scooped him up, cradling him in my arms like a baby. "It's you and me again today, buddy," I said.

He purred and snuggled closer. At least *someone* appreciated me.

I climbed upstairs and deposited Prime on the foot of my unmade bed, right on top of my white comforter. I dressed, braided my long blond hair, and flopped down beside him. From the window over my bed, I could see clear across my yard to the MacAllister House. Generation upon generation had expanded the original house, each trying to outdo their fathers before them, and had turned a standard eighteenth century farmhouse into something huge, sprawling, and entirely out of place in a Pennsylvanian mountain town. It stood three stories tall, with a wraparound porch, wavy-paned windows, and a steeply pitched roof dotted with gables. White paint peeled from the wooden clapboard siding, and the roof sagged slightly in the middle. A low stone wall bordered with rose bushes separated their yard from ours.

The window directly across from mine opened, and the boy from last night rested his elbows on the windowsill and stared out toward my house.

Toward me.

I yanked the cords for the blinds and threw myself flat onto my bed, my face hot with mortification. Prime opened one eye and glared at me.

"Oh, shut up," I told the cat, but he had already gone back to sleep.

Had he seen me staring at his house like some kind of creep?

The way he was staring at my house?

What was he, some kind of creep?

I sat up and peeked through the blinds. The guy still leaned out the window, but he had one hand pressed to his ear and waved the other around. He was talking, but with the glass in my window and the few hundred feet between us, I couldn't hear a thing.

He was on the phone.

Not spying on me.

"He's not a creep," I said to Prime. "Crisis averted."

I watched him for a few seconds longer. Who he was speaking to? His parents? A friend? His girlfriend?

The first few notes of AC/DC's *TNT* erupted from my desk. I scrambled for my own phone, nearly falling off my bed in the process. My mom's face lit up the screen. "Hello?"

"Amelia, honey, can you do me a favor?"

I stretched out on my bed and stared at the ceiling. "What is it?"

"I spoke with Ms. MacAllister, and she has a few things she'd like to donate for the anniversary. Would you mind picking them up and bringing them to me?"

I glanced at the blinds covering my window. "Uh, sure. Yeah. Right now?"

"The sooner the better."

Three

The wooden steps groaned under my weight as I hurried up onto the porch and knocked on Ms. MacAllister's light blue front door.

I stepped back and waited. The light breeze rocked the two battered chairs on my left and whispered through the wind chimes that hung from the eaves. The porch was wide and clean, though paint peeled from the railing and the wide, wooden planks underfoot were worn bare.

I knocked again, harder this time, the rap of my knuckles echoing through the door. It was kind of strange to be knocking on someone's door—this was the type of neighborhood where people shouted hello as they walked inside. Doors were only ever locked at night, and the only people who knocked were Girl Scouts peddling cookies or missionaries peddling religion.

But I'd lived next door to Ms. MacAllister for my entire life, and I'd never been this close to her house before. I wasn't going to barge in. I rocked back and forth on my toes, waiting.

Finally, after what felt like forever, the door creaked open. The guy from last night stepped out onto the porch, a cardboard box tucked under his arm. He was taller than I'd thought he'd be, tall enough that standing next to him made me realize how small I was in comparison. I wasn't even that short—five foot two on a good day—and he was easily an entire foot taller than me, all spindly long legs and arms, almost like a puppy who hadn't yet grown into his limbs.

And he was cute, with bright blue eyes and brown hair curling over his forehead. Cute despite the hipster glasses and the nose that seemed a little too big for his face. I realized I was staring at him and dropped my gaze to my shoes.

"Hey," he said. "You must be Amelia. Grams said you'd be stopping by. I'm Charlie Blue."

He stretched his free hand out towards me, and all I could do was stare at it. All of this felt too surreal—I was standing on Ms. MacAllister's front porch, speaking to her grandson. Her grandson who happened to be incredibly cute and waiting for me to shake his hand.

But then I realized it'd be strange if I didn't. I couldn't leave him there with his hand out. That would have been weird. Right? So I wrapped my hand around his, around his fingers that were cool and rough under mine. Calloused, like he played guitar. Or something.

"Amelia Dupree," I said. "It's nice to meet you."

"Likewise." He grinned at me and held the box out. "I believe this is for you."

"For my mom," I clarified. The box was heavier than I'd expected; I shifted it to my hip. "It's for this town anniversary thing."

"Cool," he said, even though it wasn't.

I took a step back. "Alright, well. Thanks."

"Wait," he said. "What about the rest of them? I'll help you carry them to your car."

"The rest of them?" I didn't follow.

He raised his eyebrows. "There are at least five more boxes in here."

"Five more boxes," I repeated. *Great*. Now he was going to think I was an idiot.

"Yep."

I didn't think they were going to fit on my bike. "Uh—"

He shrugged. "I'll help you carry them to your car."

"I don't have a car."

Charlie frowned and looked over my shoulder. I followed his gaze right to the red Jeep parked in my driveway. My father had given it to me as a gift for my seventeenth birthday last month, even though I couldn't drive it. Typical.

"I can't drive," I explained. "I don't have my license yet."

He lifted his eyebrows. "How old do you have to be in Pennsylvania?"

"Sixteen and a half." I sighed and shifted the box to my other arm. Not being able to drive was something I was eternally embarrassed about. I'd gotten my learner's permit after my birthday last May, but then Dad had left. And after the accident, I'd stopped asking. "It's complicated."

He was quiet for a moment, like he didn't quite know what to say. "We'll take my car."

"No, I can bring them home, and my mom can get them later," I said.

"It's not a big deal."

"I don't—"

"It's not a problem. It's not like I really have anything else to do, right?" He stepped back inside and reappeared with another box. His lips quirked up into a smile, and he handed it to me. "I'll grab the rest."

I waited while he dragged the other boxes out of the house and pulled the front door shut behind him. He crossed the porch in two long strides and reached his car in another three. We had everything loaded in two trips. He slammed the trunk shut, and I slid into the passenger seat.

The interior of Charlie's car smelled like the lemon-yellow pine tree that hung from the rearview mirror, and it was spotless, in stark contrast to the mess it was on the outside. There wasn't even a single crumpled up napkin on the floor or a smudge on his windshield. He slid into his seat and buckled his seatbelt. "Can you give me directions?"

I nodded. The Historical Society was easy enough to get to—it was on Main Street, tucked between Town Hall and the library. My mother had been working there since before I'd been born. Of all the places in town, the Asylum Historical Society was the closest thing I had to a second home. I could get us there with my eyes closed. I buckled my seatbelt, and the car jumped to life with a roar.

Charlie caught my wince. "Sorry," he yelled over the engine. "Something went wrong with the muffler the other day, and I'm waiting on the part."

I nodded and rolled down the window, letting my fingers trail against the wind as we headed down Laurel Street and into town. Outside, the trees faded into green and brown blurs. The Mustang was loud and fast and shuddered every time he shifted gears. I doubted it even had airbags. I should have hated it, after the accident. I should have been afraid, clutching the dashboard with white-knuckled hands.

But the tendrils that wrapped themselves around my heart and exploded through my chest weren't fear.

I leaned back in my seat. Charlie switched on the radio, and the Decemberists filled the car, over the engine. Something warm and bubbly filled my chest, and I realized I was grinning.

I thought I could like Charlie Blue.

"So," I said. "How long are you visiting for?"

"A while," he said. "I'm actually going to be living here until graduation. My dad's a minister, and he and my mom decided to become missionaries, and I didn't feel like spending my senior year in the middle of nowhere, South Asia."

"So you picked the middle of nowhere, Pennsylvania, instead?"

He glanced over at me, his blue eyes serious behind his glasses. "It's better than some places I've lived. Trust me. At least the neighbors seem nice."

"Oh, they're very nice," I said. Then I blushed, because I couldn't believe I had *said* that. I decided to change the subject. "I'm going to be a senior too."

"Maybe we'll be in some classes together."

"Most of them, probably. There are exactly sixty-one people in our class." I paused. "Sixty-two, now."

He raised his eyebrows. "Seriously?"

"Welcome to Asylum," I said.

We drove down Main Street, past the rows of stone and brick Victorian-era buildings that spilled down the mountain toward the Susquehanna River. Asylum was picture-perfect as far as small towns went, right down to the white picket fences. I managed to direct him to one of the metered spots between Town Hall and the Green, the two-acre park that served as everything from playground to farmers' market.

"Don't worry about it," I told Charlie as he dug in his pocket for change. "It's free on the weekends. Plus, I have an in with the sheriff."

"Oh?"

"I happen to be his favorite niece," I explained. "Uncle Frank is my dad's brother, and he has exactly one deputy who sleeps about eighteen hours per day. So don't worry about a ticket when you're with me."

Charlie popped the trunk. "You're sure I haven't entered some weird alternate dimension, right? This isn't the Twilight Zone or something?"

I pulled two of the boxes from the trunk and started towards the tiny, two-story clapboard building that housed the Historical Society. When I was little, my mother's office had been my favorite place in the world. It wasn't very big—smaller than her office at home—but it was packed from floor to ceiling with books and photographs, and the view was killer, overlooking the Green to where the river snaked along looming cliffs on the opposite bank.

"You know what they say about small towns," I teased. "Low on crime."

"And big on secrets," he said. He pulled out the rest of the boxes and set them on the ground. He slammed the trunk shut and fell into step beside me.

"Secrets, huh?" If anyone in this town had secrets, it'd be his grandmother. But I couldn't exactly *say* that. I set my boxes down on the porch and fished out my key ring—the Society was only open Monday through Friday, and Mom kept the door locked when she was working upstairs.

"Yeah, secrets." He shifted his box and held the door open for me. "I bet you have a ton of them."

I nearly stumbled over the step into the building. I had my share of secrets—what had happened to Mark being on the top of that list. I shook my head. "That's the thing about secrets," I said. "You don't tell them to anyone."

"On the contrary. The best secrets are the ones you share with someone else. You can trust me."

"Can I?" I blinked up at him, my face serious. "Okay, here it goes. My natural hair color is neon green. You have no idea how hard it is to get it this blond to comply with the dress code at school."

He threw back his head and laughed. His laugh was full and rich, the kind that comes from somewhere deep inside. My own lips twitched in response. "See," he said, "Doesn't it feel good to get that off your chest?"

"You have no idea." I set my boxes down on the floor next to one of the display cases. The entire front room was a mini-museum detailing our town's history from its founding in 1790 to the present. Another room, used for special exhibits, was through the doorway to the left. My mother's office and the office shared by the volunteers were upstairs, and beneath our feet was the brand-new vault, where the most valuable artifacts lived. The building was silent except for the hiss of the air conditioning. I frowned—usually when my mother was here on the weekends, you could hear whatever music she was listening to from all the way outside.

"This stuff is pretty cool." Charlie set his boxes next to mine and leaned over the case closest to him. It was one of my favorites; I'd seen it a million times before, but, like always, the gold and glittering jewels caught my attention from their soft bed of black velvet. A sparkling sapphire necklace, a painted brooch, and a pair of diamond earrings—these were things my ancestors had carried with them to Asylum. My hand drifted to the ring hanging under my shirt. When I'd shown it to my mom, she'd said it dated to the late-eighteenth century, meaning it was as old as these things here. She'd wanted to put it on display, but I'd refused.

It was mine, and it was going to stay that way.

"Those are beautiful." Charlie kept his eyes fixed on the glass.

I dropped my hand, tapping the glass over the brooch. The painted girl stared back at us, her blond hair curling over her shoulders, a tiny smile on her lips. "That's Marie-Therese Dupree. She was sixteen when they fled the French Revolution. She drowned herself in the river one winter after they received word that her beloved had been lost to *Madame La Guillotine.*"

He raised an eyebrow. "A relative of yours?"

I nodded. Tragedy seemed to run in my family. "I'm descended from her brother. They were two of the original refugees who settled here in 1790. Asylum was supposed to be this refuge from the revolutions happening in France and Haiti. Marie Antoinette was supposed to move here, before she lost her head." I cast another glance over my shoulder, towards the stairs. If Mom was here, she would have heard us by now. "I'm going to run upstairs and get my mom, okay?"

"Want me to come with you?"

I waved my hand. "Look around. There are some things that belonged to your family here too. I'll be right back."

I pushed through the beaded curtain that separated the back hallway from the exhibit space. "Mom?" I called. "Are you here?"

The second floor was silent and dark. The mini-fridge in the kitchenette hummed, but that was it. The three computers in the volunteers' office were turned off, and Mom's office door was shut tight. I tried the knob, but it wouldn't budge. Locked.

I frowned and rattled the knob again, my frustration growing.

I took out my keys. The door unlocked and swung open silently, the hinges not even squeaking. I stepped in, switched on the lights, and stopped short.

The blinds were shut, and her computer was dark. Books overflowed from the shelves along the wall, and papers covered every spare inch of her u-shaped desk. Even the pink armchair shoved in between the desk and the wall was covered in books. I'd never seen my mother's office such a mess—she was eternally organized. Every single thing had a home, a place.

I fished my phone from my pocket. No texts, no missed calls, nothing. I called, but her cell went straight to voicemail.

I hurried back downstairs, letting the door slam behind me. Was she out? Or maybe she was hurt? Maybe she'd stepped out for lunch and been hit by a car. Or maybe there'd been an accident, or... I slammed into something warm and solid. Something that smelled like pine and spice and something else. Something male.

Or rather, someone.

"Whoa, there." Charlie clamped his hands around my upper arms, keeping us both from tumbling off the landing. Bare inches separated us, and when I raised my eyes to his face, his blue eyes were filled with concern. "Is everything okay?"

"My mom isn't here," I said. "She's not here, and her office is a mess, and I don't—I don't know where she is." My voice came out strange and high-pitched and panicky, and my chest felt tight, too tight to breathe.

"Hey," he said, his grip tightening. "It's okay. Maybe something came up and she had to leave. Sit down."

I lowered myself to the closest stair and took a deep breath. "Maybe."

"Is there anywhere else she could be?" Charlie let his arms fall back to his sides and squatted down so he was low enough to look into my face.

I shrugged. "I don't know."

"Want to move the boxes somewhere safe and wait for her to get here?"

"Okay."

"Okay. Where should we take them?" His voice was soft and kind, like he was speaking to a child, or maybe a wild animal. I flushed. I didn't want him to think I was some sort of emotional freak. He was right, really—maybe she'd gone out to get a cup of coffee.

I wished I could believe that. *Calm down, Amelia.* Ever since the accident, I'd been prone to panicking at the drop of a hat. I forced myself to take another breath.

"Where should we put them?" he asked again.

"Upstairs," I said. "We can leave them in the volunteers' office."

"I can," he said. "Stay here. Where is it?"

"First door on the right."

Charlie made two trips with the boxes while I called my mom's phone over and over again. Every time it went to voicemail, my heart dropped a bit. This wasn't like her. This wasn't normal.

Charlie sat beside me, close enough that his shoulder and hip brushed mine. He didn't say anything. He rested his arms over his knees and stayed there.

After almost twenty minutes, the front door creaked open. I jumped to my feet and raced into the gallery. Mom stood next to the door, one arm over her middle while she waved goodbye to someone in the parking lot.

"Where were you?"

Her free hand flew to her throat as she whirled to face me. "Amelia! Honey, you startled me. I didn't realize you were here already."

"You *told* me to be here. With the things from the MacAllister's house?"

"I thought your bike ride would take a little longer." She forced a laugh.

I frowned. "Charlie gave me a ride."

"Who?"

"Uh, hi." Charlie waved from the back hallway. "I'm Charlie."

Mom blinked at him. She tugged at the hem of her blouse. Her buttons were done up crookedly, like she'd fastened them in a hurry, leaving one side of her shirt hanging lower than the other.

"Ms. MacAllister's grandson," I reminded her. I kept staring at the hem of her shirt.

"Of course," she said. "It's so nice to meet you. I'm Dr. Dupree."

"We were just going," I said. I turned to Charlie and jerked my head towards the door. His eyes darted back and forth between us, like he wasn't sure which one of us to look at. "I'll see you at home, Mom."

"It was nice to meet you," Charlie said as the door slammed shut behind us. I took the steps to the street two at a time. He jogged to catch up to me. "Is everything okay?"

"Yes. No. I don't know." I leaned against the Mustang and sighed. "It's complicated."

That was an understatement. Lately, everything had been complicated.

He jingled his keys in his hand. "Want to talk about it?"

I shook my head and dragged the toe of my sneaker along the pavement.

Charlie didn't press me. He got in the car and started the engine. After a moment, I opened my door and slid into the passenger seat.

"Should I take you home?" he asked.

My mom stood at the window, her hands on her hips. Watching us.

I forced my eyes from her and looked at Charlie. *Really* looked at Charlie. I took in his blue eyes ringed with dark, thick lashes, his black-rimmed glasses. His mouth, which seemed to be perpetually on the verge of a grin, the light white line of a scar across his chin. He was someone new, someone who didn't know anyone here. Someone who didn't know anything about me.

About who I used to be.

My own lips curled into a smile, and I shook my head. "Do you like coffee?" I asked.

Four

We pulled into the small gravel parking lot in front of the Asylum Coffee Company. Leah's mom's shop stood by itself, a small two-story brick building facing the Susquehanna River. Cheerful triangles of pastel fabric strung along the railing on the front porch danced in the light summer breeze. I unbuckled my seatbelt and turned to Charlie. "I'm going to warn you, my best friend can be a little intense."

His lips quirked up. "Consider me warned."

Mr. Yardley, the grocer, waved at us from his usual spot in one of the old wooden rockers. "Hello, Amelia."

I waved back. "Hey, Mr. Yardley."

"Do you know everyone?" Charlie asked as he held the door open for me. The bell jingled overhead, announcing our presence.

"I've lived here all my life, you know." The warm, rich smell of coffee mixed with fresh baked goods wrapped itself around me almost immediately, and my stomach growled. I hoped Charlie couldn't hear it over the low hum of the place; the cafe was surprisingly full for a Saturday afternoon, though there was no line at the register. Almost every seat was taken, and we—okay, *Charlie*—earned a few interested glances from people I had known all my life. My third-grade teacher, Mrs. Benson, raised her eyebrows at me from the table she shared with her husband and five-year-old twin sons. Joe LaPorte, one of my dad's high school buddies, turned and gave Charlie a long once-over that was probably meant to be menacing. But Joe was short and round and kind-faced—he looked more like he was suffering from heartburn than anything else.

At the counter, my best friend, Leah Howards, snapped her head up and grinned at me. "Hey, Brit," she called to the girl organizing the flavored syrups behind the espresso machine, "I'm going on my break. Can you handle it here?"

Brit D'Autremont, a tiny, red-haired freshman, nodded at her before turning back to the syrups. In a town this small, you pretty much knew everyone by sight, but because of the age gap, Brit and I had never been close. Leah, on the other hand, made friends easily; I shouldn't have been surprised that Brit had taken a job here.

I was more surprised that Leah, who kept me up to date on every minute detail of her life, hadn't told me. I pushed down the jealousy gnawing through my middle and waited as Leah grabbed two white mugs, filled them with coffee, and set them on a dark green tray.

"Better make it three," I said as she reached for the croissants. I pointed to Charlie. "This is Charlie. Charlie, this is my best friend, Leah."

Her red-painted mouth, the exact same shade as the crimson highlights in her black hair, made a little 'o' of surprise, but she recovered quickly, pasting on a mega-watt smile.

Leah had the bright white smile of a supermodel, with the face and body to match. She was nearly six inches taller than me and joked that she had inherited the height from her Nordic ancestors on her father's side—her Taiwanese mother stood barely five feet tall. Leah and her older sister, Taylor, had hit the genetic lottery, all long limbs and perfect olive skin and smoldering dark eyes.

"Nice to meet you," Leah told Charlie. Then she reached across the counter, grabbed my arm, and said, "Sidebar. Now."

I flashed him an apologetic look as she dragged me into the corner. "Please tell me that he is your really cute long-lost cousin that you can't date because it would be weird and illegal," she whispered.

"Erm. No. But how about he's my really cute new neighbor?" I offered.

"Neighbor? As in…"

"He's Ms. MacAllister's grandson."

Her brown eyes widened in surprise. She slid her gaze around me to Charlie. "No way."

"Be nice," I hissed.

She tucked a red-streaked strand behind her ear, not taking her eyes off him. "Oh, I'll be nice." She was practically purring. I stepped on her foot.

"Leah."

"What are you doing with him?"

I rolled my eyes. "Making friends. Which is all you're going to be doing too. Okay?"

"Just know that someone might be jealous." She pointed her finger over my shoulder. I followed her line of sight to the boy who sat by himself at a table against the wall. The light caught his blond hair as he turned and stared right at me, and for half a second, I thought I was going to throw up.

If anyone else carried as much blame as I did for Mark's death, it was Ben Liancourt. His best friend. Brit's cousin. And the boy I used to think I loved, the boy I dated right up to the night of the accident.

"I don't care who Ben sees me with," I hissed, more for my own benefit than Leah's. "We're over."

I turned my back on Ben, picked my mug up off the counter, and headed back to Charlie, who stood

A Magic Dark & Bright

with his back to us, his hands in the front pockets of his jeans. He studied the large mural on the wall behind the bar, the mural that was supposed to depict Asylum in eight panels, from the earliest times to the present. It had been painted sometime before I was born, and I'd always thought someone must have been smoking *something* while working on it, because the entire thing looked like the byproduct of a bad acid trip. Neon-orange flames burned in the forest in the earliest panel. In the latest, women in colonial dress strolled down Main Street between skateboarders and squat, boxy cars. In between were all manners of anachronisms, like the First World War-era soldier who sat on the steps of the gazebo on the Green, gun across his lap, while a poodle-skirted girl walked hand in hand with her leather jacket-wearing date.

"This is so weird," he said when I appeared beside him. "Do you know who painted this?"

I pointed to the lower left hand corner, where *R. MacAllister* was scrawled across the canvas. "Someone related to you."

"Huh." He tilted his head and frowned. "I'll have to ask Grams about it."

Leah poured steaming coffee into a third mug. "Hey, New Kid. How do you take your coffee?"

"Black's fine," Charlie said. I made a face, and he laughed. "What?"

"Gross."

"She only says that because she drinks it half-coffee, half-cream, sugar, and a shot of caramel syrup," Leah said.

"You can't taste the coffee that way," I protested. "It's wonderful."

Charlie took the mug from Leah and shook his head. We settled into the big booth under the bay window, Leah and me on one side, Charlie on the other, and the croissants on their tray between us. I spooned sugar into my coffee and stirred in cream until it turned the perfect shade of beige.

Charlie watched me take a sip and shuddered.

I grinned at him. "Delicious."

"So you work here?" Charlie asked Leah, turning his attention from my coffee.

"And live here," Leah said. She pointed to the ceiling. "Our apartment is upstairs. This shop is my parents' first baby."

"That's so cool," he said.

"It's whatever." She shrugged, though I knew she loved the cafe as much as her parents did. "But enough about me. What brings you to Asylum, New Kid?"

"Family stuff," he answered. "I'm staying with my grandmother for the school year."

"Where are you from?"

"Montana."

"What's your favorite color?"

"What's with the questions, Leah?" I interrupted.

"I'm getting to know Charlie," she said.

He tapped his fingers along the curve of his mug. "I don't mind," he said. "As long as I get to do some asking of my own."

Leah spread her hands wide. "New Kid, I am an open book."

"What about you?" Charlie turned his attention to me. "I'll only play if Amelia's in too."

"I don't give my secrets up so easily," I teased.

"I can be very persuasive." The tips of his ears reddened, and I grinned.

"Go on, then," I said. "What's your favorite color?"

"Would it be cheating if I said blue?"

I groaned. "Yeah, I think so."

"I feel like it calls to me or something, you know?"

Leah rolled her eyes at me. "He's kind of lame."

We traded questions rapid-fire, until the coffee in our cups grew cold and the cafe emptied of customers around us, until I forgot about the ghost in the woods and the fact that I was pretty sure my mother hadn't just been getting lunch with a mysterious someone and that my life was one big broken mess. Charlie propped his leg up on the seat beside him and leaned close, his elbows on the table. I learned that Charlie was an only child and his mother was a surgeon and that, in third grade, Leah had kissed Ryan LaFrance behind the gym bleachers.

"You never told me that!" I pretended—okay, half-pretended—to be mortified. "Ryan? Really? He's kind of..."

Leah's face turned as red the streaks in her hair. "Gross," she said. "I know. But it's not like I knew about the time you jumped off the roof over your garage," she added. "Fair's fair."

"So what's next?" Charlie stretched his arms over his head. "Are we going to sit here all afternoon? Not that I mind," he added to Leah. "This place is great."

I picked at my croissant. I tore it into little pieces and stacked them on my plate in front of me, eating every third or so piece. I took a deep breath. "I was thinking," I said. "Maybe we should go into the woods this afternoon."

Leah gaped at me. "You? You're going to go into the woods?"

I tore the flaky pastry into tinier and tinier pieces. "Yeah."

"I repeat: you?"

"Leah. I...I saw *her*," I whispered. I didn't look at Charlie. I didn't want to see the judgment I was sure was written all over his face. Normal girls didn't see ghosts.

Crazy girls saw ghosts.

"What?" Leah leapt from the table, nearly spilling her coffee. "When?"

Charlie held up his hands, his brow creased. "Whoa. Wait. Will someone explain to me what's going on?"

Leah and I exchanged a glance as she climbed back into her seat. "This might sound weird," she said.

"Try me."

She elbowed me, and I scowled. "You know the woods behind our houses?"

He nodded.

"They're haunted." I met his eyes, bright blue behind his glasses.

"Haunted." He repeated the word slowly, drawing it out like it was the first time his mouth had shaped around the sound.

"By a woman in white," Leah said. "Everyone thinks it's a local legend, you know? But she's there," she added quickly. "Amelia has seen her."

"You've seen a ghost?"

I nodded. Heat crept up my neck and spilled across my face. He was going to start laughing any second, and I couldn't bear it.

But he didn't laugh. He stared at me for a moment, like he was trying to figure me out. Then he nodded and said, "Okay."

Okay.

Two syllables that, for one moment, created the most beautiful sound in the English language.

Okay.

He believed me. Or, at the very least, he wasn't looking at me like I was crazy. I'd settle for that.

"Amelia hasn't been into the woods since—"

"—since last year," I interrupted. He didn't have to know about Mark. Not yet.

"What happened last year?" Charlie asked.

Leah looked, for a millisecond, like she was going to tell him. But she must have caught a glimpse of my face, because she snapped her mouth shut and picked up her mug.

"Nothing," I said firmly. "It doesn't matter. What matters is that I saw her last night, and I think it's time."

Charlie glanced back and forth between us and shrugged. "I'm in," he said. "When are we going? Tonight?"

I flinched, and Leah nearly choked on her coffee. "I don't care if you're a MacAllister," she said, leaning across the table and pointing her finger in his face. "No one goes into those woods after dark. No one. Not even you."

He blinked. "What does that even mean?"

"It means nothing except we're not going at night."

"You're kidding." He looked at me. "She's kidding, right?"

"Look at this face." Leah pointed to herself. "Does this look like the face of someone who would kid you?"

"Don't answer that," I told Charlie, nudging my shoulder against Leah's. "We only go during the day."

"Because the woods are haunted by a woman in white?" He quirked his left eyebrow, something I'd never been able to do despite hours of practice.

"Because strange things happen in the woods at night." I rubbed at my scar.

"So when are we going?"

I looked at Leah.

She sighed. "I'll go see what the schedule looks like," she said. "Don't even think about going without me."

I studied Charlie from across the table. His lips tilted up in what could be amusement, but at least he wasn't looking at me like I was crazy. "You're taking this better than I expected," I admitted.

Now a true grin stretched across his face. "It takes a lot to surprise me."

Five

The woods stretched out before us, deep and cool and green. I paused at the edge of my yard, near the spot where I'd seen the woman the night before. If Charlie and Leah noticed my hesitation, neither of them mentioned it. I wrapped my fingers around the ring that hung from my necklace and slid it back and forth over the chain. Maybe this was a bad idea.

"So," Charlie asked, "what's in the woods?"

"You'll like it," I told him. "It involves a secret."

"You know how I feel about secrets."

I laughed. Some of the tightness left my chest, and I let my hand fall back to my side. "Let's go."

I found the narrow trail that wove through the pine trees. It wasn't wide enough for us to walk side by side, so Charlie and Leah fell into step behind me, and we walked, single file, until the forest wrapped itself around us and swallowed us whole, obscuring any view of my backyard. The trees stretched high overhead, blotting out the sun, and our feet moved soundlessly over a decaying carpet of pine needles, dirt, and moss.

The path we followed wasn't anything more than a break in the trees, barely wide enough for one person to fit comfortably. Mark had come out here all the time when we were kids, but not me. I'd always been too afraid of what could happen to me out here.

This was *her* domain.

But I was here now, and I wasn't turning back. Not yet. I stepped over rocks and ducked under low-hanging branches. Charlie and Leah stuck close behind me. Their conversation had tapered off, and we moved silently, with only our footsteps and the rustle of branches betraying our presence, and only the normal sounds of the forest—chattering squirrels and the soft flutter of wings in the air—to keep us company.

We'd walked for maybe twenty minutes when the ground sloped upwards gently. I picked my way over the third dead tree that had fallen over the path in fewer than fifty yards. Dead and dying trees were everywhere: tall, skinny pines with their needles turned a brassy brown or their branches stripped completely bare, stretching towards the sky like skeletons. Other trees fought it off the best they could, turning a strange mix of green and brown.

"What's wrong with the trees?" Charlie asked. He reached out and touched the trunk of one of the dead trees, dusted with sickly white spots. His forehead creased, and he leaned closer to the trunk.

"It's the blight," Leah said. "I didn't realize it had gotten this bad out here."

"It's a disease in pine trees," I explained. "Some sort of mutant spore or something that sucks the life right out of them."

Charlie snatched his hand off the trunk and brushed it on his pants. I bit back a laugh. "Don't worry," I said. "It can't kill people."

"Yet," Leah added. She held out her arms straight ahead and shuffled towards him like a zombie. "But it's coming for you..."

The three of us dissolved into laughter that echoed through the trees.

"You should have seen your face!" Leah wiped at her eyes and gave one last giggle. "Like you could catch it from a tree."

"Yeah, yeah, pick on the new kid," Charlie said, but his eyes twinkled. "And here I thought we were already friends."

We kept moving. As we drew closer to the end of the trail, the number of blight-ridden pines grew around us until we were surrounded by brown and white, by the dried-out shells of trees, completely drained of life.

And then, without warning, the dead trees gave way to a line of pines that were lush and full and green. Goosebumps prickled my skin, causing the hair on the back of my neck to stand on end, and I was awash with a distinct feeling of *wrongness*. It wasn't until I'd passed beyond the living trees that I realized what was bothering me.

The normal sounds of the woods—the squirrels, the birds, the whisper of the breeze against branches—were missing. Not a single sound pierced the stand of trees. Everything was still, like the entire forest was holding its breath.

The question was—for what?

Leah's hand, soft and warm, found mine. Even Charlie crowded close. No one spoke, but we moved as one along the trail, until the trees ended as abruptly as they had begun, and we were spilled out into what may have once been a large clearing. Now, though, it had been reclaimed by the forest; the only hints of what it once had been stood in the fact that the trees here were younger and further apart.

We'd arrived.

Directly ahead of us stood the remains of a huge stone building, blackened with age and covered in moss and vines. Once upon a time, it must have been a mansion; this was visible in the remnants of a curved turret on the right side. It was almost as big as the MacAllister house, or, at least, maybe it had been once. The walls were completely caved in on the left side. On the remaining walls, the gaps where the windows had once been were bare, staring out like big, empty eyes. I shivered despite the summer heat. When I'd been here before, with my brother, it hadn't felt this abandoned.

It hadn't felt dead.

A tree grew in the middle of the house, towering above us, its trunk so wide that I doubted that if I wrapped my arms around one side of it and Charlie did the same on the other, our hands would touch. I glanced back at Charlie. Maybe they would, on second thought: his arms were awfully long. A few dozen yards behind the ruins, the ground started to slope gently down to where the trees gave way to a rocky incline. If I listened carefully, I could hear the trickle of water over stones. The river wasn't that far away.

Beside me, Charlie sucked in a breath. "What is this place?" he asked.

"It's MacAllister land now, but no one seems to know what it was," I said. My voice was hushed, awed. Something about this place always reminded me of church—maybe it was the stillness. I pulled my hand from Leah's and wrapped my fingers around the warm metal of my ring once more. "Asylum was a colony for French refugees. People who fled the Revolution. And this probably dates to the earliest days of the settlement, but no one remembers who actually lived here."

I stepped closer to the ruins, my feet moving silently across the ground. I reached out and brushed my hands against the stone, expecting it to topple over at my touch. But it was sturdy.

Charlie turned in a slow circle, taking it all in. "What do you mean, no one knows?"

Leah wrapped her arms around her middle. "There's no record of there ever being any house here, or anyone owning the woods out here before the MacAllisters," she said. "Amelia's mom checked the records for us after Mark found it."

Charlie focused his attention on the last part of her sentence. "Who's Mark?"

My stomach twisted, and sourness filled my mouth. "He's my brother," I found myself saying, before I could even stop it. "Was my brother," I corrected.

I waited for the gasp, for the pitying look, for the empty *I'm sorry*. Instead, his forehead creased, and he bit his lip, like he was unsure of what to say. "I'm really sorry you had to go through that," he said. "Losing someone you love is hard."

I shrugged and dropped my eyes to the ground, not trusting myself to speak over the lump in my throat.

Leah bumped her shoulder against mine, her show of solidarity. "We haven't been here in ages," she said, breaking the awkward silence. "We used to come out and try to find the ghost. Scare ourselves silly. Kid stuff, you know? Or so we thought."

I found my voice again. "We saw her for the first time out here," I said. "Standing along the tree line, there." I pointed back the way we came. He followed my gaze, like he'd see her standing there.

She wasn't.

"So you think she'll be here today?" he asked.

I shook my head. "No. But I felt like I had to come out here. Like I owed it to him, or something." I dragged the toe of my sneaker through the grass. "He'd tease me about being obsessed with her, but really—he was the one obsessed with this place. He was out here every chance he got. I think he found it peaceful or something."

Charlie stepped away from us, toward the ruined house, his arms folded across his chest. "It's kind of creepy, to be honest."

"Thank you," Leah said. "Finally, someone who agrees with me."

"I never said it wasn't creepy," I protested.

"I wasn't counting you." She flapped her hand at me. "You hate this place."

She'd meant Mark. We hadn't talked much about Leah's relationship with my brother. She'd had a crush on him for forever, and, I think, right before the accident, something had happened between them. But I wasn't ready to talk about it, about him. Not with her.

Maybe that made me a bad friend.

Still, Leah wore her cheerfulness like a suit of armor, defending herself from darkness and sadness and my moods. She stepped over the remains of a low stone wall and headed straight for the tree. I turned my attention back to Charlie. He trailed his fingers over the curtain of moss that crept from the bottom of one of this windows and turned the gray stone a light, spongy green.

He caught my gaze and gave me a small smile. "Do you bring all the new kids out here?" he asked, his tone light. Teasing.

I shook my head. "Never. I've never been out here with anyone but Leah. And Mark. No one—"

Leah's scream pierced the silent clearing, preventing me from finishing the sentence. I stared at Charlie, bewildered, before I realized that a scream like that meant something was very, very wrong.

She rested against the massive tree trunk, her face pale. She traced something in the bark, like there was something written there. She didn't even seem to notice that we'd approached, or that her hand trembled with every stroke.

"Leah?" My own voice sounded strange to my ears. Too high, too far away. "Are you okay?"

A single tear tracked its way down over her cheekbone. "Help me," she whispered, her eyes on the tree.

Dread snaked through my blood like venom. I glanced over at Charlie, who shrugged.

"Help you with what? Did something happen?"

She held out her other hand to me, beckoning. I stepped toward her until her fingers closed over my elbow, until I could see what had her so spooked.

I didn't see the letters at first. Not when all I could see was my brother's pocket knife, the one I'd given him for Christmas two years ago, jammed into the tree. I froze, unable to move, unable to breathe, unable to think. The last time I'd seen that knife had been after the accident, after Uncle Frank had returned Mark's belongings to us. His wallet. The ring I wore on a chain around my neck.

And the knife that Mark had carried in his pocket on the night he died.

"Look," Leah whispered, her voice urgent. She shook my arm, bringing me back to the present. "Amelia, look."

Six letters were carved into the bark. Six simple letters, made with my brother's knife.

I stared at them until they no longer made sense, until the letters jumbled around and formed gibberish. Until I blinked, and they appeared in their correct order, in deep, heavy slashes through the bark.

HELP ME.

Six

By the time we left the forest, the sun hung low in the sky, stretching shadows far across the yard. No one said much of anything on the way back to my house. Leah walked with her arms crossed over her chest like she was cold, even though sweat beaded on her forehead, and she didn't say a word. Not even when Charlie stopped at the spot where our yards touched. She brushed by both of us and climbed the steps to my deck. The back door slammed shut, leaving Charlie and I alone.

He rubbed his hand along the back of his neck and let out a sigh. "Is she going to be okay?" he asked.

"I think she's spooked," I answered.

"Yeah." He shivered. "Me too."

I lifted my head to look him straight in the eye. "Why are you so calm about this?"

He didn't answer me right away. Instead, he studied the toes of his sneakers, like there was something really interesting about the white rubber of his Converses. Then he shrugged. "I don't know," he admitted. "Weird things happen to me sometimes. So maybe I'm just more used to it than other people."

"Weird things?"

He shook his head. "It's nothing. But—listen. I think you're cool. Ghosts and all."

His words warmed me, flooded my chest and filled the cracks and jagged edges and left me raw. I didn't know what to say or what to do. So I took a step backwards and said, "I'll see you around, Charlie."

He smiled at me, a halfway smile, and lifted his hand in a wave. "You know where to find me," he said.

He turned and walked all the way to his wide, covered porch with his hands in his pockets. He pulled open the side door and disappeared inside.

Leah waited for me on the sofa. She had kicked her shoes off and sat with her legs drawn up to her chest. Her eyes were red-rimmed, but her cheeks were dry as I dropped down to the couch beside her.

"Hey," I said. "Are you okay?"

She rested her head on my shoulder. "I don't know." She sniffed and wiped the back of her hand along her cheek. "I'm a little freaked out."

"Me too."

She was quiet for a moment. "Do you think that Mark is out there somewhere? That he left that message for us?"

If only the floor could have opened up beneath me and swallowed me whole. I closed my eyes and pushed away the tears that threatened to fall. "I don't know," I answered honestly. "But if he is, we're going to find him."

I am fourteen years old.

I wait patiently in the foyer with Maman and my sisters, even though my dress itches and my neck aches from the weight of my hair, piled high atop the crown of my head, powdered white and twined with silk ribbons. I am not a child any longer. I am eager to show Papa how much I have grown while he has been away.

Hoof-beats thunder through the courtyard, and my heart flutters in my chest. It takes everything inside of me to keep myself from running to the door and throwing myself in his arms. Papa has been gone for nearly five years, and there were times when we did not know if he would ever return to us.

Outside, a man laughs, and others join him.

He is here.

Maman's breath catches in her throat as the footmen throw open the front doors, and there is Papa, dressed in full military regalia. She drops into a deep curtsy, and my sisters and I follow suit.

Papa crosses the room in three strides and gathers her in his arms. Maman lets out a noise between a sob and a laugh, wrapping her arms around him and burying her face in his neck. He drops kisses on her hair, and she clings to him like a common fishwife. After all this time, I suppose decency can be put aside.

He steps back from her, his face wet with tears. He takes a deep breath before he turns to the three of us, who are as still as garden statues. "Mes Filles," he says, "how grown up you all are!"

He stops in front of me. His fingers tilt my chin up, and he searches my face, as though he's reading every moment he was gone from my bones. His warm brown eyes meet mine, and now my own eyes are the ones filling with tears. "My Marin," he says. "How I have missed you, cherie."

"I have missed you too, Papa," I say.

Papa moves on to my older sisters, Jeanne and Corinne, and I am suddenly aware that he did not come inside alone. A young man, hardly more than a boy himself, stands in the doorway, clutching a black tricorn hat. He is travel-stained and dusty, but he stands tall and proud in knee breeches, silk stockings, and a bright blue coat.

He is the most beautiful man I have ever seen.

Seven

"Amelia?" Warm hands on my shoulders shook me awake. My mom's face swam into focus, and she frowned down at me. "Honey, why are you in here?"

I blinked up at her. It took me a moment to realize I wasn't asleep in my bed, but on the floor of the second floor hallway, curled up near the landing. I sat up and winced at the sharp bolt of pain that shot down my spine. In one hand, I clutched the ring that usually hung around my neck so tightly that the gold edging around the blue stone had cut into my palm, leaving a thin line of blood.

"I don't know," I said, and I didn't. "I fell asleep in my bed."

"Did you sleepwalk?" She held out her hand and helped me up. She was dressed for a run, her hair pulled back from her face, pop music already blaring from her headphones, which meant it was probably still pre-dawn. She hugged me, then stepped back, her eyes anxious. "You're freezing. Are you sure you're all right?"

The details of my dream were already beginning to slip away from me. I rubbed at my eyes. "I'm fine," I said.

She gave me a gentle push toward the attic stairs. "Go back to bed. I'll wake you up when I get home, okay?"

"Okay." It didn't take much convincing. I yawned and stumbled back into my room, where I curled up under the covers. Before my head even hit the pillow, I was swept away into a dark, dreamless sleep.

I woke up to an empty house and the gentle tapping of rain on the roof above my bedroom. It was dark and quiet, like the clouds outside had descended and wrapped their arms around the house, protecting me from the world outside. A note in my mother's looping script stuck to the refrigerator announced that I was on my own again until dinnertime, and to call her when I woke up, please. I pulled it off the fridge and dialed her cell phone while I dug around the cabinets. She answered right as I came up with a chipped white ceramic bowl and a box of Golden Grahams.

"You slept late," she said.

I glanced at the bright green numbers over the stove. It was almost noon. "I was exhausted."

"I know, honey. I'm sorry I had to run out of there, but since today's Ransom's first day, I couldn't be late."

"How's that going so far?" Ransom had been Mark's roommate at the U, and now he was my mom's new intern at the Historical Society. Why he wanted to spend his summer poring over dusty old files in a tiny mountain town instead working in a museum in New York or D.C. was beyond me.

"I think he'll be fine once he settles in," she said. "It'll be nice to have some help this summer." She paused, like she was trying to figure out what to say next. "I wanted to tell you that I spoke to Ms. MacAllister again this morning. She thinks she might have some more things for the exhibit up in the attic. She's put Charlie to work and was wondering if you'd mind giving him a hand. You seem to get along well with him."

"Mom," I groaned. A variety of scenarios flashed through my head, like one of those old newsreels on fast-forward: Charlie and I in an attic filled with spiders. Charlie and I uncovering a dusty trunk and finding a human skull inside... I pushed that last one out of my mind. "I–"

"She'll pay you." My mother threw down her trump card. "Fifteen dollars per day."

I ran my hand over my face. Money of my own would be nice–it wasn't exactly fun asking my mother to advance my allowance every time I went to the movies or to the mall with Leah. "Fine," I sighed. "I'll do it."

I ran as quickly as I could between the raindrops to the wide front porch of the MacAllister House. Ms. MacAllister opened the door right after my first knock. Almost instinctively, I took a step backwards. Thunder crashed overhead, drowning out anything she might have said.

She filled the doorway, a tall, willowy figure dressed head to toe in black, from the flowing, ankle-length skirt to the short-sleeved blouse. A wide black band held her light brown hair, streaked with gray, back from her face, and her blue eyes, Charlie's eyes, seemed to take in every inch of my rain-dampened figure.

I wished I had thought to grab an umbrella.

Under her scrutiny, I remembered why it was so easy to believe she was a witch: Charlie's grandmother was terrifying. I froze, unsure of what to do. Make a break for it?

But then her face softened, and she stepped back from the door, giving me room to pass. "Amelia, honey, you're soaked through!"

I pushed my bangs off my forehead. "It's not that bad."

"Nonsense. Come in, and I'll get you something to dry off with."

She bustled me into the foyer. That's what is was, too: not an entryway, or a vestibule—a *foyer*, two stories tall, paneled in squares of rich, dark wood, and dominated by a giant staircase on one side. Large paintings in gold frames hung at regular intervals around the room; most featured middle-aged men in old-fashioned clothes who stared down at me with familiar bright blue eyes. Doorways on either side of the room led off in different directions, and a hallway stretched towards the back of the house. My tennis shoes squeaked on the black and white marble floor, and I winced.

"Wait right here," she said. "And take off those shoes."

She hurried down the hallway and disappeared from sight. I slipped my sneakers off and tucked them under a bench beside the front door. My socks had stayed dry, at least. Outside, thunder crashed over the house. The chandelier overhead flickered, but stayed on.

The French doors to my left stood open. The light in the room was turned on, throwing a cheerful square of yellow light onto the tiles. I peeked inside and saw a living room that looked a lot like my own grandmother's had: an overstuffed floral sofa topped with what looked like a homemade afghan, two leather recliners, and a collection of framed photos on the wall. The room even smelled like my grandma's house, a mix between cookies and flowers and that thing I could never put my finger on, that thing that smelled like old people.

I stepped into the room to get a better look at the photos. All featured the same three people, over and over: an old man with an enormous white beard, a younger woman with a wide smile and brown hair worn in a variety of styles whom I assumed to be Ms. MacAllister, and a stern-faced little girl with raven's wing curls. There wasn't a single picture more recent than the mid-eighties, judging by Ms. MacAllister's hair, and more surprisingly, there wasn't a single photo of Charlie.

My own grandmother's house had been filled with pictures of me and my brother and cousins in every stage from adorable to awkward. Every room had at least one—my grandma had had to surround herself with us all the time. It struck me as sad, kind of, that here he was, having to live in this house, and she couldn't even be bothered to put up a picture of him.

"There you are."

I whirled around. Ms. MacAllister stood in the door with a fluffy blue towel in her hand.

"I was looking at the photos," I said. "Is that you?"

She handed me the towel and smiled. "You can't tell? It wasn't that long ago," she said. "That's my father," she added, pointing to the man. She stepped closer and ran her finger around the edge of the frame. "And my daughter, Laurie."

"Charlie's mother?" I asked.

Her lips pressed tightly together, and her eyes flashed with something familiar. Grief. She nodded once, then said, "Dry off. Charlie will be down in a moment."

I squeezed the towel around the end of my ponytail. Footsteps thumped down the stairs in the foyer, accompanied by the scrabble of paws over hard wood. A moment later, a tan and brown blur slammed into my shins, knocking me to the ground. A weight settled on my chest, and a long, slimy tongue licked up the side of my face. I'd seen Ms. MacAllister's dopey old Basset Hound before, sleeping in the sun on the front porch or trotting through the backyard. It had never occurred to me that he could move that quickly.

"Minion!" Charlie grabbed the dog by the collar and hauled him off me.

"I don't know what's gotten into him," Ms. MacAllister said.

I sat up and wiped at my face. "It's okay, really," I said. "I like dogs."

"He's too old to be jumping around like a puppy." The dog looked up at her with liquid brown eyes and thumped his heavy tail on the floor. He whined softly. "Don't look at me like that," she told him. "You know better."

Charlie snickered and reached down to me. "You okay?" he asked. He wrapped his hand around mine and pulled me to my feet.

"Fine, thanks," I said. I pulled my hand free and crossed my arms over my chest.

"Amelia's going to be helping you in the attic," Ms. MacAllister told him. She stepped back into the foyer, but kept talking. "I'd explain everything to her, but I've got to run and open the store. I trust you can show her what's going on?"

"Sure, Grams." Once she was out of sight, Charlie stepped over to me and touched my arm. "She's not going to eat you," he whispered.

"The jury's still out on that one," I whispered back.

He laughed then, a full, rich laugh. He threw back his head and wrapped his arms around his middle and laughed so hard that I had to start laughing too, even though I wasn't sure what exactly was so funny. He had the kind of laugh that was contagious.

Mrs. MacAllister stepped back through the doorway, her own mouth twitching in a smile. "Here," she said, and handed me two bills. "Fifteen dollars per day seemed fair."

"Thank you, ma'am."

"And you'll manage while I'm gone?" She turned her attention back to Charlie.

Charlie held up three fingers in salute. "Scout's honor."

"You were never a Boy Scout," she replied, her eyes crinkling at the corners. She leaned down to clip a leash to Minion's collar and wagged her finger at Charlie. "Behave. There are leftovers in the fridge if you get hungry."

"Thanks, Grams," Charlie said. "We can handle it."

And then she was gone, and Charlie and I were left in the living room alone.

"C'mon," he said, "I'll give you the tour."

I followed him back into the foyer and up the stairs.

"So," I said, pointing to the portrait hanging on the wall next to us. The stone-faced, middle-aged man I'd noticed earlier stared back at us with Charlie's blue eyes. "Who's that guy?"

"My great-great-who-cares grandfather, Henry MacAllister." Charlie leaned against the banister. "As you can see, Grams is really into the whole family history thing." He motioned up the stairs to the other portraits of similarly stern-faced men.

"What a cheerful looking bunch."

"And they all lived in this very house. Imagine! Two centuries of MacAllisters stood right here." The sarcasm in his voice wasn't hard to miss.

"Is it weird?" I asked. "To live in the same house as all of them," I clarified when his eyebrows drew together.

"I try not to think about it."

A Magic Dark & Bright

Thunder shook the house again, and heavy rain lashed against the stained glass window above the landing. I shivered, less from the thunder and more from the fact that my hair was dripping down the back of my shirt.

"Are you cold?" he asked.

"A little."

"Come on," he said. "I'll get you a sweatshirt."

And that's how I ended up in his bedroom, pulling a soft, hunter green hoodie with *Frontier Valley Soccer* plastered across the front over my head. It was huge on me—the hem hung down over my thighs like a dress and the sleeves draped down over my hands. There was nothing to be done about the length, but I rolled the sleeves up over my wrists, and had a look around.

Charlie's room was on the second floor, on the side of the house closest to mine. In fact, from his window, I could see clear across to my yard. The room was small and tidy, despite the fact that he was clearly still unpacking. The walls were painted a light gray and completely unadorned. His double bed, shoved in the corner, had one of those old-fashioned carved wooden headboards with the spindles, and a patchwork quilt that looked warm and soft covered the bed. An old metal lamp and a weirdly assorted stack of paperbacks—Kerouac, Dickens, Sanderson—topped the nightstand. Across the room, a small desk stood covered by his laptop and a set of speakers. He closed his laptop and leaned against his desk.

"Better?"

I turned towards him. "Much. You play soccer?"

"Played," he said.

"You should try out for our team here," I said. "They're actually pretty horrible, but—"

"Past tense. As in not anymore," he interrupted.

"Sorry," I said quickly. "I didn't mean to offend you."

The tips of his ears turned pink. "No, I shouldn't have snapped. It's not a big deal."

He stepped back out into the hallway, and I followed him. The upstairs hallway was much darker than the entryway downstairs, even with the glow of the overhead lights. The wood-paneled walls were a dark, unpainted wood and lined with more paintings of Charlie's ancestors.

"The attic is this way," he said. He led me down the hall, past several closed doors and under the still eyes of even more MacAllisters. He stopped at the very last one and pushed it open. "I'm warning you, it's a mess up there."

"I think I can handle it," I said, and followed him through the door.

The only light came from a small window set in the wall, made up of tiny panes of wavy, old-fashioned glass. The room was tiny—maybe three feet wide, and another seven feet long. It was more like an enclosed corridor than a room, actually, and completely empty. Another door was at the far end, firmly closed.

"Weird," he said. "I left this open."

I tried the knob. It turned, but the door refused to budge. "It's locked," I said.

Charlie stepped past me, his shoulder brushing against mine. I stepped out of his way quickly, all too aware of him in this tiny space. He wrapped his hand around the knob and rattled it.

It stayed shut.

"I have to go get the key," he groaned. "Stay here."

Before I could say anything, protest or agree or whatever, he was gone, and I was left standing in the doorway, gaping after him.

The rain pounded against the window, and somewhere above me, thunder crashed so loudly that the entire house shook.

The light in the hall flickered once, twice, then went out, leaving me in half-light.

Shit.

I fought back the panic growing in my chest—what was he *doing?*—and took a deep breath. I knew I was being irrational, but the longer I stood there, the more uncomfortable I became. Every creak of the house turned sinister—every rattle of the glass in the windowpanes had the hair on the back of my neck standing on end.

Minute by minute, the sky outside grew darker; my shadow climbed the wall across from me. I wrapped my arms around myself, avoiding looking at the portraits lining the hall. I could imagine all of their eyes turned on me, watching me.

Judging me.

Finally, I heard Charlie's footsteps in the hall. He held a flashlight, switched on, in one hand, and an old-fashioned-looking key ring in the other. Relief flooded me. I stepped closer to him and said, "The power's out."

Luckily, Charlie was too nice to tease me about it. "It took me a while to find this in the dark. Are you okay?"

"I'm fine," I said. He handed the flashlight to me and held up one of the keys on the ring: a long, slender skeleton key.

"Do you want to wait until the power comes back to check it out upstairs?" he asked.

I shook my head. "Let's take a look," I said.

He slipped it into the lock and turned until it clicked. The door swung open soundlessly. I stepped close behind him, shining the flashlight into the space beyond.

Narrow stairs twisted up into the darkness. Charlie reached down and touched my wrist, urging me forward. My heart beat a frantic tattoo against my ribs; I wasn't sure whether it was from his touch or nerves from the thought of heading up into the darkness.

I had the flashlight, so I went first. The stairs groaned under my weight, and I climbed slowly, focusing the yellow beam of light on the steps ahead of me until we reached the top and had nowhere else to go.

The rain was louder up here, pounding on the roof like an entire troop of tap-dancers. I swung the flashlight around, trying to get my bearings. The light danced over white-draped furniture, old-fashioned steamer trunks, and piles and piles of newspapers tied into neat bundles. The small rectangle of floor closest to the stairs was completely clear already. Lightning flashed, throwing the attic into such a bright light that I had to blink, and...

My breath caught in my throat. It couldn't be. She never left the woods.

"What is it?" Charlie was right behind me.

I stepped closer, not trusting myself to speak. This time, with the flashlight focused solely on it, the silhouette of a dress form took shape, and I let out a shaky laugh, right as the thunder rolled overhead. "A dummy," I said. "Just a dress dummy."

"Did you think...?" He let the question trail off, and I shrugged. "Can you believe all of this stuff?" he asked.

I handed the flashlight back to him and lifted the corner of the sheet-covered lump next to me. An old rose-colored tufted sofa was underneath, a large rip in one of the cushions. "This all looks like..."

"Junk," Charlie finished. "It's all a bunch of junk."

I plucked a large feathered hat from one of the piles closest to me and set it on my head. I posed in the dim light, fluttering my eyelashes at him. "Junk?" I pretended to be outraged, throwing one hand to my chest. "Why, Mr. Blue, how dare you? This here is one of the finest hats to ever grace this blessed Earth."

He laughed. "I take it back," he said. "That is a lovely hat."

I stuck my tongue out at him, and he grinned. Feeling brave, I decided to venture deeper into the attic to see what else I could find. I'd only gone a few steps when I stepped on something that was definitely *not* floor. I gave a shriek as my feet went out from under me.

I threw out my arms, grabbing at the stack of boxes beside me, trying to keep my balance. That did nothing. In fact, I hit the ground in a heap, the boxes sliding down on top of me in a pile of dust and tiny plastic pieces.

Charlie was beside me in an instant. "Are you okay?"

"I think so," I said, struggling to sit up. "Just clumsy."

The boxes were all long and thin. Board game boxes. Some had opened in the fall; a cascade of faded Monopoly money and a few lonely pieces of Clue spilled across the floor. I pushed the boxes off me and stacked them neatly to one side.

Charlie leaned down to help me, tucking the flashlight under his arm. He picked up the pieces of the games on the floor and set them into the right boxes. "Look at these," he said. "They're ancient."

I picked up a plain black box, almost the size and shape of the others that hadn't opened during the fall. I shook it gently. Something light rattled around. "I wonder what's in here."

He shone the flashlight on the box as I lifted the lid and set it aside. Nestled inside was a board covered in letters and a white triangle about the size of my palm. I picked the triangle up, running my fingers over the smooth, cool wood.

"Is that an Ouija board?" Charlie asked. He dropped to the floor beside me, sending up a cloud of dust. His long legs sprawled out, brushing against mine.

"I think so," I answered. I pulled the board out and set it on the floor between us. "Leah and I tried this once." It was one of my only clear memories of the days following Mark's funeral: sitting in his bedroom, surrounded by his things, trying so hard to get him to speak to us. To me. "We couldn't get it to work." I turned the planchette over in my hands.

He locked his eyes with mine. His smile was slow and sweet, and it made my heart flip in my chest. "We could give it a try."

"Now?" I couldn't help the shiver that marched down my spine. Outside, the storm raged.

"What are you afraid of?" Charlie set the flashlight in his lap and reached over and plucked the planchette from my grip. He set it on the board, then looked up at me, his eyes dancing in the dim light.

Everything, I wanted to say. Instead, I scooted closer to him so my thigh pressed against his. "Fine," I said, but I hesitated before putting my hand next to his on the planchette. Would I be able to handle it when it didn't work?

Would I be able to handle it if it did?

But then my fingers brushed his, and all of my concerns disappeared. I was so aware of him—maybe more aware than I should have been. I rested my fingertips on the wood beside his, my touch featherlight. He cleared his throat. "So. Now what?"

"Now we open ourselves up to the spirit world," I said, putting on my best fortune-teller voice. "And we ask them questions and wait for them to talk to us."

"What should we ask?"

I thought about it for a moment. "Is there anyone here with us right now?"

Nothing.

"Let me try," Charlie said, scooting closer to me. "Can anyone hear us?"

Under our hands, the planchette twitched, inching towards *yes*.

"Not funny," I said. "You can't move it yourself."

He was breathless. "I didn't."

"Then who did?"

The guide twitched again, moving across the board.

"Charlie, stop it," I said. The uneasy feeling I'd had before returned, stronger this time, and I snatched my fingers away.

"That wasn't me, I swear," he answered. He caught my hand and placed it back on the wooden guide. "Come on." He raised his voice. "Who are you?"

The minute my fingers touched the planchette, it darted to the left, then stopped. M.

"M," Charlie said. "Is that...does your name start with M?"

The planchette twitched again.

A. I couldn't breathe. The sounds of the storm faded away outside, and all I could focus on was the board in front of us and the sick feeling growing in my stomach. *Mark*.

"I don't like this," I said, but I kept my hand on the guide this time, and it moved again. R.

I was done playing along. It wasn't funny. I closed my eyes, and all I could see was the trees rushing towards us, the sound of metal and glass and wood crashing together. *Mark*.

I sat back on my heels, ready to snatch my hand away, when the planchette moved again.

I. Not K. I. I couldn't stop the disappointment, hot and thick, that flooded me; I was frozen, unable to move, unable to stop myself from feeling like I had lost him all over again.

Then, finally, N.

"M-A-R-I-N," Charlie said. "Marin. What does that mean?"

"Why don't you tell me?" I snapped. I sat back, rubbing at my arms. I suddenly felt cold and wanted to be anywhere but in this attic. I stood up and headed for the stairs, stumbling in the dark.

Charlie scrambled up after me. "Hey," he said. "Amelia, I swear it wasn't me. I swear it."

The walls and ceiling seemed to be pressing down on me, trapping me. Keeping me here. I had to leave. I yanked the money Ms. MacAllister gave me from my pocket and shoved it into his hands. "I can't take this."

I fled down the stairs, and Charlie followed me. The beam of the flashlight cut through the darkness like a knife. I stumbled my way through the upstairs hall, then down the front stairs, and crashed out onto the porch. I caught myself on the banister and gripped the wood, like I could crush it in my hands.

The storm had passed, leaving the air cool and summer sweet. I breathed deeply and let it fill my lungs and tried to stop the tears that fell, thick and hot, from under my lashes.

Charlie wrapped his arm around me slowly. Hesitantly. Like he didn't know quite what to do with me, with this crazy girl who saw ghosts and cried like a baby on his front porch. He pulled me to him until my face was pressed against his chest, and my fingers curled into his dust-streaked Led Zepplin t-shirt, and I was surrounded by him and the smell of pine and spice and boy.

He rested his chin on my head and moved his hand in slow circles over my back. He didn't say anything—he didn't make me promises or lie to me or say things like *it'll be okay* or *it'll get easier* or *there's nothing to be crying over*—he just held me until my tears were spent and the front of his shirt was soaked through.

"It wasn't me," he said again once my shoulders had stopped shaking and I'd cried myself dry. "I swear, Amelia. It wasn't me."

I uncurled my fingers from his shirt and stared up at him. "If it wasn't you," I said, "Then who was it?"

Eight

Leah practically died when I told her what had happened.

"I knew it!" she squealed, throwing her arms wide and flopping back onto my bed, her hair blazing black and red against my bright white comforter. "Just say it, I'm always right. You like him."

I looked up at her from my seat on the floor, where I was painting my toenails an electric shade of green. "I don't like him. I barely even know him."

She rolled to face me and held out her hand. "Please. You let him hold you. While you were crying. You like him."

I wished that I had left that part out. "Can we go back to the Ouija board, please?" I couldn't stop thinking about the guide moving over the letters. Or the message carved into the tree in the ruins.

She waved her hand. "In a minute. We need to talk more about this embrace." She waggled her eyebrows, then glanced at the bottle of nail polish in my hand. She wrinkled her nose. "Are you sure about that color?"

"I don't know." I looked down at my toes, wiggled them, and frowned. I'd picked out the polish because it had looked bright and cheerful, but now that it was on, it did look a bit toxic. I sighed and reached for the remover and cotton balls. "It was kind of nice."

"You know what's not nice, besides that shade of green?" I knew she didn't really want me to answer, so I waited until she continued. "You, withholding information from me."

"We're just friends."

"With benefits, am I right?"

I snorted and threw a cotton ball at her.

Leah slid off the bed and settled cross-legged on the rug in front of me. She picked up my shoebox full of nail polish and rooted through it, settling on a bottle of lavender almost the same exact color of my bedroom walls.

"Hey, Leah?"

She looked up at me, brow furrowed. "What's up, buttercup?"

I chewed on my lip, unsure of how to approach the other subject that had been bothering me for days: Brit D'Autremont. "Have you been hanging out with Brit a lot? I mean, since she's been working with you?"

She swiped the polish on my newly paint-free toes. "Yeah, I guess," she said. "She's been working a lot. But she's pretty cool, for a freshman."

Jealousy dug thorns around my chest, and I fought to keep it from my voice. "I didn't even know you needed help at the cafe."

She froze, the brush poised over my big toe. "Wait, are you mad?"

"Not mad. Just... I don't know. I could have worked with you. You didn't even ask." I hated how small my voice sounded.

Leah sighed. "Millie, how was I supposed to know you wanted it? You've been kind of closed off lately." She must have caught the look on my face, because she added quickly, "Which is totally understandable. Given everything. I didn't think to ask because I didn't want to put another burden on you."

"So you're not replacing me?"

She threw back her head and laughed. "With Brit? Are you kidding me?" She finished up my other foot and capped the bottle. "You're still BFF numero uno. And as *your* BFF numero uno, I don't think we're done with our previous conversation regarding a certain new hottie next door. I think you should make a move. You haven't dated anyone since the asshole who shall not be named, and Charlie's really cute."

While I appreciated the topic shift, I had to groan. Ben was cute too, and in the end, he'd broken my heart. After the past year, I wasn't sure that I had enough of a heart left for anyone else to break. "I just don't want to get my hopes up, okay?"

"It's the summer. Our last one before we graduate and leave this craphole town. Live a little." She sat back on her heels and stared up at me. "Sometimes you just have to say yes to life, you know? Before it's too late."

I let my head fall back against my desk chair and fought down the flutters that appeared in my middle. "I guess you're right."

"Of course I am. You should call him and invite him over."

"I'm not allowed to have boys over when my mom isn't home."

She pouted at me.

"Leah."

"Your mom likes him. And you were allowed over to *his* house unsupervised."

I raised my eyebrows.

She sighed. "Okay. *Fine.* At least invite him to my party?"

"The party I'm not going to?" We'd been arguing about this for weeks. Leah's older sister Taylor was home from college for the summer and throwing a party after the Anniversary Festival.

The last time I'd gone to a party, Mark had ended up dead. My fingers drifted to the scar on the back of my arm, but if Leah noticed, she didn't comment on it.

"Come on, Millie. You can't stay home." She pouted at me.

"I can. I'm not going. Everyone from school will be there. You'll have more fun without me."

"False. You're my best friend, and there's no way I can have a good time without you." She clasped her fingers under her chin and rose to her knees. "Please?"

The knock on the door saved me from answering her. For a heartbeat, we stared at each other, neither of us moving. After another knock, I climbed to my feet, careful of my wet polish. Leah was faster, and by the time I was in the hall, she was already leaning against the half-open door, her head tilted to the side. "New Kid," she drawled. "What a surprise."

I froze. *New Kid* could only mean one person, and I wasn't exactly sure what that person was doing here.

Charlie's voice drifted down the hallway. "Hi. Uh, I'm looking for Amelia. Is she home?"

"She might be. Hold on." Leah looked at me from over her shoulder. "Are you home?"

I was going to kill her, no doubt about it. I hurried to the door, nearly slamming into Leah. I bumped her out of the way with my hip. "Hey," I said.

His eyes sparkled with barely contained laughter. "Hi," he said. "Is this a bad time?"

"Not at all," Leah said before I could answer him. "I was just telling Millie that she should invite you to my party. You aren't busy the night of the festival, are you?"

My mouth fell open, and all I could do was stare at her. Once she closed the door, I was going to murder her.

But Charlie leaned forward, like he was actually considering it. He wasn't considering it, was he? "I don't exactly know what this festival thing is, but I do know that my social calendar is pretty much clear all summer."

I made a strangled sound in the back of my throat.

He slid his gaze to me. "Are you okay?"

I was definitely not okay. I was going to melt into a puddle of embarrassment right here on the porch. "Fine," I said. "What are you doing here?"

Leah stomped down on my foot, hard. I winced.

Charlie's cheeks turned pink. "Oh. Just stopping by to see if you were okay. After yesterday. Which it looks like you are, so I guess I'll just get going." He took a half-step backwards, like he didn't really want to go.

I sighed. Being bitchy because Leah was being, well, Leah, wasn't going to help if I wanted Charlie to be my friend. "Wait," I called after him.

He stopped, his Adam's apple bobbing in his throat.

"We were going to go swimming in a little while. Why don't you come with us?"

Leah drove like she did everything else: manically. I was secretly relieved that she had relegated Charlie and me to the backseat; she'd packed the passenger seat full of "necessities"—towels and sunscreen and a backpack full of snacks. We zoomed around the twisting mountain roads. Charlie's big hand rested on the seat between us, and I fought the urge to take it in my own. Instead, I let my hand fall next to his, our fingers barely brushing. After a minute, he reached over, wrapping his hand around mine. I smiled and rested my head against the glass.

Leah slammed to a stop on the shoulder and cut the engine. Once I made sure I'd arrived in one piece, I pulled my hand from underneath Charlie's and stepped out into the sunshine.

The river was only a few minutes' walk from the car. I picked my way downhill, sticking to the narrow path that wound between the trees and over wide, flat rocks until we reached the river bank and the Standing Stone came into sight.

Charlie let out a long, low whistle. "What *is* that?" he asked.

"The Standing Stone," Leah said, walking up to it and laying her hand flat against the smooth blue-gray surface. It dwarfed her—it was even taller than most of the houses in Asylum—and cast a long, rectangular shadow out over the water.

The Standing Stone stood right in front of a slow, deep pool in the river, perfect for swimming. For whatever reason, this spot was always deserted in favor of the broad, sandy beach along the town's edge; Mark was the only reason that Leah and I knew that this place even existed.

"It's always been here, as far as we know," I added. Every time we came here, it took my breath away. How could something this magnificent, something so much larger than life, exist in nature? I was always half-afraid that I'd come back here one day and it'd be gone, just a figment of my imagination. But there it was, unmoving, unchanging, twenty-five feet of perfect Susquehanna Bluestone among the green of the forest and the gentle *shhh* of the river twisting around its base.

Charlie mimicked Leah and laid his hands flat against the rock. His blue eyes fluttered shut, and a strange expression, something almost like longing, flickered across his face. The rock shimmered under his touch, so much that it looked like his fingertips sank into the stone. *Impossible.*

I shut my eyes, and when I opened them again, the rock was solid and Charlie's hands were at his sides.

I must have imagined it.

"Are we just going to stand here, or are we going to swim?" Leah asked. She had already dropped her dress to the ground, revealing a tiny black bikini. A red gem winked from her navel as she stretched her arms over her head. "It's hot as balls out here."

I scrunched up my face. "You really have a way with words."

Leah stuck her tongue out at me and splashed into the water, leaving me on the shore, alone with Charlie.

He pulled his shirt over his head and dropped it onto his backpack in that utterly unselfconscious way boys have. His glasses were next, then his shoes, and I had to stop myself from staring at him: he was thin, but not scrawny. His arms were muscled and freckled, and he had a dusting of dark hair across his chest, and this line of dark hair leading down from his belly button that made me think of things I probably shouldn't be thinking of, and, well...

Charlie was hot.

There.

I said it.

He was totally hot.

I was suddenly too aware of him, and I felt embarrassed stripping down to my bathing suit. I was worried about what he would think, especially with Leah here for him to compare me to. She was lean everywhere I was soft, and while I wasn't totally uncomfortable in my own skin, I wasn't totally comfortable like she was, either. I was just... I was just *me*. I had never really cared before what other people thought of me, but now...

I wanted him to think I was pretty.

He must have noticed me staring at him, because his face was bright red, and he cleared his throat. "Are you coming in?"

I blushed and set my things down. "Yeah," I said. "Hold on."

I undressed quickly, first making sure the ties on my bathing suit top hadn't come undone. I set the locket down on top of my dress and stood. I crossed my left arm over my chest and tried to cover my scar with my hand. It was thick and red and angry. Ugly. But if Charlie noticed it—and I was sure he did—he didn't comment on it.

I moved carefully over the moss-covered rocks until I reached the water's edge. I dipped my toe into the water rushing by and winced as the current flowed over my skin.

It was freezing.

Leah splashed at us, sending a glittering cascade of water our way. "You'll get used to it!"

I tried again and shook my head. "Maybe I'll just sit out—" My words dissolved into a shriek as strong arms scooped me up; before I could process what was happening, Charlie had thrown me over his shoulder. I flailed around, terrified that he was going to drop me, but his arms wrapped firmly behind my knees.

"Put me down!" I beat against his back. "Charlie!"

He was laughing too hard to listen to me. He waded into the river and gasped as the cold water hit his knees, his waist, and then the water hit *me*, and I shrieked again.

"Toss her in!" Leah crowed, splashing again.

"Don't you dare!"

He wouldn't.

Charlie spun us in a circle, and I clung to him. "Charlie, don't you—"

He dunked under the water, taking me with him, and the icy cold cut into me like a knife. I was too surprised to hold my breath; the water rushed into my nose and mouth, burning a frigid path into my lungs. Below the surface, he released me, and I came up, sputtering and coughing, my lungs burning. The river was too deep for me to stand here, and he paddled just out of reach.

I pushed my hair out of my eyes and lunged at him, my legs scissoring. "You'll pay for that," I growled.

He darted backwards with a splash. His long arms pulled him quickly away from me. "You'll have to catch me, first."

"Bold words," Leah said from where she treaded water a few feet away. "Should I tell him, Millie, or shall you?"

"Tell me what?" Charlie squinted at me, his head tilted.

She snorted and let her limbs sprawl out in the water. "I don't know..."

I knew what she was going to say. While she distracted Charlie, I slipped under the water and swam towards him as fast as I could. My hands closed around his ankle, and I tugged right as he kicked, pulling him under.

We broke the surface at the same time; this time, I was the one grinning. Leah dissolved into giggles, and I paddled backwards, out of Charlie's reach.

He coughed. "You're an all-state swimmer?"

"Another one of my secrets," I teased. I treaded water, even as he drifted closer to me.

"I like him," Leah announced. "Keep him."

Charlie arched an eyebrow. His fingers closed on my arm, and he pulled me to him. Suddenly, we were nose-to-nose, our bodies pressed together under the water. This was different from yesterday on his porch. Then, he had been comforting. Solid. Steady. Now, his touch raised shivers chased by goose bumps along my skin. His arms wrapped around my waist, and he blinked his dark blue eyes at me. "*Keep* me?"

Leah stilled, watching us. I didn't know what to say—I didn't know if he was serious, even though he suddenly looked serious. I didn't know what I *should* say, so I grabbed his shoulders and pushed him underwater again.

Leah's cackle echoed over the water, and I swam away, out of his reach. I flipped on my back and paddled just enough to keep myself afloat, allowing the gentle current to carry me downstream. I floated past the Standing Stone, past the wide, flat rocks where we'd left our belongings, out to where the river was wide and shallow. My legs bumped against the rocky bottom, and I climbed to my feet, intent on wading into deeper water and swimming back upstream to where Leah and Charlie splashed each other along the shore.

A gust of wind whipped my sodden hair over my eyes and pushed a heavy gray cloud over the sun. A chill worked down my spine, and I shivered, unable to warm up as the frigid river rushed around my knees. Without the sun, it was too cold to even think about getting back into the water. So I turned toward the shore, eager to reach my bag and pull out my towel.

From the corner of my eye, I caught a glimmer of light coming from the weeds along the bank. I stopped, unsure of what I'd just seen. I squinted at the shore, but didn't see it again, so I shook my head and kept walking. It was probably trash, nothing more. Still, I allowed myself one more glance, just in case.

Nothing.

The ground beneath my feet switched from rock to mud, and I slipped. I shot my hands forward and grabbed at the nearest tree roots, trying to steady myself. I used the roots to pull myself up out of the water, and as I rolled onto the bank, I saw another glimmer—this one the unmistakable glint of light on metal—coming from the murky inlet on my left.

I stood, legs shaking, and stepped closer.

Blood roared in my ears, drowning out the river, as I realized what I was seeing.

A silver bracelet, wrapped around a slim white hand, fingers tipped with chipped pink polish. A hand belonging to a small red-haired girl tangled in the weeds along the bank, her blue eyes open and staring straight into forever.

My knees buckled, and my stomach lurched. "Oh God," I whispered. I jumped back into the river and waded over to her. Every step sent water rippling towards her in a wave that rocked her gently, like she was asleep in a cradle of weeds.

I had to get her out of the water. Perform CPR. Call 911. I had to...

And then I touched her outstretched hand, felt her ice-cold skin.

And I realized that Brit D'Autremont was very, very dead.

Nine

I was going to be sick.

I fell to my knees in the shallow water beside Brit. I had to be wrong. There was no way, no possible way. Yesterday, she had made me a latte. And today...

I felt her throat, desperate to find a pulse. Any sign of life. But her skin was like marble under my fingers, cold and stiff and utterly lifeless, her lips tinged blue.

Mark's lips hadn't been blue. Mark had been white, deathly white, like the snow falling from the sky. And then red.

Everywhere, red.

I closed my eyes and tried to sift between the past and present. Between the reality in front of me and my memories of the accident that played like a video on fast-forward.

"Amelia?" Leah's voice rang out over the screech of tires echoing through my head and the roar of the river rushing around my knees. "Millie, where did you go?"

"Over here." The words stuck in my throat, so I swallowed. Tried again. "I'm over here!"

"Are you okay?" Leah crashed through the brush. "You sound like you've seen—ohmyGod."

I turned my head enough to see Leah, her hands clapped over her mouth. She swayed on her feet, and for a second, I worried she'd faint. But Charlie was there, and he reached out to steady her.

"Is she... is she...?" Leah's breath left her in tiny gasps, like she couldn't fill her lungs with enough air. "Amelia, is she...?"

I nodded, unable to speak over the tears clogging my throat. Leah moaned softly and sank back against Charlie, who struggled to keep her upright. His face crumpled, and for a moment, I thought he was going to burst into tears too. But he took a long, deep breath and managed to hold it together.

"We need to call 911."

In the end, Leah was the one who called the police. Charlie coaxed me out of the water and wrapped my hot pink beach towel around my shoulders. He knelt in front of me, his hand on my knees. "You're going to be okay," he said gently. "Amelia? You hear me? You're going to be okay."

I didn't answer him. I couldn't. I could hardly breathe over the sobs that tore their way through my chest. We hadn't moved Brit out of the water—Leah had panicked at the thought of touching her—and I couldn't stop staring at her from my seat on the riverbank. She looked so small and fragile, almost like a doll.

I was vaguely aware of Charlie stepping away and speaking to someone behind me, but it wasn't until my Uncle Frank bent over me and gathered me in his arms that I realized help had arrived. He pulled me to my feet like I weighed nothing, and I collapsed against the wall of his chest. I didn't even care that the sharp corner of his sheriff's badge pressed against my cheek.

"Sweetheart, I need you to calm down." He stroked my hair, which only made me cry harder. "Shh, Amelia. You're all right. You're all right."

"I tried... I tried..." I tried to save her.

"I know." He pushed me back far enough to study my face and used one thumb to wipe the tears from under my eyes. "I need you to tell me what happened."

I managed it in fits and starts—how I had drifted downstream and how I'd found her totally by accident. By the time I finished, his forehead had creased, and he nodded, his lips pressed into a firm line.

"Okay," he said. "I'm going to need you to go sit over there with Leah. I'll be right back."

I scrubbed my hands against my face. "Okay," I whispered.

He patted my arm and pushed me gently toward the Standing Stone, toward where Leah and Charlie sat huddled together. Neither of them spoke when I slipped in between them. Leah rested her head on my shoulder, and Charlie wrapped a long arm around me. We sat in silence as we watched Frank speak with his deputy, Dave Brune. Dave was barely older than us— he'd been one of Mark's friends and had dated Leah's older sister for almost a year. He usually trailed Frank like a second shadow, eager to do my uncle's bidding.

Right now, Dave's face had taken on a greenish cast, but he nodded in response to whatever Uncle Frank had told him. Frank patted Dave's shoulder, almost exactly the way he'd patted mine. He left Dave standing guard over Brit and walked over to us, the radio on his belt crackling with life.

"Backup is on the way," he told us, even though he didn't have to. "Dave's going to stay here with the vi— with Britney," he corrected himself. "And I'm going to take the three of you home."

Every other Saturday, Mom and I dressed up and took flowers to Mark's grave. I'm not sure why we always had to put on nice clothes to visit my dead brother, who used to complain about wearing jeans instead of sweatpants, but this time I wore a calf-length pink sundress that he would have teased me for. I could almost hear his voice saying *"God, Millie, why do you have to be such a* girl?" Like it was the worst thing imaginable that his sister was, in fact, a girl.

I think Mom would have preferred to take me with her more often, but I hated the cemetery, with its neat, tight rows of granite headstones. We followed the curving gravel path all the way to the edge of the new quadrant at the back, away from the old stones that stood like gaping teeth near the entrance.

Mark's grave was simple, made of the same sparkling Susquehanna Bluestone as the Standing Stone, and carved with just two lines that read: *Mark Francis Dupree, Beloved Son and Brother,* with the dates of his birth and death.

I hated that too.

The spot was nice enough, as far as spots for graves go. A massive oak tree stood nearby, spreading its branches wide, keeping us cool even under the late June sun. The grass, thick, green, and lush, carpeted the ground, interrupted only by the stones. Benches dotted the path every so often, just in case you felt like sitting and admiring the view.

I wandered off while Mom knelt and murmured words just for him, too soft for me to understand. She ran her hands through the grass in front of his headstone, like she was actually touching him. But Mark wasn't there.

I mean, he *was*, technically. Physically. Whatever. But his spirit, his soul, his *Markness* wasn't there. It seemed so pointless to visit this sad, empty place full of sad, empty bodies rotting away under the earth. Mark had only been here twice in his life, for our grandparents' funerals. Both times, we had been too young to understand what was happening, and we'd played hide and seek behind the mausoleums and obelisks and carved, weeping angels that the living used to mark the dead. He'd tripped over a headstone that had been worn down to little more than a nub in the ground and cut his knee so badly that he'd had to get stitches and a tetanus shot.

Down the hill, mourners clad in black, their heads bowed, gathered around a fresh grave.

My stomach twisted. Brit's funeral was today. Mom had asked if I wanted to go, but I'd refused. Finding her had been bad enough; the last few days had been almost unbearable as whispered rumors and theories spread around town. Yesterday's headline had summed it up perfectly: Asylum Teen's Suicide Devastates Close-Knit Community.

That's what the coroner had ruled it—a suicide. I'd heard Uncle Frank discussing it with my Mom when he'd stopped by for breakfast this morning. No sign of a struggle or foul play. No bruising, no scratches, no injuries. It was like she'd just walked into the river and let herself drown.

I wiped at my eyes as I made my way over toward the older quadrants, my sandals crunching on the gravel path. My skirt fluttered in the light breeze. In the shade, it was just cool enough to make me wish that I'd grabbed a cardigan out of my closet. I stopped at my maternal grandparents' graves and pulled out a few weeds that had sprouted from underneath. I picked up a sad bundle of brown stems and decomposing tissue paper and carried everything over to the trash can.

Losing a son had turned my mother into a neglectful daughter. But she had nothing on my father; losing a son had caused him to abandon the living along with the dead.

My father's parents and grandparents and great-great grandparents were all buried together in the Dupree mausoleum at the very edge of the cemetery. Dad had wanted to stick Mark in there too, but my mother had refused. She didn't like the thought of Mark spending eternity in some dank, dark vault with grandparents he had never met. Or maybe she'd wanted to be able to visit him in private, without having to pay attention to the ex-in-laws who had never liked her much, anyway. Or maybe she'd just wanted to stick it to my dad.

If that was the case, I definitely couldn't blame her.

I stopped in front of one of larger statues and ran my fingers along the rough granite base. A six-foot-tall angel carried a girl—either dead or sleeping, by the loll of her head and the limp cast to her arms—in his arms, his face turned towards the sky. Someone must have paid a fortune for the statue—the mastery and craftsmanship were apparent in the soft curve of the girl's lips and the delicate feathers of the angel's wings. Even weatherworn and darkened with age, it was breathtakingly beautiful.

A bundle of yellow roses rested against the bottom of the grave, tied in a bright yellow ribbon. They were so perfect that I didn't think they were real—and if they were, they were freshly cut; the blooms hadn't wilted at all. I bent down and touched one of the flowers, careful to avoid the wicked-looking thorns. It was just as silky and soft as it looked. Real.

I read the metal plaque attached to the base. In large, bold letters, the grave proclaimed:

A Magic Dark & Bright

Winnifred M. MacAllister
April 11, 1904 – June 1, 1918
*You are not dead to us
But as a bright star unseen
We hold that you are ever near
Though death intrudes between.
non oblitus vestri sacrificium*

Fifteen. She'd only been fifteen—the same age as Brit. I let my fingers trace the last line. I didn't know any Latin, but even I could parse out that the last word meant *sacrifice*. I wondered about this girl's family, about what had happened to her. Was she somehow related to Charlie?

Had Ms. MacAllister left the roses?

Footsteps crunched on the gravel behind me. I stood and turned, pink skirt swishing around my knees. My heart pounded in my chest, like I'd been caught doing something illicit, like I was going to get in trouble.

The path stood empty and still in both directions.

I blinked and shook my head. The last few days had really gotten to me if I thought I was seeing ghosts around every corner.

Still, I left the statue behind and kept moving. The graves crowded closer together and grew more and more elaborate as I moved backwards through time until I reached the mausoleums of the oldest families in Asylum. They stood separated from the rest of the cemetery by a swath of lush green grass, seven small stone buildings arranged in a semi-circle before an elaborate fountain that someone had erected sometime during the early parts of last century. The fountain was supposed to represent the founding of Asylum and featured a generically-faced couple dressed in Revolutionary War-era clothing. He pointed off into the distance while she clung to him, a swaddled baby tucked under her arms. Water bubbled around their feet, like they were standing on the shores of the Susquehanna. It struck me as strange to have this memorial here when none of the original settlers were actually in these vaults.

The buildings were nearly identical, made of squat granite blocks with heavy iron doors. Each mausoleum had the family's name carved in the stone above the door—LaPorte, Ovet, Talon, Liancourt, D'Autremont, and Dupree—in tall, wide letters. The MacAllister vault was off to the left, just downhill from the others. Even in death, the MacAllisters stood apart. Another bundle of yellow roses rested against the door, as fresh as the others. I bent and ran my fingers over the silky soft petals, then stood. I didn't want my mother to worry about me.

But my mother wasn't alone when I reached her. A boy stood next to her, his hand on her shoulder. The sun glinted off his perfectly blond hair, and the sight of him—even now, with his cheeks hollow and dark circles ringing his eyes—stopped me in my tracks.

Ben.

Just a few months ago, my heart would have been somersaulting at the sight of him. Just a few months ago, I would have run right up to him and thrown my arms around his neck and pulled his mouth to mine.

Before-Amelia would have done a lot of things.

But I wasn't that girl anymore. I couldn't be.

"What are you doing here?" The words tumbled out of my mouth before I could stop them.

My mother and my ex-boyfriend turned as one. "Look who I ran into!" Mom said, like we were standing in the cereal aisle of the supermarket and not over Mark's grave. She reached up and tucked her hair behind her ear. "Isn't this nice?"

I crossed my arms over my chest. "No."

His mouth tightened, but he didn't say anything.

Mom glanced back and forth between us, her forced cheerfulness falling away. "Millie, honey—"

"What are you doing here?" I asked again.

He ran his hand through his hair. "Brit's funeral was today, and I thought..." He trailed off, spreading his hands wide. "Can I talk to you?"

I stared at him.

My mother took a step backwards. "I'll go wait in the car."

"Mom, no," I protested, but she waved me off and started down the path alone. I turned to Ben. "I'm sorry about Brit, Ben. But I have nothing to say to you."

"Wait, please—" His voice shook as his hand closed around my elbow. "Just give me two minutes."

I pulled my arm free. I wanted to turn on my heel and leave him standing alone, but...

I'd loved him once. And he'd just buried his cousin. "Two minutes," I agreed.

"I just..." He swallowed. "Life's short. Too short. So I wanted to tell you again how sorry I am."

Something hysterical bubbled its way up from deep inside me, and it took everything I had to not let it loose. "You're really going to do this? Here?" I pointed to Mark's headstone. *Beloved Son and Brother*. "After everything you did?"

"He drove the car that night, Mils. Not me. And not you."

"Is that what you wanted to say to me? Really?"

"No. Yes. I don't know." He dragged his hand through his hair, making the edges stand up. He didn't say anything for a moment, but when he did speak again, his voice was somber. Resigned. "He was my best friend. I'm allowed to grieve him just as much as you are. You aren't the only one who lost him. I lost him too. I lost you both. And now I see you running around with this guy that no one knows—"

"Ben." The walls around my heart hardened. If they'd been stone before, they were reinforced with iron now. Strong. Unbreakable. This wasn't about me, or about Mark, or even about Brit. It was about Ben being jealous. "You lost your right to have opinions about what I do and who I hang out with."

"I don't want you to get hurt."

"I'm going to leave before I say something I don't want to say," I said. "I'm sorry about Brit. I really, really am. But I'm done with this. With you. Remember that."

I spun on my heel and left. Every nerve in my body screamed at me to hurry, but I forced myself to walk calmly to the car. I settled in the passenger seat and managed to close the door without slamming it. Mom started the engine, and I buckled my seat belt with shaking hands. She gave me a long look, but didn't say anything as we drove slowly out of the cemetery, down the road that wound, snakelike, through the graves. I rested my forehead against the cool glass of the window, my eyes skipping over the identical rows of granite until I found the wild, broken stones that marked the very first deaths here in Asylum, Pennsylvania. They were separated from the others by a rusted iron fence, the names all but worn away. Alone. Forgotten.

Ten

That Monday, I found Charlie sprawled on his front porch in the late-afternoon sun, one arm tucked behind his head and a book propped up on his chest. His red t-shirt rode up, exposing a sliver of skin and the waistband of his jeans.

Lord help me.

I plopped down next to him, close, but not too close, and wrapped my arms around my knees. "Hey, stranger."

"Hey," he said. He sat up and set the book down on the porch between us. *Catch-22*. "Ready to go work?"

"Let's do it," I said, relieved to get back to normal.

"You won't be afraid?"

"It can't be that creepy in the daylight. Can it?"

"Don't worry," he teased. "I can protect you."

I pushed him. "I'm perfectly capable of protecting myself, thanks."

He threw his arm across my shoulders, pulling me snugly against his side. "That's good," he said, lowering his voice to a conspiratorial whisper. "Because you might need to protect *me*."

Sunlight streamed through the dormer windows, catching dust particles in the air and making them shimmer like glitter. The cloth-draped furniture and dress dummy and boxes no longer looked threatening, just worn and sad.

The room was medium-sized, above the center of the house. Two walls had dormer windows looking over the front or back yards, two each, with window seats built beneath them, the kind I'd always wanted as a little girl. The walls and floors were finished, if dirty and worn. Faded blue wallpaper peeled at the seams, exposing the bone-colored plaster underneath, reminding me of Cinderella after her ball gown turned back into rags. Every few feet, the walls were dotted by old-fashioned sconces, the kind you put candles in, the mirrored glass pitted and darkened with age. To my left, a door with a crystal knob led off to who knew where. Probably another room as filled with junk as this one. The wall opposite had no matching door that I could see, but it was lined with so much junk that I doubted I could get close enough to tell for sure. I knew one thing: it didn't seem like this room had always been used for storage.

The Ouija board sat where we had left it, the planchette knocked off to one side. In the light of day, it looked harmless. The storm had made my imagination run wild. Still, I pushed the planchette even further away from the board with the toe of my shoe, just to be safe.

"This place is a mess." Charlie stood with his hands on his hips, looking a little overwhelmed.

"When's the last time anyone was up here?" Everywhere I looked, there were piles and piles of the paraphernalia people tend to accumulate over their lifetimes.

Charlie shrugged. He stepped over the pile of board games and lifted the lid of a large, dinged-up piece of furniture that looked like the buffet we had in our dining room. He let out a whistle. "This is a record player." He crouched down next to it and slid open a door along the front. He pulled out a record and turned it over in his hands, then held it up, grinning at me. "The Stones."

I pulled the cloth from the pink sofa and settled down on it, sending up a puff of dust. Its springs creaked under my weight as I leaned over and picked up a book from a nearby pile and flipped it open. Rows and rows of black and white photos stared back at me in all their 80s-haired glory.

I held up the book in my hands. "I think I found your mom's high school yearbook."

He was at my side in an instant. "Seriously? She never talks about living here."

I flipped through the pages. I stopped on one page with half-page photos—there was my mom, small and blond and grinning in a cheerleading uniform, her arm thrown around a tall, thin girl with a huge perm. Over the top left of the photo, my mom had written: *Love ya! Best friends forever*.

"That's my mom," Charlie pointed to the tall girl.

"Our moms were best friends, apparently." I traced the words with my fingertip.

"She never told me that," he said, and I didn't have to look up at him to know that he was frowning. "She always made it sound like she never had anyone here she could count on."

"That's not what it looks like here," I said. "I wonder what happened."

Charlie shrugged and turned back to his pile. "It was a long time ago, wasn't it? Things change. People change."

The next few hours passed quickly. We uncovered another sofa and a blue wing-backed chair and dragged them over to the center of the room, arranging them across from the velvet couch. Interesting stuff—yearbooks and hatboxes full of photographs and letters—went into a pile, and junk—wadded up newspaper and moth-eaten blankets and rotting cardboard boxes—went into heavy-duty black trash bags.

The junk outnumbered the interesting stuff.

We talked about everything and anything. With Charlie, talking was easy. Every now and then, I'd glance up and catch him watching me, making my heart flutter. He'd look away quickly, the color rising in his cheeks, and I'd smile and keep working.

The next few days passed in a blur of dusty boxes and aching muscles. I worked myself into an exhaustion so bone-deep that I couldn't actually keep my eyes open at night. I slept for the first time in months.

Charlie fit so easily into my new routine—I'd let myself into the house every morning, and we'd spend a few hours cleaning before joining Leah at the Asylum Coffee Company for lunch. Then we'd be back in the attic for another hour or two, though more often or not we'd spend the afternoon sprawled on the two sofas up there, talking or playing board games. We didn't touch the Ouija board again, and we definitely didn't talk about Brit or Mark or the Woman in White.

For the first time in a long time, I was happy.

I am sixteen years old.

I am wrapped in my blue velvet cloak as I make my way to his rooms above the kitchens, my slippered feet stepping silently on the marble floors. I raise my hand to the door and knock softly. I'd thought that I would be nervous or afraid. I've dreamt of this nearly every night since Papa brought him here, since I was a girl and he was seventeen, freshly returned from the war in the Americas.

And now it is happening.

The door creaks open. Robert stands there in his shirtsleeves, his blond hair curling around his shoulders, and as always, my breath catches in my throat at the sight of him. His blue eyes, dark with desire, sweep over me once before he pulls me into the room. He locks the door behind us, and for a moment, we just stare at each other.

He breaks the silence first. "I did not think you'd come." Two years here and his French is still heavily accented, showing his Scottish roots. He steps close to me, picking up a dark brown curl from my shoulder and rolling it between his fingers. "I had almost hoped you wouldn't. You will be my downfall, Marin."

"I am no one's downfall," I reply. I let my cloak fall to the floor. I'd picked out my prettiest nightgown for tonight, made of soft silk and ribbons, and it has the desired effect on him. A muscle twitches in his jaw, and his fists clench the silk at my back as he draws a ragged breath.

He's so close to giving in, I can feel it.

And he will be mine.

"If you love me, Robert, you won't refuse me." My voice is soft as I run my fingers along the curve of his jaw. His eyes flutter shut.

"I have a mind to refuse you because I do love you," he says. "You do not understand what you are asking of me. Marin, your father will never allow us to be wed. You know that. You're too valuable to waste on someone like me."

"He owes you his life," I say, my temper flaring. "Is one daughter worth more than the air in his lungs, the beat of his heart in his chest?" I stand on my toes and press a kiss to his cheek. "You underestimate your worth, my love."

He stares down at me for a moment more, seemingly fighting a battle within himself. But then he lowers his face to mine, and I smile against his lips.

I have won.

I look down at the gardens from my bedroom window, where Robert and Papa walk slowly. Papa is waving his hands around the way he does when he's trying to prove a point. Robert listens with his head bowed. Every so often, he glances up toward my window.

Toward me.

Are they speaking about me? I smile, replaying every night of the last week over in my mind. Truly, he belongs to me now, and I will never let him go. Perhaps Robert is asking for my hand at last. And because of the debt my father owes him, he will have no chance but to accept. I can't help the giddiness rushing through me at the very thought—Robert's wife. Everything has gone according to plan.

I need to hear what they are saying. I press the fingers of one hand against the glass. In my other, I clutch the golden ring I usually wear on my right ring finger, saying the words of the spell under my breath.

I'd learned long ago that the words do not matter as much as the intent and the power behind them do; Maman can cast without speaking a word. I'm not there yet, but I should be, soon.

I let the dark torrent of magic fill me. Like always, it threatens to overwhelm me, to pull me under, but I struggle against it, forcing it to shape itself to do my bidding.

Under my fingertips, the heavy glass of the window shimmers and goes soft. I hear what my father and lover are speaking of as clearly as if they are beside me.

"I worry about finding her a husband, Robert. She's so willful and stubborn—what man wants that in a wife? Perhaps my wife and I have been too soft on her—she is the baby, after all, and used to getting her way."

"Any man would be lucky to have her," Robert replies.

My heart is nearly beating out of my chest. This is the moment when everything will change. I can just imagine the words leaving his lips, his perfect lips...

"Stop that this instant, Marin." My mother's voice behind me is cold. I spin towards her, clutching the ring to my chest. The glass in the window returns to normal.

Maman steps close to me and grips my chin. Her fingers dig into my flesh, and I squirm, trying to loosen her grasp. She stares down at me, her dark brown eyes boring into mine. "What a selfish child you are," she hisses. "What have I told you, time and time again? Your gift is to be used to help others, not to lurk and spy and serve yourself."

I step backwards, wrenching myself free. "What good is my power if I am never allowed to use it? You are a coward, Maman."

"You don't know what you speak of," she spits. "One day, your arrogance will be your undoing."

As always, time proves my mother wrong. My arrogance will not be my undoing.

Love will.

Eleven

The shrill wail of the alarm screamed through the house. I snapped awake, and the ring, burning hot against my palm, clattered to the ground. I clamped my hands over my ears and crouched down, squeezing my eyes shut against the noise that seemed to pulse in time with the beating of my heart. *I'm not crazy. I'm not crazy.*

Light flooded the room, and the sound cut off mid-siren, leaving only a ghostly echo in my ears. Slowly, I opened my eyes and lowered my hands.

Mom and Leah stood in the living room in their pajamas. They stared at me. I blinked at them.

The night before came crashing back to me at once—Humphrey Bogart and banana splits and faded portraits and Leah, deciding to spend the night.

Mom's hand was still on the panel for the alarm, her face creased with worry. She sighed, then crouched down next to me. She ran her fingers through my tangled hair before she wrapped her arm under my shoulders, helping me to my feet. She steered me toward my bedroom, her hand on the small of my back.

"Again?" she asked, her voice soft.

I nodded, too exhausted and disoriented to protest. I crawled into my bed and pulled the covers up to my chin. Mom turned out the light and stepped back into the hallway. She and Leah talked in low voices too soft for me to hear for a few moments before the door opened again and Leah slipped inside. The mattress dipped under her weight as she crawled into bed beside me and snuggled against my back. Waiting for questions that never came, I drifted off into an uneasy sleep.

The next time I opened my eyes, Leah was already awake and dressed. She sat in the big cozy chair in the corner, her legs tucked up under her. She chewed on her lip the way she did when she was deep in thought and turned something over and over again in her hands.

I sat up, pulling my knees to my chest. "Morning," I said.

She gave me a quick smile before returning her gaze to whatever it was she held. "You doing okay?" she asked.

I nodded. The entire episode seemed like it too had been part of my dreams—already, it was soft and fuzzy around the edges, the details beginning to drift away. "I'm sorry about last night," I said.

She shrugged. "You've been walking in your sleep?"

I ducked my head. "This is the second time," I admitted.

"Why?"

It was my turn to shrug. Instead of looking at her, I looked down at my toes, which were painted a bright blue. "I don't know. It's... it's so strange. I don't remember anything—one moment, I was falling asleep up here, and the next, I was setting off the alarm."

And the dream. I remembered the dream, the continuation of the one from the last time I'd walked in my sleep.

"You dropped this." Leah held up my ring, causing it to glint in the morning light.

I leaned forward, palm out. She frowned, but dropped it into my outstretched hand. The minute it touched my palm, my entire body relaxed, and I sat back, wrapping my fingers around it.

"Where'd you get that, anyway?"

"Found it," I said, running my fingers over the faceted front.

"Found it *where*?"

"Why do you care?" I couldn't stop the harsh words from spilling out of my mouth. I flushed, embarrassed.

She stared back at me. "I'm your best friend. Of course I care."

I dropped my eyes. "But why do you care about this?"

She rolled her eyes. "You wear it everywhere. I'm curious. Sue me."

"I just—" I had nothing to say to that, no answer. I really didn't know *why* I wanted to keep this hidden from her, so I sighed. "Mark had it," I said. "He had it in his pocket the night of the accident."

She was quiet for a long moment. When she finally spoke, her voice shook. "Do you think—do you think that he has something to do with this? With the sleepwalking?"

I bit my lip, remembering the words carved into the tree in the ruins with Mark's knife, which was now locked safely in my desk drawer. "I don't know," I said honestly. "It's probably just stress or something, right?"

She sighed and stood. "Right," she said, grabbing her backpack.

I sat on my bed long after she left, thinking. It had never occurred to me that these dreams would be a message from Mark. None of it—the dreams, the sleepwalking—so much as whispered *Mark* to me. I didn't think that the dreams were my brother trying to tell me something.

But that didn't mean it couldn't be someone else.

Prime jumped up onto the bed and rubbed against my legs. I scratched between his ears and he purred. At least *he* still loved me.

Mom tapped her knuckles against my door. "Knock knock," she said. "Can I come in?"

She didn't even wait for me to answer before settling down on the end of my bed. Prime climbed into her lap instantly and closed his eyes, while I looked anywhere but at her.

"I was thinking," Mom said slowly. "Maybe we should make another appointment with Dr. Gibson. I'm worried about you."

Dr. Gibson. I'd seen him off and on since the accident. The only shrink in Asylum, as ironic as that sounds. He was actually a pretty nice guy, but that didn't mean I wanted to go. "I'm fine."

"Sleepwalking isn't fine, so you're going," she said. She petted Prime, looking directly at me. "I wish you'd talk to me more, honey. You can tell me anything, you know that."

"I know." She must have sensed I was holding something back, because she tightened her fingers around mine, waiting. I had to say *something*.

"You were friends with Charlie's mom, weren't you?" I thought back to the picture in the yearbook. Mom had looked so young, so happy. So much like me.

"Once upon a time," she said, and she sounded a little sad. She stood up, pulling away from me and pushing the cat from her lap. We both watched Prime grumble before he found a new spot and settled back down. "It was a long time ago, before she left."

I was dying to ask *why*, to learn what had happened. But she was already halfway to the stairs. "I'm going to be late for work," she said. "I'll see you later?"

Before I could answer, she'd disappeared downstairs.

***

Three days later, on Thursday, Charlie knocked on my front door.

"I have something to show you," he said, as soon as I peeked outside. He rocked back and forth on his toes, his hair falling into his eyes.

"Oh?" I stepped out onto the porch.

"Yeah," he said. "Come on." He grabbed my hand and pulled me down the steps. All the way across our yards, he kept his fingers wrapped around mine, all the way inside his house, all the way upstairs.

He turned at the bottom of the attic stairs, capturing my other hand in his so we faced each other. He was close, so close, close enough that I could see his pulse jump against the skin of his throat, close enough that if I rose up on my tiptoes, I could—*nope*. I wasn't even going to *think* about that. I bit my lip and took a half-step backwards, dragging my eyes up to his.

Only he wasn't really looking at my eyes, either. I cleared my throat.

Pink smudged his cheeks, and he dropped my hands. "So," he said, "I couldn't really sleep last night, and I decided that I may as well get some work done, right?"

"Okay?" I wasn't sure where he was going with this.

"I thought I'd work on the side room, since we haven't touched that yet. I started to sort some things when I found something I thought you'd like to see."

"More yearbooks?"

"Better," he said. "You're going to freak out when you see this."

He flipped the switch for the light, and we climbed the narrow wooden stairs. It looked exactly the way we'd left it last night—a row of bags filled with trash waiting to be taken downstairs on one side and piles of boxes waiting to be put away on the other.

Except.

A large, cloth-draped rectangle rested against the pink sofa. Charlie practically bounced over to it. "Ready?"

"What is it?"

He pulled the cloth off with a flourish that would make a stage magician jealous, and I almost teased him about it, until I saw what was under the cloth and the words died in my throat.

The woman in the portrait was breathtakingly and stunningly beautiful, even though she was painted in the same style as all of those funny-looking portraits of Marie Antoinette. She was pale, with a high forehead and a straight, aristocratic nose. Her black hair that was swept up and curled elaborately, and she stared at the painter with a look of bored, entitled indifference.

And I knew her.

She was the girl from my dream the other night.

Impossible.

My knees felt weak, and I reached out, brushing my fingers against the canvas.

It was real.

And on her right hand was a golden ring topped with a sparkling blue stone.

It couldn't be.

It *couldn't*.

The ring hanging against my chest seemed to warm in response. I unclasped the chain and held it up, letting the blue stone shimmer in the fluorescent light. I laid it flat on my palm, and Charlie and I looked at each other in stunned silence. He reached out, picked it up, and turned it over and over in his fingers. My mind raced through a million questions in the space of a minute.

How? *How?* How did the ring from that portrait, a ring that was apparently over two hundred years old, end up in my brother's pocket the night he died? And why was her portrait in Charlie's house?

And who was she?

Charlie stared at me expectantly, and I knew there was something else.

"I have one more thing to show you." He sounded as spooked as I felt. "Look at the back of the painting."

"What?"

"Just do it."

I turned the painting over. The wooden back of the frame had rotted away over the years, exposing the back of the canvas. There, written in a spidery hand, was the name *Marin Laurent Genevieve de Lusignan.* 1790.

The letters from the Ouija board. M-A-R-I-N.

Marin.

We were staring right at her.

"What does this mean?"

I reached out and closed his fingers over the ring.

"It means we need to go ask some questions."

Twelve

Charlie helped me fasten my necklace around my neck. I held up my hair while he fumbled with the clasp, his knuckles brushing my skin, and then he grabbed my hand and held it the entire way to the Mustang. He dropped my hand to open the passenger-side door for me, and he didn't reach for it again once he slid into his seat and started the car. He kept both hands firmly on the wheel for the entire drive into town.

My mother's Toyota was parked outside of the Historical Society when we arrived. Mrs. Edy, the volunteer on duty in the gallery, gave a little wave when we came in the door. I waved back and crossed to the sign on the wall that listed the original settlers. I scanned the names quickly. No Marins or de Lusignans, though there were at least five different Maries, including my relative who had owned the brooch in the display case.

"She's not there."

"We could ask her." Charlie tilted his head towards Mrs. Edy, who watched us with a curious look on her face.

"I doubt she'd know," I whispered.

"It won't hurt to try." He leaned over the case that held the original surveyor's map of the settlement. "You never know."

I left him with the map and crossed to Mrs. Edy's desk. "Hey, Mrs. Edy," I said.

"Is that your young man, Amelia?" Mrs. Edy might have been many things, but *quiet* wasn't one of them. Her voice boomed through the tiny space. "I heard you were going with that MacAllister boy."

I laughed and threw a glance over my shoulder. Charlie's ears turned red, and he looked at me, like he was waiting for me to answer.

"Mrs. Edy, this is my *friend*, Charlie. Charlie, this is Mrs. Edy."

She peered up at him from behind her bright pink glasses. "Well, ain't that just a shame. He's too handsome to stay a friend for long."

My mouth opened and closed again, and I shot Charlie a desperate glance.

"We were wondering if you knew anything about the original settlers here. The refugees," he said. "The ones from France."

She sat up a little straighter in her chair. "I know many things, young man," she said. "What are you interested in?"

He leaned against the desk and gave her a heart-melting smile. He really *was* handsome, especially when he smiled like that. "We were going through some things at my grandmother's house," he said, "and we came across this name. It was kind of unusual, and we just wondered if it was maybe connected to the settlers."

"It's possible," Mrs. Edy said. She smiled back at him. She pulled a thick book from one of the shelves under the desk and flipped it open. "What name was it?"

"Marin de Lusignan," I said. "M-A-R-I-N."

Her hand stilled on the edge of the book. Some of the color seemed to drain from her already pale face, and her eyes darted to the large picture window that looked out onto the empty street. "I don't think I heard you right, dearie. What was that?"

"Marin," Charlie said.

She slammed the book shut and shook her head. "No, I'm sorry. I can't help you."

Charlie and I exchanged a glance. "Are you sure?" he asked.

"Quite sure." She took a deep breath. When she released it, the color had come back into her face, and she wagged her finger at me. "You'd better make your move on this one, Amelia, before someone else gets her claws into him."

It was my turn to blush. "Well, thanks. We're going up to see my mom," I said, and dragged Charlie out of the gallery to the back hall. I pushed through the beaded curtain and buried my face in my hands. "Oh my God," I groaned. "Sorry about that."

"I liked her," Charlie said. "She thinks I'm handsome."

I decided to change the subject. "Did you get the feeling she was lying to us?" I asked.

He nodded. "Definitely. But why?"

"I don't know," I said. I started up the stairs to Mom's office. "I can't figure it out."

The hall upstairs was empty. The volunteers' room was dark, but light spilled from Mom's open door. An old woman's voice carried down the corridor.

"Lilian MacAllister is nothing but trouble," the woman was saying, "and asking her to help with the festival will be a disaster, mark my words."

Charlie grabbed my arm and stopped me dead in my tracks. "Is she talking about my grandmother?" he hissed.

My mother leaned forward and rested her elbows on the desk. "The MacAllisters were among the founding families, Marie, and they deserve to be included. Lilian has been my friend for a long time."

The woman in the chair had to be Marie Ovet. She was descended from one of the original families in Asylum and was one of my mother's most dedicated volunteers. Her ancestor, Pierre Ovet, had been the first mayor of Asylum, a fact she liked to bring up in almost every conversation. But she donated large sums of money to the Society every year, so my mother was obligated to put up with her.

"And then she goes and brings that grandson of hers to live with her. A young MacAllister! I thought I'd seen the last of them when his no-good mother left, but no." She wagged her finger at my mother. "Robert Yardley told me you were letting your Amelia run around town with him willy-nilly. I'm not one to tell another woman how to raise her children, you know. But you need to keep her away from him, keep her from getting mixed up in all that. You know as well as I do that nothing good happens when there's a young MacAllister in this town. They're cursed."

At my side, Charlie stiffened and made a small sound in the back of his throat.

My mother fixed Mrs. Ovet with a flat stare. "I'll put up with a lot, Marie, but I draw the line at superstitious nonsense. The MacAllisters are not cursed, and Lilian's grandson is a lovely boy. You worry about your family, and I'll worry about mine."

"You think you'd worry more, after what happened."

My mother's left eye twitched. "Excuse me?"

I'd had enough. I grabbed Charlie's hand and tugged him towards the door. "Mom," I said. "Charlie and I need to talk to you."

Mrs. Ovet, tiny and ancient, looked up at me from one of the two pink armchairs in front of my mother's desk. "Your mother and I were in the middle of a conversation, child," she said.

"Actually, Marie, we were done." Mom stood and motioned to the door. "Shut the door behind you on your way out."

"Well, I—"

"Goodbye, Marie."

Mrs. Ovet stood, adjusted her skirt, and left without a noise of protest. She slammed the door so hard that the framed photo of Mark that sat on Mom's desk fell over with a thud.

Mom sighed and ran her hands through her blond hair. "How much of that did you hear?" she asked.

"Enough," I replied. I threw myself down into the chair that Mrs. Ovet had just vacated.

"Charlie," Mom said, "I'm sorry you had to hear that. There's some bad blood between Mrs. Ovet and your grandmother. It's nothing you need to worry about."

"What did she mean, that we were cursed?" Charlie settled himself in the chair next to me.

Mom waved her hand. "It's nothing. It's a silly rumor started by small-minded people with too much time on their hands. People like Marie Ovet," she added. "The nerve of that woman astounds me."

"It didn't sound like nothing," Charlie said.

"It's nothing," my mother repeated. She reached for the fallen frame and set it back up on her desk. "Now. What brings you down here? I thought you were cleaning the attic?"

"We were wondering if you could answer a question for us," Charlie said. "Was a woman named Marin among the original refugees?"

Mom blinked at us. "Where did you hear that name?" Her voice betrayed only the smallest quiver, but it was enough to let me know that something was wrong.

"Mom?" I leaned forward in my seat.

"Where?" Her eyes flashed with something I didn't recognize.

"We found a painting," Charlie said. "The name was on the back of it. It seemed old-fashioned and unusual, and we thought–"

"You thought wrong," she interrupted. Color rose in her cheeks, and she fought to keep her voice steady. "There was no one here by that name. Ever. Do you understand me?" She took a deep breath and laid her hands flat on the desk. "Go home," she said. "Go home, and forget all about this."

"Mom?" I repeated.

"Go," she said. Her tone left no room for argument, so we left. I pulled the door shut behind us, and we hurried downstairs and outside.

Mrs. Edy had lied to us, and so had my mother. I was sure of it.

The question was, why?

Thirteen

Over the next week, I barely saw my mother. She left before I woke up in the mornings and came home late in the evening, and I spent every waking moment possible with Charlie and Leah. I came home to shower and sleep and to keep watch for the woman in the woods, who hadn't reappeared. I wasn't fighting with my mother, not exactly, but things were definitely strained between us.

For the first time in a long time, I felt like a normal teenager.

On the tenth day, I was surprised to see her Toyota parked in the driveway when Leah dropped me off. I dropped my purse down next to the sofa and patted Prime on the head. "Mom?" I called. "Are you home?"

"Back here, honey." Her voice came from upstairs.

Mark's room.

I found her sitting cross-legged on his bed, staring down at the purple sweatshirt in her hands. I paused in the doorway and watched as she traced the white letters that spelled out 'Scranton Cavaliers' with one finger. There was a black trash bag on the bed next to her and several plastic bins at her feet. I clenched my fingers hard against the wooden doorframe.

"Mom?" I hated the way my voice wavered over those three simple letters. "What are you doing?"

She looked up, her cheeks dry. "Sit down." She set the sweatshirt down and patted the bed next to her.

I curled up and let her arm slip around me. She pressed a kiss to my forehead. "I thought I'd try to put some of these things away before Ransom arrives. Since we have the bedroom, it may as well get put to use."

"Ransom?" I couldn't have heard her correctly. Why would her intern—Mark's *roommate*—be coming to stay with us?

"His housing situation changed." She ran her hand over her face and sighed. "I'm not exactly sure on the details. Apparently there was some structural damage to the building and they can't allow anyone to stay there."

"So he's staying here."

"It was that or lose him right before the Quasquibicentennial."

I opened my mouth to argue, but after getting a good look at her face, I shut it again. Dark circles shadowed her eyes, and a few gray strands streaked her normally perfect blond hair. "Where?"

"Where do you think? We've got one empty bed, honey."

I shot to my feet, out of her grasp. "No."

"Amelia..." She seemed so calm, so together.

So resigned.

I hovered in the doorway, my arms crossed over my chest, feeling the opposite. What if, by clearing away Mark's things, she severed any connection he had to the house? To me? My stomach twisted, and I closed my eyes, willing my lunch to stay down. "We don't have to do this, Mom. He can sleep on the couch downstairs. Not... not here."

She didn't even stand up to stop me. "Either you're helping or you aren't."

A Magic Dark & Bright

The thought of her here alone was almost worse. I inched back into the room one baby step at a time.

She seemed to take that as surrender, and thrust the black trash bag into my hands. "Start with his desk."

I dropped into the chair and rested my elbows on the glass surface. Sticky notes, wadded up loose leaf, and chewed pens fought for space alongside candy bar wrappers and dried up, useless highlighters, each an artifact, each proof of Mark's existence. I picked up a pencil with a broken tip and no eraser. I twirled it in my fingers, imagining him sitting here, doing the same thing. If I threw this out, would another piece of him cease to exist?

The thought made me sick.

Mom's hand came down on my shoulder. "It's garbage, honey. Let it go."

The pencil went into the bag, along with the candy wrappers, the sticky notes, the loose leaf covered in his slanted scrawl. Everything, until it was gone.

I turned my attention to his dresser. It wasn't so different from what I'd been doing every day in Ms. MacAllister's attic—sorting. I tucked his swim team medals in a box alongside his high school diploma and acceptance letter to the University of Scranton, while my mother boxed up his clothes to be taken to Goodwill. And with every inch of space I cleared, my head felt lighter. Freer.

Mom snorted with laughter. From her spot on the floor in front of the closet, she held up a tattered gray Lafayette High Swim Team hoodie. Half of the front pocket was detached from the body and a long blue stain covered the left arm. I had a matching—and *cleaner*—one tucked in my closet. "Do you know how many times I tried to throw this away?"

A grin tugged at my mouth. "At least five."

"More like a million."

"He broke his arm wearing that," I said. "While we were snowboarding."

"I'd hoped they'd have to cut it off him so we'd have an excuse to get rid of it."

"It's disgusting," I said.

"Incredibly," she agreed. She folded it and put into the pile of clothes she was keeping, a pile that seemed pathetically small beside the box of things to be given away.

Mom checked her phone for the millionth time over dinner. I poked at the food on my plate—food that was cold because Mom had insisted that we wait for Ransom before eating. Almost an hour had passed before I rebelled and loaded lasagne and salad on my plate and carried it to the living room. She followed after a few minutes, though she didn't pick up her fork even once.

The doorbell rang. Mom jumped up, smoothing her hands down over her hair. I followed her to the door, plate in hand.

"Dr. Dupree?"

The boy filled the doorframe completely, just as tall as Charlie but twice as broad. He carried an army-green duffel bag in one hand and a laptop case in the other. His short brown hair was parted on the left, like he was some sort of old-time movie star. He looked like a movie star too, with straight white teeth and a strong jaw and cheekbones that could cut glass.

Mom stepped forward and held her arms out for a hug. "I'm glad you made it in one piece, honey."

"I'm sorry I'm late. My ride ended up getting lost."

"Don't worry about that. You remember Amelia, don't you?" she asked, motioning to me.

"Hey," I said. I gave a little wave.

"How could I forget?" His gray eyes crinkled at the corners. "Nice to see you again, Amelia."

"Just drop your bags here, I'll give you the tour. Have you eaten? Are you hungry? How was the drive?" Mom steered him from the room, her questions rapid-fire.

He must have answered the questions to her satisfaction, because when I stepped into the kitchen a few minutes later, he was eating a plate full of lasagne at the table. Mom was nowhere in sight, though the door to the laundry room stood open. I rinsed off my plate and loaded it into the dishwasher, unsure of what to do. Sit down and make small talk? Ignore him? Anything but stand there and stare at him, right?

He paused between forkfuls. "So, Amelia," he said. "How's it been?"

"Fine." What else was I supposed to say? *I know the last time I saw you, we were burying my brother, but don't worry, life's been just awesome since then!* Luckily, my phone buzzed in my pocket, sparing me from any further conversation. Charlie. "Sorry," I said to Ransom. "I'll be right back."

I ducked into the hallway and answered. "Hello?"

"I was thinking maybe we should just run some string between our windows and communicate via tin can."

I smiled. "It would certainly cut down on phone bills."

He laughed. "Are you doing anything tonight? Grams is at some charity thing and left me twenty bucks for pizza."

"You just don't want to be home alone," I teased. "Are you afraid?"

"You did promise to protect me." He paused. "We could—I don't know. Watch a movie or something. Just us."

Just us. Warmth bloomed in my chest even though I tried my hardest to squash it down. "Only if there's popcorn."

"What do you take me for, Dupree? Some sort of barbarian? Of course I'll have popcorn."

I hung up and practically skipped back into the kitchen. My mother sat at the table across from Ransom, hands folded in front of her. They both looked up when I came in the room. "I'm going over Charlie's," I said. "Is that okay? I think we're just going to watch a movie or something."

"Sure, honey," Mom said. "Why don't you take Ransom with you? I'm sure he'd have fun hanging out with you and your friends."

The spark of excitement fizzled. "Uh–"

"I wouldn't want to intrude," Ransom interrupted.

"You wouldn't be," she replied. "Would he?" She directed this to me. I blinked at her.

"I guess," I said. "I mean, I guess not."

"Dr. Dupree–"

"First," my mother said, turning to him and holding up a finger, "while you're living in my house, you'll call me Issy or Isabelle. Not Dr. Dupree. Second," she added, "go and have a good time. I'll put you to work tomorrow." She turned to me. "Text Charlie and see if it's all right."

I sighed, but I did what she asked. Maybe he'll say no, I thought. I almost imagined telling my mother, 'Sorry, no, Mrs. MacAllister doesn't really want strangers in the house'.

He texted back, **sure.** Then, **why dont u ask Leah too?**

Butterflies completely gone, I did what he suggested. It looked like we were having a party.

Ransom trailed me across the yard. The sun sat low in the sky, and the cicadas were already out, chirping in the humid summer air. "I really don't want to intrude," he said again.

I waved him off. "It's fine. I thought I'd spare you from hanging out with a bunch of high schoolers."

"It's not like I have a full social calendar. It's fine."

Charlie waited for us on the porch, his arms folded over the railing, face turned towards the sunset over the mountains. He lifted his hand in a wave as we approached. "Hey," he said.

My flip-flops smacked against the wooden steps. "Charlie, this is Ransom. He's, um, a friend of the family, and he'll be interning with my mom for the rest of the summer. Ransom, this is Charlie."

Charlie pushed his glasses up with one hand and held out the other. "Nice to meet you, man."

Ransom shook it with enthusiasm. "I'm sorry if I crashed your date," he said.

Charlie's face turned red, and he turned to stare at me, open-mouthed. I forced a laugh, even though my stomach dropped. "Date?" I choked out. "Who said anything about a date?"

"Oh. I just assumed..." Ransom trailed off and spread his hands wide.

"We're not dating," I said, trying to do damage control. What if Charlie thought I'd said something to Ransom, like some sort of creepy stalker neighbor girl? "We're friends. Right, Charlie? Just friends."

Something flashed in Charlie's eyes, but before I could figure out what that could even mean, he grinned at Ransom. "Just friends," he repeated. He pushed open the door and waved us inside. "Are you guys going to come in, or what?"

"Where's Minion?" I asked. The old dog usually greeted me with a bark and a sloppy kiss, but tonight, the foyer was still.

"Grams is at a fundraiser for the Humane Society. Canine-friendly," Charlie added. "She put him in a bow tie."

Ransom stepped between us, his brown leather oxfords clicking on the black and white marble. He craned his neck, taking in the paintings lining the stairwell. "Nice dead white guys," he said.

"Be nice. Those dead white guys are Charlie's relatives," I teased.

Ransom seemed impressed by this. "That's pretty cool, that you still have them," he said to Charlie. "Most people can't look their ancestors in the face like this."

"My family's lived in this house for two hundred years. I don't know how we'd manage to lose them."

"You're kidding. It's that old?"

"Parts are," Charlie said. "The kitchen is the oldest room in the house. The rest were added on later."

"Incredible," Ransom murmured, running his hand over the carved wooden bannister. "I've lived in Los Angeles for a long time. Buildings out there aren't old, not like this."

"I can show you around if you'd like."

Ransom's entire face lit up. "Really? You don't mind?"

Charlie lifted one shoulder, as if he offered tours to random strangers all the time.

And so I trailed behind the boys, upstairs and downstairs, all over the house. Our first stop, the small study on the first floor, caused Ransom to go into full-blown geek mode. He picked a leather-bound volume off a shelf at random and flipped through it. "Incredible," he repeated, more to himself than anyone else. "I never thought..." He shook his head. He replaced the book and crossed to the fireplace that dominated the far wall. He picked a small glass orb up off the mantle and rolled it back and forth in his palms.

He wanted to explore every room. He peeked under the table in the formal dining room and stepped into each of the three unused guest rooms. He opened curtains, ran his hands over the ancient, wavy windowpanes, and tilted his head to stare at the portraits lining the walls in the corridor. He had started down the hallway toward the door to the attic when the doorbell rang.

"That must be Leah," Charlie said.

Ransom paused. "What's down there?" he asked, pointing down the hall.

"Another bedroom, stairs to the attic." Charlie didn't wait for him to comment before he turned and started downstairs. "Come on."

We exchanged a glance on the landing. He raised his eyebrows at me, and I shrugged.

Leah burst into the foyer, an extra-large pizza in her hand. "Special Delivery?"

She passed the pizza to Charlie and pocketed the money he handed her with a grin that turned from friendly to flirty as Ransom came down the stairs behind us. "Well, hello there," she said. "Blue, have you been hiding your brother from us all summer?"

"He's not my brother," Charlie said.

"Cousin?"

I decided to intervene. "You remember Ransom, don't you? Mark's roommate? He's interning with my mom."

"Right. Duh. Of course." Leah slid her gaze back and forth between them, and shrugged. "But you guys kind of look alike."

Charlie snorted. I hadn't noticed it before she'd said anything, but she was right; they did resemble each other. Superficially, at least. Both were of a similar height, brown-haired, light-eyed. But that's where the similarities ended—Charlie was slim where Ransom was broad. Charlie's hair was a mess of curls, while Ransom's laid combed neatly over his scalp, and Ransom's skin was a shade or two paler than Charlie's. Close enough to have shared a grandparent or great-grandparent at the least, but I didn't think anyone could mistake them for brothers.

Ransom's eyes sparkled with laughter, but he only allowed himself a smirk. "You must be the lovely Leah," he said. He stepped around Charlie and took her hand. He bent low over it and pressed a kiss to her knuckles like some sort of Victorian gentleman.

Leah let out a noise between a squeak and giggle. "Oh," she said.

Oh. I rolled my eyes and followed Charlie into the living room.

It was going to be a long summer.

Fourteen

The movie was terrible, and I loved it. Ransom took the recliner, and I sat on the couch with Leah's feet in my lap and Charlie's fingers wrapped in mine. He'd slipped his hand around mine during the opening credits, his thumb dancing over my knuckles, and for once, I'd decided to let myself go with the flow. I could pretend to be a normal girl, hanging out with her best friend and a boy she liked, in the dark, watching a dumb action movie.

After almost an hour, Charlie leaned close. "About that popcorn," he whispered. His lips brushed against my ear, and I shivered against him.

Yes. I could *definitely* be a normal girl.

"Did someone say popcorn?" Leah asked from the other side of me. "I could really use some popcorn."

"We'll get it," I said. I pushed her legs off me and pulled Charlie up off the couch. Her gaze fell onto our joined hands, and she grinned at me.

"Yeah, Millie," she said. "*Get* it."

I glared.

She winked.

I gave her the finger.

Charlie held my hand all the way to the kitchen. He bent low and opened the cabinets until he found the ancient air popper. I tried to let go, but he kept his grip. "I like holding your hand," he said.

Warmth bloomed in my chest, so quickly it almost hurt, so quickly that all I could do was stare at him.

"Even if we're just friends," he added.

The warmth fled. "Charlie, I–"

"Don't worry about it." He gave my fingers a light squeeze. "I'm patient."

He pulled the air popper out with one hand and set it on the counter. He plugged it in, tugged me across the kitchen to fetch the jar of popcorn kernels. Measuring cups came from the drawer next to the refrigerator. He held the cup steady while I poured out the kernels. He set it aside, flipped the switch on the popper, and smiled down at me. "Now we wait until it heats up," he said.

I was frozen, glued to the ground. He stepped closer. His free hand brushed my hair back from my face, his warm fingers whispering against my cheekbone.

Charlie Blue was going to kiss me.

A million images flashed through my head in that instant—Charlie pressing me back against the counter, his eyes fixed on mine, his kiss unhurried and perfect. Or maybe it was fast, just a brush of his lips against mine. Or maybe, maybe...

He leaned close, so close that our noses touched, and I stopped thinking. We weren't holding hands anymore; my hands rested on his chest, his heartbeat swift and erratic, mirroring my own, under my fingertips, his hands cupping my jaw, his thumb brushing over my bottom lip. My eyes drifted shut, and I lifted myself to my tiptoes, tilting my face up to his.

"Is there a bathroom around here?"

I whipped around. The heat that had been pooling in my belly rushed to my cheeks, and I covered my mouth with my hand.

Ransom stood in the doorway, hands in his pockets, head tilted. "I'm sorry," he said, though he didn't sound sorry. He sounded amused, his lips curling up at the corners into something that was not quite a smile. "Was I interrupting something?"

Charlie pointed to the hallway. "You just passed it."

Ransom saluted and sauntered off.

"That guy..." Charlie trailed off, shaking his head.

I busied myself with the popcorn. I dumped the kernels into the top of the machine and waited for them to explode. Charlie pulled down bowls, and we waited, side by side, not speaking over the popping coming from the plastic chamber in front of us. When the popcorn finally spilled from the top and the popping slowed, I grabbed the bowl and practically bolted out of the kitchen.

I had nearly kissed Charlie. *Kissed* him. And then he just stood there, nonchalant, like nothing had happened between us, even though something had. Something like a kiss could ruin everything. We'd go from being friends to being Something Else. And I didn't do Something Else, not anymore.

Leah barely looked up when we rejoined her in the living room. Ransom was already on the couch next to her, in the spot where Charlie had been sitting, and I didn't think she'd have noticed if I'd painted myself bright pink and started dancing the Macarena in front of them—she was too busy showing Ransom something on her phone, her fingers flying over her touch screen.

Ransom didn't seem interested. "Awesome," he said, digging into the popcorn. "Do you have any hot sauce?"

Charlie, who had just lowered himself into the recliner, made to get up. "Yeah, it's—"

"Dude, I got it. Just tell me where it is."

"Pantry," Charlie said. "It should be on the back shelf."

Once Ransom was out of earshot, Leah's attention zeroed in on me. "I'm calling it," she said. "Dibs. I have dibs."

"On him?" I tried not to roll my eyes. I may have failed. "All yours."

Before she could respond, a crash echoed from the kitchen, followed by a thump and a faint moan.

"Ransom?" Charlie was on his feet in an instant, and Leah and I were right behind him.

We found him on the floor of the pantry, covered in flour and surrounded by cans of food, one hand clutching his forehead and the other gripping a bottle of hot sauce.

"Oh my God." Leah stepped into the pantry, macaroni crunching underfoot. "What happened? Are you okay?"

"Yeah," he said. He sat up and dusted flour from his hair. "I think there's something wrong with that wall, Blue."

While Ransom climbed to his feet, largely intact except for the egg growing on his forehead, Charlie found the switch, and the bulb overhead blazed on, throwing the pantry into a harsh white light. It was probably the largest pantry I'd ever been in, even bigger than Leah's walk-in closet. Shelves lined every wall, filled with jars of fruit in syrup, boxes of food, muffin tins and serving dishes and cookie sheets. All except the void where the back wall should have been. The center of the wall was gone, the contents of the shelves strewn over Ransom and the pantry floor. Cool, stale air drifted out from the door-sized opening.

"Figures you'd have a secret passage in your kitchen," Leah said to Charlie. She picked up a piece of macaroni and tossed it into the blackness beyond the door. It hit something almost instantly and skittered along what had to be a floor. "Is everyone just going to stand there, or are we going to investigate, Scooby-style?" She tossed her hair. "I'm Daphne," she explained to Ransom. "You can be Fred. Which makes these two Shaggy and Velma."

"I like Velma," I said, shrugging. When we were kids, Leah had *always* been Daphne. I'd had time to get used to being the mousey sidekick. "She never needs rescuing."

"Fred can rescue me any time," Leah said, sending Ransom an exaggerated wink. The tips of his ears turned pink in response.

If Charlie had any objections to being cast as Shaggy, he didn't voice them. He produced a flashlight from the cabinet under the sink—the same flashlight we'd used the day of the storm. Leah went to grab it from him, but he held his free hand up, stopping her. "It's my house," he said. "I should go first."

"It's your grandmother's house," I reminded him. "It might be dangerous."

He flicked on the flashlight. "Remember, I'm a MacAllister," he said, his lips tilting into a grin. "I don't have anything to be afraid of. Not in this house."

And then the darkness swallowed him up.

Fifteen

The beam of the flashlight cut through the darkness like a knife. "It's a second stairwell," Charlie called back to us. The light swung wildly over the floor, walls, and ceiling. "I don't think there's a light."

I went next, testing the floor carefully. The space behind the pantry was actually a small landing, not unlike the one upstairs that led to the attic. The air was musty and stale, and dust danced under the yellow light.

"Where does it go?" I craned my head up and peered into the black above us.

Charlie stepped gingerly onto the first step and shone the flashlight up to where the stairs curved in on themselves. "Up," he said.

"Thanks, genius."

He pointed the flashlight under his chin and grinned, turning his face into a ghoulish mask. "Coming?"

The stairs creaked underfoot as I picked my way up, fingers clutching at the ancient banister.

"Careful," Ransom called from the doorway. "You don't want to fall through."

He was right. Charlie and I moved slowly up the stairs. Leah and Ransom trailed behind us, our way lit only by the narrow beam of the flashlight. Cobwebs stretched overhead like a gauzy curtain, and every footstep raised dust. The walls crowded close, forced us to climb single file.

"What was this, do you think?" Leah's voice broke through the gloom.

"Servant's stair, most likely," Ransom answered.

Ahead of me, Charlie stopped on a small landing. To his left, the stairs curved ninety degrees before continuing upwards. But he shined the light to his right. A doorframe, complete with hinges but missing the door, was set in the wall. The opening was boarded over from the opposite side with narrow strips of wood over plaster. Charlie switched the light off, plunging us all into darkness.

"What the hell, Charlie?" Leah gripped the back of my shirt. "This isn't funny. Turn the light back on!"

"Look," he said.

Light streamed through tiny cracks in the doorway, each as thin as a sheet of paper. Charlie pressed himself against the wall. "It's my bedroom," he murmured. "This is right over my desk."

Icy fingers trailed down my spine. "Like a peephole?"

He stepped back. He found my arm in the dark and guided me to the wall. I had to stand on my toes to see out, but the crack was wide enough for me to see his unmade bed, the pile of dirty laundry in front of his dresser. My breath caught. "This is so weird."

"Very creepy," Leah agreed from over my shoulder, her breath tickling the back of my neck. "Can we turn the light back on now?"

Charlie obliged. I blinked against the sudden glare. He looked pale, almost ghostly in the half-light. I reached out and grabbed his hand, squeezing his fingers once. He smiled down at me.

We climbed the next flight of stairs. Each of us moved more quickly, though I wasn't sure if it was because the stairs had been sturdy up to that point or because everyone else was as unnerved by the spyhole into Charlie's bedroom as I was.

On the third floor, the stairs opened up to a small landing. The flashlight danced over the splintery wood floor, the cracked plaster walls. A small round window in one wall was covered over with black paper.

Ahead of us was a door. Not a boarded-up frame like the one below us, but a proper door with a cut glass knob, like the one that led to the room off the side of the attic.

Charlie tried the knob.

Locked.

"Why would anyone do that?" Leah asked.

Charlie didn't answer, but he didn't let go of my hand right away. Instead, he walked me a few feet away, handed me the flashlight, and gave my fingers a quick squeeze before letting go. Then he threw himself at the door, shoulder first.

He hit it with a dull thud and dropped to the floor in a heap, dust rising around him. He rolled onto his back and hissed with pain.

I dropped to my knees beside him. "What's the matter with you?" I grabbed his good shoulder and shook him. "Are you crazy?"

He sat up and winced. "It looks easier in the movies," he said. "That really hurt."

"We're breaking down the door?" Leah asked from the top step. "Is that really the best idea?"

"Do you have a key?" Charlie asked. He climbed to his feet stiffly, rubbing his shoulder.

She shrugged. "Fair enough."

"Let me try," Ransom said. "Step back."

He raised his foot, and with one expert kick, the wood around the knob splintered.

He did it again, and again. Finally, the latch broke away from the rest of the door with an earsplitting crack, and the door gaped open. Ransom stepped back and grinned down at us. A thin layer of sweat and dirt mixed with the flour that covered his forehead, turning him an odd shade of gray.

"Ladies first?" Charlie asked.

"You're just chicken."

He leaned down, his hand on the small of my back, his lips brushing against my ear, sending a chill down my spine that had nothing to do with whatever was waiting for us behind the door. "You did promise to protect me."

I leaned forward and gave the door a firm push. With a creak that sounded almost like a sigh of relief, the remaining wood gave way, and the door swung open. I shined the flashlight into the darkness beyond.

The narrow beam bounced over a small and crowded room, even smaller than Charlie's room downstairs. Paint peeled from the ceiling and walls and covered the floor. Everything was covered in layers of inches-thick dust. Sheets of paper, tacked to the walls, moved softly as I moved into the room, giving the sensation that the room was alive. A narrow bed in the corner lay stripped bare, the sheets and blankets crumpled at its foot. Long tears rent the mattress, exposing the springs underneath, like someone had taken a knife to it. On the floor next to the bed, a pillow lay in shreds on a cushion of feathers. The hair on the back of my neck prickled, and I was glad when Charlie's hand slipped into mine.

"Looks like someone was angry," Ransom said from behind us.

Books spread across the floor, like they had been flung off the low shelves that ran along the bottom of the walls. Dust-covered candles stood on the desk, the top of the chest of drawers, the nightstand. Wax had melted and hardened into pools in several spots on a narrow writing desk tucked under one of the dormer windows. The drawer was pulled out and turned over, its contents strewn around the floor. The chair lay on its side nearby, its cushion ripped, just like the mattress and pillow. I stepped closer to the desk. I'd barely moved when the ground crunched beneath my foot.

"What's this?" On the floor, a picture frame lay face down. I picked it up carefully and winced when shards of glass tinkled to the floor. The silver frame had turned black with age, but the picture was in almost-perfect shape. It was one of those stiff and posed early-twentieth century portraits where everyone stared so seriously at the camera. Two of the three people in the picture had Charlie's clear eyes and long, straight nose. The girl wore a straight, ankle-length dress and had light hair piled on top of her head and a ghost of smile on her lips. Boys in a black suits sat on either side of her, one with fair hair parted down the middle. His face was serious, eyes cold. The other boy's head was missing, the paper torn out. "More ancestors?" I handed it to Charlie.

"Maybe." He frowned down at the frame and set it back on the nightstand. "Why would someone lock all of this away?"

I leaned closer to the writing desk. Strange symbols and patterns were burned into the wood. I fought back a shiver. "Maybe you should ask your Grams."

"Yeah, I can see that conversation now. 'Hey, Grams, you know that room hidden behind the wall in the attic, behind the secret passageway in the pantry? Why was it trashed and sealed up?'"

"You think she was the one who did this?"

He shook his head. "This room has been shut for a long time. Longer than she's been alive, maybe. She might not even know about it."

Ransom stepped close to the wall. "Can I have the light?"

My fingers tightened on the plastic handle for half a heartbeat, but I passed it to him. He shone it close to the wall, close enough that we could see each of the sheets of paper was covered with a blood-red scrawl. Goosebumps crawled over my skin.

"What does it say?" Leah hovered in the doorway. She still hadn't set foot in the room. Not that I blamed her.

Ransom cleared his throat. "It's a poem," he said. "Or at least the beginning of one."

"Come on, read it."

Ransom's voice was clear and cold as he read from the wall. "She walks in beauty, like the night / Of cloudless climes and starry skies; / And all that's best of dark and bright / Meet in her aspect and her eyes: / Thus mellow'd to that tender light / Which heaven to gaudy day denies."

"That's Byron, isn't it?" Leah asked.

"You just know that off the top of your head?" Charlie asked. He sounded impressed.

She lifted one shoulder in a shrug. "I like poetry," she explained.

"Byron sounds about right," Ransom said. "But I think it's only the first stanza."

He moved the light on to the next sheet of paper. A strangled sound came from deep in his throat, but he continued. "She walks in beauty, like the night." The light scanned the wall, over the fluttering scraps of paper. He handed the flashlight back to me. "They all say the same thing."

"So someone was really into poetry. No big deal," Leah said. "Why don't we go back downstairs?"

I picked up a book covered in green leather from the pile on the desk. It was heavier than it looked and stiff from years of disuse. The binding creaked as I carefully opened it to a page in the middle, marked with a scrap of faded brown ribbon. Neat, boxy script flowed in two columns down the page. Delicate vines and red and white flowers twisted along the edges of the pages, and smaller red petals drifted down around the text. I looked closer, trying to decipher the writing. But it was in French—heavily abbreviated French, at that—and despite three years of Madame Harper's best efforts, I couldn't read it.

Charlie leaned over my shoulder. "Hands," he said, tracing the illustrations with his finger. "Those... those are hands."

He was right—they weren't flowers after all, but arrangements of severed hands made to look like flowers, dripping blood. Not petals.

The book hit the floor with a dull thud. My skin crawled, and I stepped backwards, right into Charlie. His hands closed around my arms to steady me, even as the walls and ceiling seemed to press closer and closer.

Ransom threw open heavy curtains that I hadn't noticed, and his breath caught. "Holy shit."

Pale moonlight filtered through the glass, covering everything in the room in a soft glow. The yard spread out beneath us, right up to the edge of the forest.

Right where *she* stood, a pale white wraith, dress twisting around her ankles. She didn't flicker this time, she didn't flit from tree to tree. She seemed more solid, somehow. More real.

She raised her arm and pointed up at the house. Up at the window, where we stood.

Up at me.

The ring hanging from my necklace grew hot against my skin, and I clawed at it, trying to get it away from me before it burned me.

"Are you okay? Amelia? You're shaking." Leah's voice sounded like it came from far away. She stepped toward me, arms outstretched.

I lurched away from her and fled the room. I made it as far as the second-floor landing before my legs gave way and the floor rushed up to meet me.

Sixteen

I was moving.

Okay. Technically, I supposed, I was being *carried*. Strong arms cradled me under my knees and shoulders, and my head rested on a warm chest. We moved slowly down the stairs, one step at a time.

"Is she okay? Did she hit her head?" Leah sounded frantic. "Should I call her mom? Or call 911?"

My head. Sharp pain sliced through my skull with every step, and a whimper escaped my lips.

We stilled. Light flashed in my face, and I closed my eyes, turning my face into the warmth surrounding me, inhaling spice and pine and Charlie.

Charlie.

The arms tightened under me. "Just give me a minute," Charlie said. His voice rumbled through his chest. It was a nice voice. And a nice chest, if I was being honest.

Then light was overhead, everywhere, and spots danced over my eyes. I shut them against the glare, and when I opened them again, I was being lowered to the sofa in the living room. Charlie's face hovered inches from mine, our noses almost touching.

His blue eyes snapped to mine. "Hey," he said, voice soft. He had grime smudged down the side of his face, right under his cheekbone. I reached up and rubbed it away with my thumb. His breath hitched, but he didn't move away. "You all right?"

My mouth felt dry and cottony. "Did I faint?" I managed to croak out.

"Yeah."

"I'm sorry."

Confusion danced across his face, and he laughed softly. "Don't be sorry," he said. "I just want to make sure you're okay."

"I think so," I said. "Where's Leah?"

"She and Ransom are cleaning up the pantry."

He was so close, his arms still wrapped around me, my hand still on his face. Awareness prickled my skin. His mouth was right there. Right above mine. If I sat up, just a little bit...

He seemed to come to the same realization. His eyes darkened. His tongue darted out, wetting his lips. "You scared me, you know."

Memory crashed through me. I jumped to my feet, knocking him over. He reared backwards, out of my way.

"The woman," I said. "She was there."

"Amelia—"

"What if she's still there?"

Charlie caught me in the doorway. He grabbed me around the middle, stopping me before I could go any further. "She's gone," he said. "Ransom checked already."

"She was watching us," I said. I turned in his arms so we were facing each other. I let my head fall forward until my face pressed against his chest. I breathed in deeply and tried to remember why that was so important. But whatever I'd been thinking was gone, so instead I said, "You smell really nice. Is it your body wash? What kind do you use?"

His hand stroked through my hair. "Uh, I don't know. Soap?"

"I think it's nice."

"And I think you're concussed. You should lie down."

I smoothed my hands over his shoulders, down his arms. "You could lie down with me."

"Oh yeah?" He quirked his eyebrow at me. "And why would I do that? I'm not the one who fainted."

"Because you like me," I said. "That's why you're always touching me. Always looking at me like that."

His breath caught. "Amelia—"

"It's okay," I said. "I like you too."

And then I kissed him.

Or, at least, tried to kiss him. But the ground lurched under my feet, and I missed. My mouth brushed the corner of his lips and landed on his cheek, my forehead pressing against the frame of his glasses.

He laughed softly. "Come on, Casanova," he said. "Why don't we get you back on the couch? I think Leah was right, we should call your mom."

I tried to pout at him. "Don't you want to kiss me?"

Charlie led me to the sofa. My knees hit the upholstery, and I let myself fall. He lifted my feet up, tucked a pillow under my head, pulled a blanket over me. He leaned down and pressed his lips to my forehead. "More than you can know," he whispered, so softly I was sure I'd imagined it.

The rest of the night was a blur—Mom showed up and bundled me into the car, and the next thing I knew we were at the emergency room and a young doctor was asking me a million questions and shining a light into my eyes.

"Definitely concussed," he said to my mom. "Make sure she takes it easy for the next week or so. No sports, no activities, no computer. I don't even want her reading. Her brain needs to rest."

And so I spent the next seven days, the entire week leading up to the Quasquibicentennial Festival, camped out on the couch, binge-watching entire seasons of TV shows and old movies. Uncle Frank spent his lunch breaks with me, bringing takeout bags filled with greasy burgers and fries for us to eat. He'd eat dinner with us too, cooking simple meals for me and Mom, the way he had in the days after Mark died.

Leah kept me company in the afternoons, sprawled out on the hideous orange shag carpeting in downstairs. The den in the basement was the one room in our house my parents hadn't remodeled before the divorce, and now that Dad was gone, I wasn't sure my mom had the energy to tackle it on her own. So it remained in all of its 1970's burnt orange glory.

Every night, I tried to stay up and watch the woods, to see if the ghost would return, but, without fail, my eyes grew heavy, and I fell asleep long before I'd catch a glimpse of her.

Charlie had somehow been roped into helping Mom, Ransom, and the rest of the Historical Society with last-minute preparations. Each evening, he'd walk over after dinner and spend an hour or so with me after Leah had gone home for the day. We'd eat ice cream and play Uno and talk about anything and everything except for the fact that we'd almost kissed.

Twice.

And then there was Ransom. Always on the periphery, always moving around the edges, always there but not quite joining us. He talked more with Leah and Charlie than he did with me. While I was in the ER, they had explained the story of the woman in the woods to him. When I asked Leah how he'd taken it, she shrugged and struck a pose in the middle of my bedroom. "Fine, I guess. Mark must have told him about her already. He didn't freak out or anything. What do you think of this dress for the party? Too short?"

"It looks great on you," I said.

She rolled her eyes. "Not for me, dummy. For you."

"Me?"

The dress *was* pretty—dark green fabric flowed to mid-thigh. It wasn't a dress I'd have ever picked out for myself; the skirt was short and the sweetheart neckline dipped low in the front and the back was nearly nonexistent, thanks to the halter-style top. My scar would be on full display.

"For the party?" Leah raised her eyebrows. "Come on, Mils, you didn't hit your head *that* hard."

"I don't know."

She slipped the dress off, utterly unselfconscious, and wiggled back into her shorts and tank top. The dress landed in my lap. "It's going to look great on you. Don't even."

"My mom might not let me go," I said. "She's freaking out over this," I added, pointing to my head. "And the last time she let me go to a party, well..." I trailed off. I didn't have to finish that sentence.

Leah dropped to the bed beside me and slipped her arms around my shoulders. When she spoke, her voice was soft. "Losing Mark was awful," she said. "But he'd want you to go. Don't let the fact that he's gone turn you into a ghost."

Tears, hot and heavy, prickled at the corners of my eyes. "Leah—"

"She's going to let you go," she said. "I already talked to her."

"I don't know if I can do this," I whispered.

She rested her head against mine. "We'll do it together," she said.

And that was that. I was going to her party.

Since I was under strict brain-resting orders, I couldn't do much of anything over the rest of the week. I was stuck inside, wasting time, while everyone else seemed busier than ever. My mother was like a slave driver, and as the week wore on, Ransom and Charlie started to give off this frantic energy, like every second spent sitting and doing nothing was a second wasted.

I went back to the doctor the morning of the festival. Mom tapped her foot in the waiting room and checked her cell phone constantly. After a few questions and a quick exam, he cleared me to return to normal life, and she bundled me into the car.

"Just in time," she said. She checked her lipstick in the mirror, frowned, and flipped the visor closed. "Marie's left me sixteen voicemails." She glanced over at me, took in my knit shorts and Lafayette High Swimming t-shirt, and sighed. "Will you be okay getting changed at the Society?"

"I could ride my bike," I said. I'd packed a bag just in case, but I much preferred getting ready at home in my room to the cramped bathroom in the basement of the Historical Society.

She sighed. "No. You can't. You just had a concussion, for Christ's sake—"

"A week ago—"

"Your brain bounced off the inside of your skull. You're not ready."

"The doctor just said I was ready," I protested. "What are you going to do, make me wear a helmet all the time?"

"I haven't ruled that out yet," she said. "You should consider yourself lucky that I'm even entertaining the idea of letting you go to Leah's party tonight."

"You don't have to let me go," I said. Part of me almost hoped she'd say no so I would have an excuse to stay home instead of facing the people who'd be there. Mark's friends, home from college. The girlfriends I'd drifted away from after Mark's death, when I'd shut everyone out except for Leah. Ben.

But Charlie would be there too. And maybe Leah was right—maybe it was time I started trying again. "I just—I don't know. I just want things to go back to being as normal as they can be, okay?" I made my voice as small as I could. "I don't want to be that girl with the dead brother. I want to be me again."

Her face softened. "Fine," she said. "You promise that you won't do anything stupid?"

Stupid, like the last time. I fought against the sick feeling in my stomach and turned away from her, back to the window.

"I promise."

Mom looked at me for a long second, then sighed. "It'll be good for you to be with your friends. But no drinking. And call me if you need anything."

As if I'd ever even *think* about drinking after what had happened. I'd learned my lesson. I held up my hand, pinky facing hers. "Done," I said.

She wrapped her pinky around mine, like she had when I was a little girl and a promise from my mom could fix anything.

If only things could be that easy again.

Seventeen

I leaned against the window in my mom's office and watched the crowd on the street below. The Anniversary Festival was always a big deal in Asylum—we had a parade, speeches, and ended the night with fireworks over the river. This year—the two hundred and twenty-fifth anniversary of Asylum's founding—was an even bigger deal than normal. Tents spanned the Green, filled with crafters and people selling funnel cake and cotton candy. People milled about below, dressed like they'd just left Marie Antoinette's court, with tall powdered wigs and elaborate costumes. Once upon a time, our ancestors had dressed like that, before heads had started rolling in the streets and they'd been forced to flee here, to the place where they'd be safe, tucked in the wilderness of a brand-new country. They were refugees, and this town was called Asylum for a reason.

People took their history *very* seriously here.

This time last year, Mark had been with me. He'd opened the window and leaned as far out as he could go, smoking a cigarette. He'd graduated only two weeks before and had spent almost every night partying with his friends, taking advantage of the fact that Dad had moved out and was working for his former law school roommate in DC. Our parents hadn't mentioned the 'divorce' word yet, but they didn't have to. Both of us had known it was coming—that's what happened when your dad started sleeping on the pull-out couch in the den and dinner was eaten in icy silence.

Mark had chosen to rebel. He'd stay out all night long, racing his car along the twisted mountain roads, smoking weed in the woods with his buddies. He went through an endless parade of girls who were 'just friends'. I, on the other hand, tried my best to be perfect: I had perfect grades, made all-state on swim team, and snagged the beautiful and popular boyfriend. I didn't know what I'd expected to happen—that my parents would be so proud of me, the child they'd raised, that they'd remember they used to love each other?

Mark had hated Pennsylvania, hated these mountains, hated Asylum. "This town," he'd said, flicking ash down onto the street below, "is a grade-A shithole."

Two short weeks later, he would move into his freshman dorm at the University of Scranton, only an hour away. Our mom was on the faculty there—she taught two classes a year—which meant Mark would go for free. I'd always wondered why he hadn't even thought to apply anywhere else if he hated it so much here, but he wasn't like me, with a perfect GPA. He wasn't dumb—he was an average student. He just didn't try.

I'd gotten mad at him that day. I remembered that, even if I couldn't remember exactly what I'd said to him. He'd shrugged it off like he always did. He hadn't been one for fights. But I was. I'd yelled at him, crossed my arms over my chest, and marched out, right into Ben's arms. They'd had words at the party that night, and Mark had stumbled up to me, eyes glossy and speech slurred, to apologize. I'd forgiven him, of course. I always had.

I trailed my hand over the windowsill where he'd perched, scowling down at the crowds below. I hadn't realized it then, but just because Mark had hated the place where we grew up, hated this town, didn't mean he'd hated *me*.

A soft knock on the door had me turning, my soft green skirt fluttering around my thighs. I'd worn the dress that Leah had picked out for me, but I'd topped it with a yellow cardigan to cover my scar. Some things were better off hidden away.

Charlie stood in the doorway, hands tucked in his pockets. His red and white checked shirt was open at the throat and rolled up at the elbows, and he had on a pair of dark jeans and brown leather boots. Paired with his messy hair and Buddy Holly glasses, he looked like some sort of indie rock star, not a teenage boy. "Hey," he said. "Your mom said you were up here." He scanned my face and frowned. "Is everything okay?"

I smiled at him. "Just remembering," I said. "Sometimes I forget that he's gone, you know?"

"Your brother?" Charlie's voice was soft. We hadn't discussed Mark very much beyond what I'd told him in the ruins the day we'd met. He hadn't asked, and I hadn't felt like sharing. Not yet.

I wrapped my arms around myself. "I know it's silly. But sometimes I like to pretend that he's on a really long vacation or something. That I'll turn around and he'll be standing here, smoking a cigarette and making fun of all of the people down there."

Charlie didn't say anything. He leaned against the door and looked at me, waiting for me to continue.

But I wasn't going to. I wasn't going to let today be ruined by ghosts, real or otherwise. I reached for my brown leather purse and slung it over my shoulder. I grabbed his hand, wrapping my fingers around his. "Shall we?" I asked.

The gallery downstairs was still, lights turned off. In a few minutes, my mother and the mayor would make their speeches, and the parade would begin. Then the doors would open and the crowds would rush in. Mom, Charlie, and Ransom had worked so hard to put together the exhibit over the last week. The founding families were represented in the large cases in the center of the room, each designated by their coat of arms. Some of the items, like the Dupree Brooch, were familiar. Others I had never seen before. I took my time, lingering over each item. Charlie leaned against the case closest to me. "What do you think?" he asked.

It was magnificent. Handwritten letters lay beside sparkling jewels and iron tools. Tiny miniatures, exquisite in their detailed brushstrokes, represented a member of each of the families. A card next to each painting gave the name of the subject and the date and location of their birth and death. The items grouped around the miniatures, the personal effects of those depicted and items used by their descendants, were labeled as well.

"This is what you were working on all week?"

He nodded, his grin wide. "Did we do a good job?"

"Charlie, this is incredible," I said. Pride swelled in my chest. I knew he'd been helping my mother, but I had imagined him moving boxes and cleaning, not arranging the delicate artifacts in the exhibits. "You should be proud of yourself."

He stared down at the MacAllister case. They were the only family without a coat of arms, represented instead by a swatch of red and green tartan. A small boy, rosy-cheeked and raven-haired, stared back at us from the painting. "Would you believe that's one of the guys hanging in my stairwell?" Charlie asked.

I stepped closer to him. The child looked innocent, almost cherubic. It was hard to imagine him growing

A Magic Dark & Bright

into the stern-faced men in the other portraits. "You're kidding."

"I'm serious," he said. "Meet Henri MacAllister. This was in one of those boxes that Grams had hidden upstairs."

I tapped my finger on the glass over a set of medals arranged beside a faded yellow Western Union telegram dated 10 November, 1918. "That was one day before the war ended, wasn't it?"

DEEPLY REGRET TO INFORM YOU THAT YOUR SON, 43674 PFC. R. ANTHONY MACALLISTER HAS BEEN REPORTED MISSING IN ACTION IN FRANCE. LETTER FOLLOWS.

No letter sat inside the case.

Charlie nodded. "That was Grams' uncle. He just disappeared. Never came home. No one knows what happened to him."

I thought of the grave in the cemetery, the angel carrying the girl in his arms. Was this missing boy her brother? Cousin? I had known what had happened to my brother—it must have been torture, to wait day after day, month after month, and never know. Never have answers. At least... at least, whoever she was, she hadn't had to live through that.

The bell over the door jingled. Mom stuck her head in, saw me, and grinned. "What do you think, sweetheart?"

My smile matched hers. "It's awesome, Mom."

"Good. Come on outside, we're about to start speeches."

Charlie and I trailed her down the front steps and across the street to the Green, where a stage had been set up next to the gazebo. I kissed her cheek and stayed below, amongst the crowd, while she climbed the steps. Mr. Liancourt, the mayor—and Ben's father—was already waiting on stage. So was my Uncle Frank, wearing his dress uniform, his wide brown hat pulled low over his brow and his thumbs hooked in his belt. He saw me and winked. I waved back. His gaze dropped to my hand, wrapped in Charlie's. His eyes narrowed to slits, and he tried to look intimidating.

I pretended to ignore him and tugged Charlie further into the crowd.

Mom joined Frank on the stage. She leaned close to him, whispered something in his ear, placed her hand on his arm. He relaxed visibly under her touch and laughed at whatever it was she said. She picked up a set of notecards from the chair behind him and waited, hands crossed, while Mr. Liancourt stepped up to the podium. He tapped at the mic, getting everyone's attention.

"Good afternoon, everyone, and welcome to our–" He paused and glanced at my mother before continuing. "–Two Hundred and Twenty-Fifth Anniversary festival. Our town archivist and fearless leader of the Historical Society, Dr. Isabelle Dupree, has prepared a few words in honor of this momentous occasion. Isabelle?"

Mom stepped up to the podium, the heels of her pumps clicking on the wooden stage. She set the cards down and adjusted the microphone. "Thanks, Mike," she said. "And again, welcome, everyone, to our Quasquibicentennial Celebration. Two hundred and twenty-five years ago, a group of sixty-three men, women, and children, haunted by revolution and hunted by their own countrymen, escaped their native land and fled across the ocean to begin life anew. They faced many horrors along the way: loved ones imprisoned and executed for the crime of carrying a family name; weeks of hunger and storms on ancient, creaking ships; and an uncertain future in a new world.

"They came here refugees, fleeing a broken land. They came here, to a place set aside for them by a friends in a brand new Congress, a safe haven in a fledgling nation tested by blood and driven by freedom.

"They arrived impoverished, ragged, and starving, these men and women who had once lived in the most extravagant court in all of Europe. They arrived, noble men and women—a count, a duchess, a prince—and ventured into a harsh and unforgiving wilderness. They arrived in a place where their very survival was uncertain. They arrived here, two hundred and twenty-five years ago, and they did the unthinkable: they thrived.

"Over the past two centuries, the tiny settlement once called French Asylum has become a town with a deeply rooted past. We are a proud, hardworking people, people who embrace their history and the place that our ancestors carved out for us in this brave new world.

"Life has not always been easy for the citizens of Asylum." Mom's eyes fell on me for half a heartbeat. "Not even six years after our founding, a terrible winter and a devastating fire reduced half of the settlement to ashes. But our ancestors survived. They picked themselves up and rebuilt, stronger than before.

"Asylum has survived times of war and times of peace. Our young men and women have given their lives on lonely battlefields all over the world. We have, as a community, made sacrifices time and time again. We are a noble, honorable people. We are a strong people. We are a proud people. We are the citizens of this French Asylum, and today we celebrate ourselves and, more importantly, those who came before us. Thank you."

Applause rumbled through the crowd. I dropped Charlie's hand and clapped loudly. Mr. Liancourt took the podium again. His speech was short, mainly thanking people again for coming out and outlining the schedule of events. Behind him, Uncle Frank and my mother hugged.

The rest of the afternoon sped by. Charlie and I wandered through the stalls set up on the Green. He bought a funnel cake, and we sat on the low stone wall along the river and shared it. We found Leah' sister, Taylor, at a table in front of the Asylum Coffee Company, selling iced coffee, tea, and lemonade. Taylor was even taller than Leah, nearly six feet barefoot. She handed me a lemonade and pushed a black curl out of her face. "Who's this? The boyfriend?"

"Taylor, this is *my friend*, Charlie. Charlie, this is Leah's sister, Taylor."

Taylor glanced down at our clasped hands. My palm itched, and I thought about pulling free, but Charlie clamped his fingers tight around mine. "It's great to meet you," Charlie said.

"Uh-huh." She shrugged. "You guys will be there tonight, won't you?" she asked.

"Like Leah takes no for an answer," I said. I tried to play it cool and looked up at Charlie. "You're coming, right?"

His fingers squeezed mine. "Of course," he said. "It's a date."

I gaped at him.

He grinned at me, dimples flashing, and pulled me back towards the green.

Taylor threw her head back and laughed. "See you two around, Millie," she called after us.

"A date?" I squeaked. "Tonight is—I don't know what it is. But it isn't a date."

"Would it be so bad?" Charlie asked. He dropped my hand and stepped in front of me. "Is it really that horrible of an idea to you? Going on a date with me?"

I nearly dropped my lemonade. "I—I—"

He didn't stop to listen. "Because I think it might be kind of nice, actually," he said. "Maybe I'd like to take you out on a date."

"Charlie, I–"

He waved me off. "Forget it," he said. "If it makes you feel better, tonight isn't a date."

That didn't make me feel better. I held up my hand, ready to tell him as much, but he just shook his head. He leaned in and kissed my cheek. "I'll pick you up at eight."

And then he was gone, and all I could do was press my fingers to the place where he'd kissed me and watch as the crowd swallowed him up.

Eighteen

I cradled my cell phone between my shoulder and chin and sorted through my makeup. "I can't do this," I said. "Why did you make me do this?"

Leah sighed into the phone. "Because it'll be good for you. I want you to be able to have fun again."

"I'm able to have fun." I glanced over at my laptop. *The African Queen* was paused on the screen, leaving Katherine Hepburn scowling. I knew how she felt. I'd been frowning since Charlie had left me at the festival. Mom had dropped me off almost an hour ago before heading back out. The house was quiet, and I was half-tempted to just put on my pajamas and crawl into bed.

"Staying inside and watching old movies doesn't count as *fun*, and you know it."

I crossed my arms over my chest, even though Leah couldn't see me. I had one card left to play. I sank to the bed and dropped my voice. "Leah. Everyone from school will be there."

"And what better way to show them that you don't care? You can't let other people dictate your life for you."

I didn't think she was trying to be ironic, so I let her comment slide. Dictating was one thing that Leah was *very* good at.

"You don't leave me much of a choice, you know."

I could almost hear her smile over the phone. "I know." She hung up, and I dropped the phone to the bed and ran my hand over my face.

I could do this. I just had to finish my makeup and wait for Charlie. I used to go to parties with Leah all the time, back when we were sophomores and Mark and Taylor were seniors. And in the beginning of last year, when we'd joined the ranks of upperclassmen and I'd started dating Ben. Right up until Mark had been home on spring break and I'd begged him to take me to a party at Josh Wayne's hunting cabin in the woods even though it was snowing.

Before.

I took a deep breath, pushing down the tightness in my chest, the burning behind my eyes, the rush of blood in my ears. If I started crying now, I'd never stop.

I could do this.

At exactly 8:01, Charlie knocked on the front door. I pulled it open right away, so quickly that he still had his hand in the air.

"Hey," he said. He shoved his hand in his pocket. His eyes didn't leave mine.

"Hi." I didn't know what to do, or if he was still mad at me. I didn't know if it mattered. My chest felt tight again. My hand, almost of its own volition, drifted up and brushed the ring hanging at my chest, and I swallowed. If I had to stand around and chat for another five seconds, I'd freak out and be back in my bed, watching *The African Queen*, faster than I could say *Bogart*.

"Ready?" he asked.

I nodded.

He didn't reach for my hand, just spun on his heel and hurried down the steps. I pulled the door shut behind me and followed him to the car.

He paused, one hand on the car door. "Is everything okay?"

I gave him a tight smile and slid into the seat. "Fine," I lied.

He raised an eyebrow, like he didn't quite believe me. He shut the door and walked to his side of the car. He waited for a few seconds, his fingers on the handle, before shaking his head, opening his door, and climbing into the driver's seat. The engine rumbled to life, and he shifted into reverse.

We didn't speak until I had to point out the road that led to the Standing Stone. He turned down it, and we bumped along until we started to see other cars parked in the grass. Charlie slowed down and pulled off behind a red pickup truck that I knew all too well. He cut the engine and switched off the lights.

I fixed my gaze on the truck's bumper. My hands curled into fists at my sides, and I bit my lip, hard.

Of course *he'd* be here. It was silly to think that he wouldn't. He was here, just like the last time...

I couldn't do this.

Charlie hadn't moved yet either. "Amelia?"

"I'm fine," I repeated, pulling at the door handle. The overhead light switched on.

Charlie blinked at me from behind his glasses, concern written across his face. "Are you sure?"

The weight on my chest was even heavier, threatening to crush me. "That's my ex-boyfriend's truck," I said.

He stared at me. "We don't have to stay. If you want, we can go somewhere else."

Somewhere else. I nodded, my response stuck in my throat.

Leah was going to kill me.

He stared at me for a second more. He sighed and turned the car back on. "Where to?"

I buried my face in my hands. "No," I said.

"No? Tell me what you want to do. I can take you home, I can take you somewhere else, or we can go to the party and try to have a good time. It's up to you. I'll do whatever you want."

Whatever I wanted. I closed my eyes. I wanted a lot of things—I wanted to be home in bed. I wanted my brother to be alive. I wanted to figure out what was happening between Charlie and me.

I wanted to see if we were more than just friends.

I wanted him to kiss me.

I took a deep breath, squared my shoulders, and unbuckled my seat belt, ignoring the tremor in my hands and the weight of my heart in my chest. "Okay," I said before I could change my mind. "Let's do this."

Nineteen

A thumping baseline and the acrid tang of burning wood filled the forest around us as Charlie and I walked the half mile to the Standing Stone. The last rays of the evening sun threw shadows over the narrow footpath. It was just wide enough for us to walk side-by-side—close, but not touching. I crossed my arms over my chest and concentrated on my feet moving over the uneven ground. I stumbled once, and Charlie reached out to steady me. He smiled down at me, and my heart slipped a little more.

Already, a bonfire burned on one of the wide, flat rocks along the water, and music poured from a set of speakers hooked up to the front of someone's four-wheeler. A few people sat on fallen logs around the fire, and a small group danced nearby. Some even splashed around in the shallow water close to shore, stripped down to their bathing suits. Most people, though, were gathered around the keg.

I stopped walking and stared at the people just below us. Now, they were my classmates. Once, most of them had been friends. A low, cold feeling snaked its way through my belly and wrapped icy tentacles around my veins. If I closed my eyes, I could pretend that this was a different party. That I was different.

Warm fingers on the bare skin of my wrist brought me back to the present. Outlined by the setting sun, Charlie stood as the most visible reminder that things had changed.

"Ready?" He stretched his other hand toward me slowly, like I was some sort of wild animal, ready to bolt. Which, I guess, really wasn't that far from the truth. His fingers were warm and solid, and somehow, sometime over the past few weeks, I'd gotten used to this, used to his hands wrapped around mine.

We walked hand in hand down the beach and joined the others. It looked like all sixty or so members of Lafayette High's rising senior class were here, plus a few juniors and most of the class that had graduated in June.

Leah appeared the moment we set foot on the beach and threw her arms around me. She smelled like sweet pea body lotion and cheap beer. "You're here!" she said. "I made the right call on that dress." She turned her attention to Charlie and gave him a long, sweeping look. "You clean up well, New Kid."

"You don't look so bad yourself," he said, and Leah preened. She wore a short white dress, her red and black hair curling halfway down her back, her skin practically glowing. Ransom stood behind her, his hair neatly combed to one side, wearing a vest and slacks. Even with his sleeves rolled up and a red cup in his hand, he looked like some sort of golden-age film star. Already, a gaggle of girls trailed behind him, clustered together and giggling.

"You have an entourage," I told him.

He sighed and tipped back his cup, finishing his beer. "Don't remind me," he said. "They'll get over it eventually."

I recognized one of the girls, a sophomore named Yvette Montrose, from swim team. I thought about waving, but judging by the wrinkle of her nose when she took in the sight of me, she wasn't very interested in renewing our acquaintance. I turned to Charlie. "I'll go get us drinks," I shouted over the music. "Leah can introduce you to everyone."

"We can wait until you get back," he said.

I shook my head. "Trust me," I said. Yvette still stared at me; I could feel her gaze focused on the back of my head like a laser beam. "You're better off without me."

"I'll come with you," Ransom said. He wiggled his cup in front of him. "I could use a refill anyway."

The line for the keg curved around the beach. I skipped it and went straight to the table someone had set up off to the side and filled two cups with Coke. Ransom surprised me by filling his cup with soda too.

At my raised eyebrows, he grinned and pulled a tiny silver flask from his vest pocket. "Rum?" he asked.

I shook my head. "None for me. And none for Charlie, either," I added. I snatched the cups from the table. "He's driving."

Ransom tipped the flask into his cup. "Smart girl." His gaze flicked to my chest, and I fought the urge to lay my hand across the cleavage the dress revealed. I was going to kill Leah. His gray eyes sparkled like chips of steel in the half-light. "That's an interesting necklace."

"This?" I picked up the ring and turned it over in my fingers. The orange light from the fire caught in the sapphire, causing it to blaze bright blue. "Mark gave it to me."

"It's very beautiful," he said. He brushed his fingers against my shoulder. "I miss him."

"I do too." I let the necklace fall back against my skin and turned back to the party, where Leah and Charlie stood encircled by Yvette and her friends. Yvette had her hand on Charlie's arm and laughed and tossed her long, white-blond hair at something he'd said. Something hot and sour rose in my stomach, and I squashed it down. Charlie was allowed to speak to whomever he wanted. Leah and I were practically the only people he knew here, so it stood to reason that other girls would be interested. They could be as interested as they wanted to be.

I was more worried about Charlie being interested in *them.*

Charlie looked up, his eyes catching mine across the clearing, like he'd known I was thinking about him. His smile set my heart fluttering in my chest, and he shrugged out of Yvette's hold. He jogged the few steps to me. I handed him his cup, and he bent down and kissed my cheek, right in front of everyone.

I blinked up at him. "I got you a Coke," I said.

"Thank you," he said. He grabbed my free hand and tugged me over to Leah. Thankfully, Yvette and her friends had scattered.

I shared my soda with Leah, who filled us in on the latest gossip up until the music changed suddenly. "Oh my God," she said. She dropped my cup to the sand and threw her arms in the air. "I love this song!" She wrapped her hands around Ransom's arm. "Let's go dance."

He let her pull him across the sand. Charlie and I stared at each other for half a heartbeat.

"Do you–" he began.

"I guess you wouldn't–" I said, at the same time.

We laughed. "Do you want to dance with me?" he asked.

I bit my lip, trying to hide my smile. "That'd be nice," I said.

He set his cup on the ground and pulled me after Leah and Ransom. The song was fast and upbeat, and when we found our place in the crowd, he put his hand around my waist.

"Is this okay?" he asked, leaning down so I could hear him over the music. "Too much like a date?"

I stepped closer to him and wound my arms around his neck. "I'll allow it."

Leah pulled Ransom up beside us and slithered against him, her highlights burning brilliantly in the firelight, all reds and coppers and golds. We started dancing, moving in time to the music, our bodies swaying together. With every beat of the music, we seemed to get more in tune, more in sync with each other. Charlie's eyes found mine in the darkness, and we stayed locked together.

Then Leah reached out and grabbed my arm, breaking the spell between Charlie and me. I stepped back, away from him. My arms fell to my sides. Her eyes narrowed, and for a moment, I thought she was mad at me. Then I realized she was looking behind me, to someone over my shoulder. "Amelia, behind you."

I whirled around and came face to face with Ben.

This time last year, we'd come to this party together. This time last year, he had been mine.

Right now, though, he didn't look anything like the boy who had taken me to junior prom, the boy who had been my first kiss, my first love. He didn't look anything like the boy who had pleaded with me at the cemetery.

He looked *pissed*.

He stepped close to me, his arms crossed over his chest.

"You have some nerve, showing up here."

My mouth fell open, but Leah came to my rescue. "Back off, Ben. Leave her alone."

"I wasn't talking to her. I was talking to him." He pointed at Charlie. "You're really hanging around with a MacAllister, Amelia?"

Charlie didn't back away. Instead, he leaned close, putting his hand on my waist. "Is there a problem?" he asked.

Ben's eyes went to Charlie's hand, then his face, then flicked back to mine. "Yeah, buddy. There's a problem. You."

"Screw you," I said. My face grew hot, and I balled my hands into fists at my side. "Charlie's here with me."

Behind me, Charlie tensed. "I don't want any problems with you, man."

"Then leave Amelia alone."

Charlie's fingers tightened on my waist. "I don't think that's your call to make," he said, his voice low. I could feel the anger radiating from his touch, and the last thing I wanted was a fight between my ex-boyfriend and my... whatever Charlie was.

I reached behind me and grabbed Charlie's hand. "Let's go, Charlie."

I slammed my shoulder into Ben, and he staggered back. The beer from his cup sloshed over the edge and spilled down my dress, soaking me.

"Hey!" he shouted, but I wasn't listening. "What do you even know about this guy, Mils? Huh?"

I kept my hand wrapped around Charlie's and dragged him off the beach, out to the edge of the woods, away from the party, back to the car. The cool night air wrapped around us. My anger evaporated, and suddenly, I felt like I was going to cry. I just wanted to go home—until I saw that the dirt road where we'd left the car had turned into a parking lot.

"Seriously?" Charlie kicked at Ben's tire. "They seriously had to park right here?" Charlie was completely parked in, with a dark-colored Toyota practically kissing the Mustang's bumper. And we were too far from home to walk in the dark.

I pulled open the passenger side door. "Let's just wait in the car," I said. "Someone has to leave eventually, right?"

The inside of the car was dark, quiet, and warmer than the air outside had been. I went to close the door, but Charlie's arm was in the way. He bent down. "I can't open the driver's side door," he said. "The other car's too close. I'll have to climb in the back."

"Oh," I said. I climbed out of the car, and we traded places, suddenly awkward around each other. He folded the passenger seat down and spread out across the back. Then I was the one standing outside of the car, looking in.

I was pretty sure that somewhere along the way, my mother had warned me about getting into cars with boys.

But Charlie wasn't any boy.

And maybe... maybe I felt like getting into trouble.

To hell with it. I climbed over the passenger seat, shutting the door behind me, and ended up in the backseat, practically in his lap. He shifted out of the way quickly, and I adjusted my skirt. "It'll be easier to talk this way."

His eyes were wide behind his glasses in the moonlight, and they seemed to be fixed on my lips. "Yeah," he said, "We can keep talking."

I scooted closer to him, still feeling bold. "Or not talking," I said.

Charlie closed his eyes. His Adam's apple bobbed in his throat. "Amelia," he said, almost pleading. There was something new in his voice. "I think we need to talk."

I froze. "You have a girlfriend," I said, horrified. "Oh my God, you have a girlfriend."

"What?" His eyes flew open, and his hands found mine in the dark. "No. No. I don't have a girlfriend."

"Oh."

"Did you really think I'd..." He trailed off and shook his head. "There's only one girl I'm interested in."

Oh. I stared at him. He cleared his throat.

"I take it that was the ex?"

I let out a short, bitter laugh. "Yeah. I'm sorry about him."

"It's not your fault he's an ass."

I sighed. "He's not usually like that. I mean, the way we broke up? It was horrible. But I think he honestly thinks he's looking out for me. I'm not really all that popular in school anymore. Maybe... maybe it'd be better if you stayed away from me. You'd make more friends."

He rubbed his thumb over the back of my fingers. "Why would I want to be friends with a guy like that?"

I shook my head. "You don't understand. He can make your life hell."

"I have all the friends I need," he said. "Come here."

He held out his arms, and I fell into them, my head tucked under his chin, my hands spread across his chest, his heart thumping beneath my fingers. "We broke up the night Mark died," I said, after the silence between us had stretched to minutes. I traced my finger in a circle over the fabric of his shirt. "We were at a party, kind of like this. All of the same people were there. Mark was playing some game downstairs. He was taking shots," I explained. "We'd all been drinking." If I closed my eyes, I could almost see it—Leah, perched on Mark's lap, his purple baseball cap on her head. Her arms, winding around his neck.

Charlie's arms tightened around me, bringing me back to the present. "Anyway, I went upstairs to use the bathroom. And I opened the wrong door."

The images came in a flash. Opening the door to the only bedroom in the cabin. Erin West, stretched out on the bed, wearing a hot pink bra. My boyfriend, on his knees in front of her, easing her jeans over her hips.

Her smirk as her eyes met mine, her lips mouthing, *Get out, bitch.*

"Ben was in there with some girl." My voice was small. "So I did what any jilted girlfriend would do. I dumped my beer over his head and ran."

"What a dick," Charlie said.

I closed my eyes and took a deep breath. I was going to tell him all of it. Everything.

All of my secrets.

"I went downstairs, and I found Mark," I said. "I pulled him away from Leah and begged him to take me home. Never mind the fact that he could barely stand up straight, or that he'd been drinking for hours. I made him get in the car."

"Amelia—" Charlie's voice was soft.

"You can't like me. I don't deserve that," I blurted. "I killed him."

It was the first time I'd said it out loud, ever. I'd thought that there would be more tears, more wailing. Instead, an eerie calm settled over me. My fingers found the scar on the back of my arm, the skin so new and pink, the reminder that I'd lived when Mark hadn't. I closed my eyes, and suddenly, I was right back there, lying in the cold snow on the side of the road, the blood running hot down my arm. The night around me had been too still, silent except for the sound of the wind rustling through the branches overhead and my own screams. I still didn't know how I'd ended up there, feet away from the car—if I had crawled out of the wreckage. "It's my fault he's dead."

"Hey." Charlie shifted beneath me. His hand cupped my jaw and tilted my face up to his. His eyes, fierce behind his glasses, glistened in the half-light. "It's not your fault, Amelia."

"Of course it is."

"It isn't."

"I made him do it."

"He chose to do it," Charlie countered. "It was an accident."

I stared at him, my mouth moving soundlessly.

"An accident," he repeated. "It was nobody's fault."

"Drunk driving is always somebody's fault." I couldn't stop the tears, not this time. I curled into Charlie, into the place where his neck met his shoulder. He pressed his face to my hair and let me sob into his shirt. "I miss him so much."

Charlie didn't say anything. He smoothed his hands over my hair, down my back, over and over until his shirt was soaked through and my sobs had subsided into hiccups.

When I spoke next, my voice was so thin and wavering that I barely recognized it. "So when we used that Ouija board, and the letters started spelling out... when I thought..."

I finally looked up at him. His mouth hung slightly open, and he tugged at my hand, pulling me close. He wrapped his arms around me, and I sighed against him. "M, A, R. You thought it was him," he said. His voice rumbled through his chest and echoed through me. "And you thought I was—"

"I know that's not true," I interrupted. "You'd never do that. I know that. For a second, I thought maybe it was him, trying to talk to me. Trying to tell me everything was going to be okay." I took another deep, shaky breath, inhaling Charlie's scent of pine and spice and boy, and curled my fingers into the soft fabric of his shirt. "Telling me that he forgives me."

"You deserve to be happy," he said, tracing his fingers down my spine. "I'm not going to stop whatever this is just because you're blaming yourself over an accident. Because that's what it was. An accident. Your brother—I didn't know him, Amelia. But from what you've said, it sounds like he loved you. And I don't think he'd want you to punish yourself like this."

Charlie was right. Deep down, I knew it. Something tender blossomed in my chest, unfurling and filling me with something warm and new.

Hope.

Hope that the Woman in White would lead us to Mark.

Hope that we'd help him find peace.

Hope that he'd forgive me.

We lay like that for a while, just the two of us, together in the darkness, surrounded by only the sounds of our hearts, thumping like the bass at the party we'd just left.

Twenty

Somewhere behind us, a car door slammed. A bright white light flashed through the window, and I scrambled out of Charlie's lap, blinking against the harsh glare.

"Amelia Rosalind Dupree, that had better not be you in there."

Shit.

I'd have known that voice anywhere. I crawled up to the front seat and climbed out into the cool night air. Uncle Frank waited between Charlie's car and the big brown and yellow SUV that served as the official transportation for the Asylum Sheriff's Department, still wearing his dress uniform, arms crossed over his chest. He stared down at me over his long nose, looking so much like my father that I nearly stumbled. Dave stood behind him, his thumbs tucked under his belt. But instead of a stern frown, he gave me a wink.

"Hi, Uncle Frank," I said. "Hiya, Dave."

"Hi Amelia," Dave said, ever so polite. I thought he was going to say something else, but Uncle Frank glared at him, and he dropped his gaze to the ground.

"Don't 'hi, Uncle Frank' me, little girl. That's the MacAllister boy in there with you? Does your mother know you're here tonight? Is that beer I smell, young lady?" His voice rose with each question, so by the time he was done, he was shouting and I was staring at him, open-mouthed.

Charlie climbed out after me, unfolding to his full height. He grabbed my hand. "Sir," he said, "I can explain."

Uncle Frank fixed him with a withering glare. "Hands to yourself, son."

Charlie let go of me and raised his hands in the air.

"And I don't want a word from you," he said. "My niece here was just going to tell me what was going on. All it takes is one word from her, and I'll have you in the station so fast—"

"Uncle Frank!" I stepped between them, hands outstretched. "Nothing happened."

"You two stink like a brewery, and he had his hands all over you in the backseat of his car. Doesn't look like nothing."

I didn't back down. "Ben Liancourt spilled his beer on my dress. He didn't like the fact I'd brought a date," I explained. "He's still not over me."

Frank seemed to mull this over.

I took a deep breath. "We were trying to leave the party once it got wild, and we were parked in. It's too far to walk, and we figured we'd wait in the car. That's it. Please."

"You could have called your mother," he said.

I held up my cell phone. "With what service?"

He sighed, rocking back and forth on his heels like he was about to do something he really didn't want to. My heart plummeted. "Go get in the truck, Amelia. And take the boy with you."

"Are you kidding me?" I grabbed his arm. "You're arresting us?"

He shook free from my grasp. "Don't start that. I ain't arresting you. We got a call from the party that we need to check out. Just wait in the car." He fixed

Charlie with a stern gaze. "Dave here is going to make sure that you keep your hands to yourself, son."

Charlie gulped.

Frank turned to Dave. "Make sure they don't get into trouble."

Dave straightened his shoulders. "Yes, sir," he said.

"And keep your radio on. I'll call you if I need you."

Frank waited until Charlie and I were settled into the back of the SUV before he headed down the path toward the Standing Stone, flashlight in hand. Charlie sat as far away from me as he could get, his hands folded in his lap. "He's not going to shoot you," I hissed.

"I don't feel like taking any chances."

I rolled my eyes.

Dave settled in the front seat and picked up a thermos and a sandwich sealed in a plastic baggie. "Don't worry about him," he said, glancing back through the partition separating us from him. "Your uncle has everything under control."

"I'm not worried about him," I snapped. I let my head fall back against the seat. "I'm worried about the fact that he may as well have handcuffed us back here. We weren't doing anything wrong, Dave."

"He just wants to keep you safe is all." Dave sipped from the thermos. "You should have seen his face when the call came in over the radio. Another body in the water."

Charlie sat up straighter in his seat. I froze. "Another body?" Charlie said.

Dave took a bite of the sandwich. "Yeah. The girl who called it in was hysterical. Could barely get a word in."

"Who is it?" I asked.

Dave shrugged. "That's what your uncle's going to find out. I think he was just relieved to find you in one piece, is all. Can't blame a man for wanting to protect his niece."

The radio crackled to life before I could respond. "I'm gonna need you out here, Dave," Uncle Frank said. "We've got a blond Caucasian female, DOA. Call it in and come help me secure the area."

Dave crammed the rest of his sandwich in his mouth and opened the door.

"Wait!" I said. I scrambled to the door and pulled at the handle. "You can't leave us locked in here. What if there's some psycho out there? Take us with you."

Dave hesitated. He looked back and forth between me and the radio in his hand. "I don't know."

"Think of all the trouble we could get in back here. Just me and Charlie and this spacious back seat..."

Dave flushed red under the overhead light. Next to me, Charlie choked. I kicked his ankle.

"I guess it's better if I can keep an eye on you," Dave said. "Just stay close. And don't touch anything."

The gentle whisper of the river along the rocky shore had replaced the party's booming music, and my classmates' laughter and shouts had faded into hushed sobs. Uncle Frank stood near the dying bonfire, his hands on his hips. He looked up as Dave stomped the last few feet down the path. His eyes met mine, and he scowled. "What part of 'stay in the car' didn't you understand?" he asked Dave.

"I didn't know if you wanted me to leave them, you know," Dave said, leaning close to Frank and dropping his voice a few notches, "*alone*."

"Hmph." Frank stared at Charlie. "Just stay out of my way, understood?"

But I wasn't listening. Already, I was looking past him to the place where the combined light from the bonfire and the four-wheelers' headlights should have faded into darkness. Instead, a soft glow enveloped the edges of the shadows, wrapping them in a warm, white light.

And stretched out on the ground below the Standing Stone, one arm left to dangle in the water, lay a small girl with long, white-blond hair.

Yvette.

"No." My stomach lurched, and the ring around my neck turned icy cold against my skin. I pushed past Frank, right to the edge of the rock. I stopped just short of reaching her—family ties could only get a girl so far. I didn't think Uncle Frank would look kindly on me contaminating his crime scene.

Rough hands wrapped around my arm and jerked me out of the way. The glow dissipated, leaving us in near-complete darkness. "This isn't staying out of my way," Uncle Frank said. But his voice was gentle, and he studied my face. "Do you know her?"

I nodded. "That's Yvette. Uh, Yvette Montrose. She's a sophomore." I said. I couldn't stop staring at her hand, jerking in the current.

Just like Brit.

I pressed my own hand to my mouth. "She was on the swim team with me."

"All right," he said. "I'm gonna need you to go sit over there with everyone else until we get this sorted out." He gave me a gentle push toward my classmates. Ben glared at me, his arms wrapped around his knees. Charlie already sat on the ground next to Leah, Ransom, and Taylor.

When I joined them, Leah wrapped her arms around me and searched my face with her eyes. "Is she...?" she asked.

I pressed my lips together and nodded.

A low moan escaped her lips. Taylor swore. Ransom only stared out into the night, a frown etched across his mouth. Charlie stared at me, his blue eyes boring into mine from behind his glasses.

"Who is it?" Charlie asked. His eyes didn't leave mine.

"Yvette," Leah whispered. At Charlie's blank look, she added, "The girl who was flirting with you earlier."

The blood drained from his face, and he glanced over his shoulder to where Uncle Frank and Dave stood huddled together. "The little one?"

Leah didn't get to answer. Uncle Frank stepped up in front of the fire. The light from the flames danced over his brown and tan uniform, causing the fabric to look like it slithered across his skin.

"Listen up." His voice boomed through the stillness of the clearing. "No one leaves here until you've talked to either me or Deputy Brune or one of the gentlemen from the county police." A chorus of excuses rose from those gathered around me. He raised his hands. "Listen," he repeated. "I ain't charging any of you with anything. Not with underage drinking, or even trespassing on MacAllister land. We just need to get to the bottom of this."

"Sheriff Dupree, is Yvette really dead?" a girl called out. Hope, one of the other girls from earlier, rose to her feet, voice shaking. Her mascara ran down her cheeks. "Like, really?"

"I'm afraid so," Frank said. "Now. Deputy Brune and I will take your names and addresses, one-on-one, after which you will be free to go. Unless we feel that you have been drinking. In that case, we'll arrange for alternative transport home."

"Yeah, in the back of a cop car," the girl next to me muttered. "No thanks."

"It could be worse," another girl said. "We could be dead. Like Yvette."

"Hey." Ben rose to his feet. "Sheriff Dupree, why do you have to question all of us? None of us killed her. We were all right here. No one left the party." He paused and turned to face me, his face innocent. "Well, almost no one. I think you need to talk to that new kid. Charlie. Yvette was all over him before he took Amelia off to—"

The crowd around us exploded into whispers, every eye fixed on us.

Charlie threw up his hands. "Are you kidding me?"

I knocked Leah's arms from me and surged to my feet. "You're an asshole," I shouted. "You know why we left."

Leah stood next to me. Her red hair blazed in the firelight. "What the hell is wrong with you, Ben Liancourt?"

"Enough!" Uncle Frank stepped forward. He pointed at Ben. "Sit down, son. We're talking to everyone." He pointed at me. "You too, Amelia. Leah. Sit."

I crossed my arms over my chest. "You can't let him—"

"Sit. Down. *Jesus.*" The radio on his belt crackled to life. He grabbed it and stalked away.

I sat. I scooted close to Charlie and put my hand on his knee. "Don't worry about Ben," I whispered. "He's just doing that to get back at me."

A muscle in Charlie's jaw twitched. He stared at Ben. "I'm not worried about him," Charlie said. His voice was strangely even, like he weighed every word as he spoke. "I'm furious."

"Charlie..." *I'm sorry.* I rocked back on my heels. "This is all my fault."

"It's Ben's fault," Leah spat.

"All right," Dave shouted. "You heard the sheriff. Everyone in two lines. Move it."

We ended up in the middle of Dave's line. Ben and his friends were in Frank's. It moved quickly—he and Uncle Frank were only taking names and addresses. It didn't stop the stares at Charlie, though, or the whispers echoing through the clearing. Jack LaPorte, one of Ben's friends, a short, burly guy with a serious case of acne and a letterman jacket, pretended to trip as he walked by. He slammed his shoulder into Charlie's.

"Get the fuck out of this town," Jack snarled. His eyes were rimmed red, like he'd been crying. But so were everyone else's.

Charlie stumbled back with a surprised grunt. His hands curled into fists at his sides, but he didn't move.

He stood, tensed and coiled, like a whip. And then I realized he was waiting for Jack to hit him.

I lunged at Jack. Ransom caught me by the elbow, hauling me back into line.

Jack stared at me. "You're really going to pick a *MacAllister* over one of us?"

"Screw you."

"Don't protect him," Jack said. His voice wavered. "Did you help him kill her? What happened, Amelia?"

Ransom released his hold on my arm. "You know what?" he said. "Go ahead. Hit him. He deserves it."

Jack's eyes narrowed. He took a step backwards into the night. "Suit yourself," he said. He spat a thick white glob at my feet and smirked at me. "Better watch your back."

Twenty-one

Once the county police showed up, Frank had Dave drive Charlie, Ransom, and me home. Taylor and Leah's mother was called, and they waited by the side of the road with almost everyone else who had been at the party. Leah lifted her hand and waved at me, her white dress streaked with dirt. The reflection of the car's taillights cast her in an eerie red glow, like she was covered from head to toe in blood.

I shivered and closed my eyes.

My mother waited for us on the front steps, wearing her pajamas. She stood as Dave pulled into the driveway, her arms crossed over her chest, her mouth pressed into a thin line. I sank down in my seat.

"She does not look happy," Ransom said from beside me.

Dave opened the passenger side door. I braced myself for the scolding I was sure to get. Grounding, without a doubt. I slid outside and stepped onto the driveway.

Before I made it to the yard, Mom rushed down the stairs and threw her arms around me. She drew me tight against her, burying her face in my hair.

"Mom?"

She stepped back and wiped at her eyes. Her hand trembled, betraying just how shaken she was. "I'm so happy you're safe."

Dave cleared his throat from behind us. "Issy, can I talk to you for a minute?"

Mom cast a quick glance at me, her lips pressed into a frown. "Of course," she said, letting him lead her to the other side of the SUV, where they talked in hushed voices.

Charlie stepped beside me. His arm brushed against mine, and I fought the urge to lean into him.

"Grams isn't home," he said. His eyebrows dipped down below the frame of his glasses. "She's never out this late."

I turned and followed his gaze across the yard. The MacAllister House stood still, every window dark, the driveway empty. The light from the full moon glinted silvery-white against the dark metal roof and cast the entire house in an eerie glow not unlike the light that had surrounded Yvette.

"It looks like something out of a horror film," Charlie said, reading my thoughts. "No wonder people think the worst about her."

I stiffened. I'd deliberately never brought up the rumors concerning Ms. MacAllister and the fear of that house that had loomed larger than life over my childhood. "No one really believes all that," I protested.

The corner of his mouth lifted so quickly I almost missed it. "Ben seems to."

"Ben's an idiot."

"You were afraid of her too. I remember." His hand caught mine. "It's okay."

I looked down at my feet. "Charlie—"

The rest of my sentence was cut off by Ms. MacAllister's car pulling into her driveway. She cut the engine and climbed out of the car, followed by

Minion. The dog bounded over to us, his wrinkled folds swaying with every step.

Ms. MacAllister picked her way carefully across the grass. Under the moonlight, her skin was smooth and pale, making her look younger and strikingly beautiful. "What's going on over here?" she asked when she reached us. "Is that Dave Brune?"

"Lilian," my mother called. "I was just about to call you."

Ms. MacAllister arched one perfectly blond eyebrow. "I hope my grandson isn't in any trouble," she said.

Charlie's cheeks reddened, and I took the opportunity to crouch down and rub Minion's belly, since he'd flopped to his back immediately upon reaching us.

Mom and Dave joined us. "He's not in any trouble, ma'am," Dave said. "There was an incident at the party, and the sheriff thought it'd be best if I gave these three a ride home."

"Three? Who else was there?"

I half-turned to introduce Ransom, but only empty air remained in the place where he'd been standing. Ransom had vanished.

"Ransom must have gone inside," Mom said. "He's my intern."

Ms. MacAllister's eyes narrowed. "What did you say his name was?"

"Ransom," Mom answered. "Unusual, isn't it?"

"Quite." She cast her gaze up toward the house. "What kind of incident?"

"Excuse me?" Dave squeaked.

"At the party. What kind of incident was cause for the sheriff to get involved?"

Dave glanced at my mother, like he wasn't sure how much he should say.

Mom didn't have any such reservations. "Another girl drowned in the river, right near the Standing Stone."

A tremor rippled through Ms. MacAllister's body. But then the cool mask slipped back over her eyes, hiding whatever she was really thinking. "How awful," she whispered.

Her gaze never left our house.

I am seventeen years old.

I sit along the river's edge, my hand resting on the slight swell of my stomach, barely noticeable beneath the layers of stays and petticoats under my dress. I am crying, heaving giant, ugly sobs that come from somewhere deep inside of me.

Robert sits beside me, his hands fisted in his hair. After what feels like hours, he whispers, "You're certain?"

Of course I am certain. I wouldn't have told him if I was unsure. I wipe at my eyes, then grab his hand and press it against me. "Do you doubt me?" I hiss at him through my teeth. "Do you accuse me of deceiving you?"

His blue eyes stare into mine, and his mouth moves wordlessly. I throw his hand off me and push to my feet. "I never took you for a coward."

He does not move from his seat along the riverbank, not when I climb onto my horse, and not when I ride away. I let my fingers trace the blue stone of my ring, and deep in my heart, my despair gives way to resolve.

My father will have no choice but to accept his offer of marriage now.

Robert does not come to me that night, nor the next. I lie alone in my bed, staring up at the patterned fabric overhead, my fingers tracing patterns on my belly.

"Don't worry," I whisper to the babe growing inside of me, "your papa will do the right thing."

Only, as the days pass, I grow less and less certain, and the secret I am harboring becomes harder and harder to conceal. My older sister Jeanne corners me in the gardens. "You've grown fat, sister," she says. "What man will want a wife like a pig?"

My face burns, and I try to brush past her, but she blocks my way.

"Perhaps I should rephrase myself. What man will want a wife who is no better than a common whore?"

"Jeanne," I whisper, pleading. "No one must know."

She looks so triumphant in that moment, like she is pleased to finally have something to use against me. "What will Papa say when I tell him?"

"When you tell him what?"

My mother's voice startles us both, and we turn to face her like children caught stealing food before supper.

Jeanne smirks at me and tilts her head. "Tell Maman your dirty little secret, sister."

Every ounce of blood in my veins runs hot, and in that moment, I hate her more than I've ever hated anyone. I slip the ring off my finger, and the magic fills me at once, roaring in my ears.

Before I can think twice, my sister's skirts are on fire. She screams, a horrible scream, and thrashes at the flames that consume the fine silk. Maman, of course, douses the burning dress with a quick flick of her hand. Jeanne collapses to her hands and knees, sobbing.

My mother stares at me then like she has never seen me before, like I am a stranger, like I am not born of her flesh, of her blood.

Like I am someone dangerous.

I spend the next months hidden away from everyone in a small cottage in the country. Papa has banished me from his sight and forbidden me all contact with Robert, the son he had always wanted and had never been given. My only company is the brook that winds through the forest and the grimoires I had secreted from my mother's study.

As the babe inside of me grows, so does my power. I can cast spells without words now, without even using my ring to channel the magic. I am becoming stronger than my mother, than my sisters. Days bleed into weeks, and weeks pass into months, and I speak to no one, see no other human being.

Late in autumn, when the scent of snow is heavy in the air and the forest around me has grown silent and still, my solitude is interrupted. Robert stands in my doorway, his shoulders hunched, his face thin.

He looks like a man haunted.

I have dreamt of this moment a thousand times, but at the sight of him, my mouth goes dry, and I cannot speak. I just stand there, mute, and stare at him.

He falls to his knees in front of me and wraps his arms around my waist, laying his head on my swollen middle. "Forgive me, my love," he begs.

"You abandoned me." My voice sounds strange when I speak aloud.

"I had no choice. I've spent the past months begging your father for your hand." His blue eyes are clouded. "Marin, your situation is dire."

I run my hand along his jaw. "But you're here now," I say. "You're here to save me."

He shakes his head. "If I do that, your father has sworn to disown you and cast me out. We'll be alone and penniless. We'll starve on the streets."

"But we'll be together," I protest.

He shakes his head firmly. "I'm here to warn you, my love. Your father is on his way. He has betrothed you to another man, and there is nothing I can do to stop it."

"You mean there is nothing you will do." I step back, away from him, but he is fast, faster than me, and he takes my hands in his. I snatch them away again. "You would willingly abandon your child, your own blood, to be raised by another man?"

He stands then, and wraps me in his arms. "No. No, Marin. Don't you see? That's why I'm here. Leave the child with me." His voice wavers. "This way, everyone will be taken care of. You will marry a rich man. The child will bear my name and be welcomed in your father's household. He promised me, my love."

"We won't be together."

He takes my face in his hands and tilts his face up to mine. The desperation that shines in his eyes mirrors the dread that snakes its way through me. "We cannot. This is the only way, Marin. This is the only way our babe can have a chance, a life."

I close my eyes and rest my head against his chest. His heartbeat thrums through me. My magic responds almost immediately, rising to meet each beat. It would be so easy, so simple, to just reach out and stop it…

I scramble backwards, away from him, so quickly that my feet go out from under me and I tumble onto the packed dirt floor. Pain shoots through my middle, causing tears to prickle at the corners of my eyes. I reach out for him, and he comes to me, completely unaware of how vulnerable he is, of how dangerous I am.

If I am ready to destroy him, I am capable of destroying anything, including the babe that is ready to make his way into the world.

If God has any mercy, he will take me now, during childbirth, and spare me from making this choice.

It turns out that God has no mercy.
Not for me.

My son comes into the world red-faced and squalling. With trembling hands, Robert wraps him in a soft blanket to keep him warm and places him at my breast, and for just a moment, I allow myself to marvel at how small and perfect he is. I study every part of him—his dusting of brown hair, his blue eyes, already so much like his father's, blinking slowly, his long, thin fingers and ten perfect toes. I press a kiss to his forehead. "Henri," I whisper, "Your maman loves you very much."

And then I do the unthinkable. I hand my newborn son to Robert, to his father, and I say only one word: "Go."

Robert hesitates, shifting Henri in his arms. "Marin—"

I slip my ring from my finger. I flip open the tiny compartment under the stone. There's a pair of sharp scissors on the bedside table, and I pick them up. I carefully snip off a lock of my long black hair. I wind it into a ball, stuff it in the ring, and snap it shut. This too I hand to Robert. "So Henri will remember me," I tell him.

He takes it and slips it into the pocket of his waistcoat. He steps toward me again, but I shake my head.

"Leave now, before I change my mind." I turn my face away from him so he does not see my tears.

After a few minutes, I hear him move away. He pauses in the doorway and says, "I will always love you, you know."

I do not answer him, and as he leaves, my heart does not break.

It turns to stone.

Twenty-two

The ring burned in my hand, searing the skin of my palm. I woke with a start and dropped the ring to the grass beside me.

The grass.

Not my bed.

I sat up with a groan, cradling my hand against my chest. The yard around me glistened in the early-morning fog; my cotton shorts and Ravenclaw Quidditch t-shirt were damp with dew.

I'd walked in my sleep.

Again.

Suddenly, I missed the nightmares I'd had about the accident, the nightmares that had haunted my sleep before Charlie had showed up. They'd been awful, but at least I'd always known where I was going to wake up. Now...

I picked my necklace up by the chain, careful to avoid the ring, and pushed myself to my feet. At least this time, Mom hadn't caught me. Somehow I'd made it outside without tripping the alarm.

Prime sat on the porch, in front of the open door. As I climbed the steps, he meowed at me and wound around my ankles. I herded him inside, closing the door behind us. The house was silent as I trudged upstairs. Mom's bedroom door was closed, and across the hall,

Mark's door—it would always be Mark's door, even if Ransom was staying in the room—was shut tight.

I took the stairs to my room two at a time and turned my computer on.

It was time to do some research.

"I thought about it, and I don't want to see Dr. Gibson," I announced, walking into the living room. "I'm fine."

Mom looked at me from over the top of the magazine she was reading. "Honey..."

I sat down next to her and spread the pages I'd just printed out over the coffee table. I'd spent hours on the computer this morning, and I'd come up with a plan: if my dreams were somehow connected to the woman in the portrait, to the ghost in the woods, and maybe to Mark, I didn't want them to stop. I wanted to help her, so I'd armed myself the best way I knew how to: with the facts.

"Look," I said. "It says right here there's no real treatment for sleepwalking. They suggest hypnosis. *Hypnosis.*" I crossed my eyes and twirled my finger next to my ear.

She set the magazine down and reached for the paper closest to her. "I still think I'd feel better if you went, especially after what happened at the party last night," she said. "There's nothing wrong with getting a little help, and seeing that girl like that..."

I don't want help. There was no way I could say that, though, so I bit my tongue. "Mom, please," I said instead, only pouting a little bit. "I'm fine, I promise. And if it keeps happening, I'll go, okay?"

She softened, just like I'd known she would, as she flicked her gaze over the rest of the pages. "Okay," she agreed. "But promise me that if you sleepwalk again, you'll tell me, and we'll go talk to him."

Fat chance of that. But I hugged her anyway and promised her that I would. She pressed a kiss to my hair. "So I talked to your Uncle Frank this morning," she said carefully. "He told me about you and Charlie."

The blood drained from my face. *Damn him*. "That's interesting," I said, "since there wasn't anything happening that he could tell you about."

"He found you in the backseat of Charlie's car," Mom pointed out, but she seemed more amused than angry.

"Nothing happened."

"Mmhmm." She leaned back against the sofa. "He's the one who drove you over there, isn't he?"

I nodded. "We went together, yeah."

"Are you two dating?"

"No," I said quickly. I felt my cheeks burn—I didn't really want to be talking about this with my mom. "I don't know."

"He's a nice boy," she said.

"He is."

Her smile was downright conspiratorial. "Cute too."

"Mom."

She spread her hands wide, the picture of innocence. "I'm just *saying*, if you were to get another boyfriend, he's a good candidate."

My phone buzzed in my pocket. Mom grinned as I fished it out, and asked, "Charlie?"

I glanced down at the screen and nodded. "He was actually wondering if we could take him to pick up his car," I said.

She nodded and reached for her purse. "I was going to stop by the office anyway," she said. "I'll drop you off on the way."

Overnight, Asylum had slipped from revelry to mourning. Black ribbons appeared hanging on doors and wrapped around on trees like they'd sprouted there in the few hours before the sun rose. By the time Mom dropped Charlie and I off at the turnoff leading to the Standing Stone, a pile of flowers and teddy bears rested against the foot of the tree that marked the dirt road. Heavy rainclouds gathered overhead, like nature itself was mourning for Yvette. "Drive carefully, Charlie," Mom said, eyeing the sky. "It looks like a storm's coming in."

"You too, ma'am," Charlie said.

She laughed. "I'll see you at home tonight, honey," she told me. "Stay dry."

We hurried down the dirt road. Last night, it had been filled with cars. Today, it stood deserted. Charlie's Mustang was the only car left. The first raindrops, big and fat, began to fall, splattering against my hair. I walked faster, eager to get inside the car before the rain soaked us.

"Son of a bitch," Charlie swore. He dropped to his knees and ran his fingers over a long, deep scratch on the driver's side door. "Someone keyed my car."

The raindrops plunked on the roof of the car, hard and cold, coming faster and faster. He kicked at the tire and swore again.

"Let's get in the car," I pleaded. "We're going to get soaked. We can't do anything about it right now."

He jabbed the keys into the lock and opened his door. He leaned across the bench seat and unlocked the passenger door for me. I climbed in just as the sky opened up above us. The rain drummed a fierce cadence on the roof, as furious as the rage in Charlie's eyes.

He slammed his hands on the steering wheel. "Who would do that?"

I shifted in my seat, unsure of what to say. He knew as well as I did that, thanks to Ben, anyone at the party could have done this. He was lucky they hadn't smashed the windows or slashed the tires.

Charlie looked over at me, his face softening. "Sorry," he said. "I shouldn't have lost my temper like that." The engine roared to life, and he flicked the windshield wipers and headlights on.

"It's understandable," I said. "It's not exactly a warm welcome."

The corners of his mouth twitched. "I already had all the welcome I needed."

I twisted my hands in my lap and fought the heat threatening to rise to my cheeks. I didn't know what to say to that, so I changed the subject. "I'm sorry about your car."

He swallowed, his Adam's apple bobbing in his throat, and rested his head against the back of the seat. "This was my grandfather's car," he said after a moment. "My dad's dad. We used to live with him, when I was little, while my mom was in medical school." He ran his hands over the steering wheel. "It's a piece of junk, but it's the only thing I have left of him."

"It's not a piece of junk," I said. I shifted closer to him and laid my hand on his arm. "I think... I think it just needs a little love."

The noise from the rain on the roof nearly drowned out Charlie's soft laugh. He turned towards me, draping one arm across the back of the bench seat. "Are we still talking about the car?"

I grinned at him. "I don't know," I said.

His gaze dropped to my lips; my breath caught. We sat so close that I could count the freckles across his cheekbones. I reached up and let my fingers trace the fine white line of the scar across his chin. He leaned forward into my touch. His eyes fluttered shut.

This was it.

I was going to kiss Charlie Blue.

It seemed to happen in slow motion. He dipped his head, and I lifted my chin, and then my lips were on his, soft and warm and firm all at once, and I felt like I would shatter into a million pieces, like everything that had been holding me together, holding the butterflies at bay, had evaporated.

He responded immediately, dropping his hand to the small of my back, and slowly, hesitantly, parted my lips with his, like he was asking permission.

He let out a little sigh against my lips, like he'd been waiting for this the same way I had.

I pressed myself closer to him and threaded my arms around his neck, and he made a small noise in the back of his throat.

Kissing Charlie was nothing like kissing Ben. Ben had been awkward, even a little aggressive, all demanding tongue and teeth and groping hands that had left me wondering what all the fuss was about.

Now, though—now, I got it.

Charlie's kisses were urgent but sweet, full of tenderness but underscored with a wanting that left me breathless, left me aching, left me leaning back into him again and again and again.

He kissed me like he was drowning and I was his air, like I was the one thing I couldn't get enough of, and I returned it in kind.

Somehow, I ended up in his lap with his hands tangled in my hair and my back pressed against the steering wheel. He left my lips and dropped kisses along my jaw and neck, and I shivered, pressing closer to him.

He buried his face in the curve of my neck and breathed me in. I closed my eyes and rested my cheek against him.

"Wow," he said after a moment. He sounded as breathless as I felt.

I giggled against his soft brown curls.

Wow indeed.

Twenty-three

"Dude," Leah said, studying the selection of ice cream in the freezer aisle. "Cue major movie moment. You made out with the super-hot boy next door in a classic car in the middle of a rainstorm. Cookie dough or triple fudge brownie?"

"Just pick one." I hefted the grocery basket in my arms. It was filled with everything we needed to have a successful girls' night: frozen pizza, whipped cream, maraschino cherries, and rainbow sprinkles. The only thing missing was the ice cream, and Leah had been contemplating flavors for the last five minutes.

"Or," she said, pulling open the freezer door and depositing two pints into the already over-full basket, "we celebrate you growing some balls and jumping his very fine bones, and get both."

"Living on the edge," I joked. I followed her almost all the way to the check-out counter, my sneakers squeaking on the linoleum floor.

Only one line was open. As we approached and the cashier came into view, I reached out and grabbed Leah's arm. "Since when does she work here?" I hissed.

She followed my gaze to the register. Erin West sat on a stool, wearing the hideously maroon-colored cashier's apron like she was modeling a couture dress. Leah tugged the basket from my hands, her eyes soft with concern. "I can handle this. You can go wait outside."

"I'm not going to run away from her," I whispered. "I can't avoid her for forever."

"She kind of ruined your life," Leah pointed out, which was something I didn't need to be reminded of. "Remember?"

Erin had hooked up with Ben the night of the accident. She carried almost as much blame as he did, as I did, for what had happened. But it wasn't Ben I was thinking about now, or even Mark. It was Charlie.

"I can handle it." I took a deep breath, squared my shoulders, and took the basket back from Leah. Maybe I *had* gotten ballsy. I'd told Charlie my secret, I'd kissed him, and the world hadn't imploded.

I wasn't afraid of Erin. Not anymore.

Erin stared at me from the counter as if daring me to run. It was almost unfair how beautiful she was, even under the cheap fluorescent lights that made me look downright ghoulish. Her dark hair hung down her back in perfect princess waves, and her light brown skin was as flawless as ever.

We had been friends once, the three of us. And then in fifth grade, Erin had sprouted boobs overnight and turned popular and left Leah and me for the wolves. And then she had stolen my boyfriend.

For once, I didn't care.

"Hi, Erin," I said, unloading the items from my basket onto the belt. "I didn't know you worked here."

She stared at me like I'd grown a second head, but she recovered quickly. "I didn't know you hung around with murderers," she said. "They say you learn something new every day."

My blood ran cold, and I clenched my fists until my nails bit into my palms. Lunging across the register and punching her too-pretty face would accomplish nothing. I fought to keep my voice steady. "You can take that up with my uncle. You know, Sheriff Dupree? He knows that Charlie had nothing to do with it."

"So you say."

"At least I know what I'm talking about."

She lifted her lip in a sneer. "Loser."

I rocked forward onto the balls of my feet, but before I could move, Leah had stepped in front of me. "Maroon is totally not your color," she told Erin. "It makes you look a little washed out."

"At least I don't look like a hipster reject," Erin snapped, eyeing Leah's short-sleeve floral dress and denim vest. "1993 called. They want their fashion back."

"Are you just going to stand there, or are you going to actually do your job?" Leah picked up a pack of gum and threw it down onto the belt. "I mean, your actual job. Not stealing people's boyfriends."

The corners of Erin's mouth twitched, and she smirked at me, but she started scanning our food. "Other girls just make it so easy," she said, and I felt myself flush. But I was over blaming myself for what had happened, and I wasn't going to give her the satisfaction of freaking out right here. I was over it. Over Ben.

Leah, though, was just getting started. It was like she'd been waiting for ages to unleash on Erin, and now that her chance was here, she wasn't going to let it go. "Newsflash, honey. *They* aren't the easy ones," she said, running her mom's debit card through the scanner so violently I thought she'd crack it in half.

"Bitch," Erin spat. She practically threw our food into bags, apparently unable to think of a comeback. I grabbed the bags and darted for the car, Leah right on my heels. I was caught halfway between feeling mortified and feeling free.

Leah draped herself over the steering wheel of her Prius. Her shoulders shook with laughter. "Did you see her face? I've been waiting *months* to say that to her."

I managed a smile, even though all I could hear was Erin's insinuations about Charlie. But I played along for Leah's sake. "She looked like she wanted to strangle you with her bare hands."

Leah adjusted the rearview mirror, then grinned back at me. "She'd have to catch me first."

I flopped back on the sofa in my basement, arms folded over my stomach. "No more food," I groaned, looking at the detritus strewn over the coffee table. "Ever." It was almost eleven, and between the amount of ice cream I'd consumed and the horror movie we'd watched, I was feeling a little ill.

Leah was sprawled out on the floor, watching as Audrey Hepburn chased Cat through a downpour. *Breakfast at Tiffany's* was our go-to movie to watch so we could sleep after we'd scared ourselves silly. "The third sundae may have been overkill," she agreed, her hands over her face. "We're going to get so fat."

"It was worth it," I said.

She rolled over, propping herself up on her elbows. "So," she said. "What was it like? Kissing Charlie, I mean."

Incredible. Amazing. Breathtaking. I picked at a loose thread along the hem of my tee-shirt. "It was nice," I said.

And it had been nice. I liked him—I knew that much from the way my insides turned into butterflies whenever he touched me, and how I felt warm all over when I caught him looking at me, and the way the touch of his lips set my blood on fire.

"Nice." Leah's voice was flat. "Puppies are nice. This ice cream? It's nice. Kissing that boy? That should definitely be something more than *nice.*"

I giggled. Like actually flat-out giggled. "It was perfect," I whispered. "I like him a lot, Leah."

"I knew you did," she said. "Just say it, I was right. Again."

"You're insufferable."

"And right."

I threw my pillow at her.

Heavy footsteps thudded down the basement stairs. "Hey, Amelia, do you..." Ransom trailed off as he rounded the corner and came into sight. "Hi, Leah."

Leah sat straight up and ran her fingers through her hair. "Hey," she said. "Where've you been all night?"

"Reading," he said. He didn't take his eyes from Leah as he spoke to me. "Amelia, do you mind if I put the ice cream away? You left it out on the counter."

I frowned. I could have sworn I'd put the ice cream back in the freezer before we came downstairs.

"She can put it away," Leah answered before I had a chance to open my mouth. "Can't you?"

I rolled my eyes, but stood up. "I'll be *right back*," I said. "So no funny business."

Ransom, at least, blushed. "I can do it." But he didn't move.

Leah grinned wickedly.

I grabbed our bowls and made sure to stomp up the stairs. "Right back!" I repeated. "I'll be gone for all of two seconds!"

"Take your time," Leah called after me.

I flipped the kitchen light on. There wasn't so much as a towel out of place, let alone a melting tub of ice cream. Despite myself, I smiled. Ransom wanted get Leah alone. Was there something in the air?

I rinsed our bowls in the sink and gazed out the window toward the MacAllister House. Charlie's bedroom light was on, and my smile grew. Maybe I'd be nice and leave Leah and Ransom alone for a few minutes.

I fished my phone from my pocket and scrolled through my contacts until I found Charlie. He answered on the first ring.

"Hey," he said. His voice was soft, like he was smiling. "I was just thinking about you."

"Oh?" I tried to play coy. "Good things, I hope."

"Always." He was silent for a moment. "I had a really good day yesterday."

"Me too." I pressed my fingers against the glass. Only about a hundred yards separated us, yet he felt so far away. "I'm sorry I didn't get to see you today."

"I thought you were having a girls' day with Leah?"

"I was. And then Ransom crashed it," I said. "I think he likes her."

"You think?" Charlie laughed. "He definitely does."

"Amelia!" Leah's voice carried up the stairs. "We have an idea!"

"Hold on," I said to Charlie. "Leah apparently has an idea."

Leah appeared at the top of the stairs with Ransom right behind her. I held my hand over my mouthpiece and waited.

"Is that Charlie?" she asked, and when I nodded, she brightened. "Perfect! We'll need him. Tell him to get over here."

"Need him for what?"

She looked back over her shoulder at Ransom. "A séance!" she said. "Have him bring that creepy old Ouija board with him."

My necklace prickled against my skin. "Did you hear that?" I asked Charlie.

"Loud and clear," he said. "I'll be over in ten."

Twenty-four

Charlie stood on the porch, one hand shoved in the pocket of his jeans, moonlight reflecting from his glasses, the Ouija board tucked under his arm. "Hey," he said.

I leaned against the door and didn't try to stop the big, goofy smile from spilling across my face. "Hey," I replied.

"Come on, lovebirds." Leah closed her hand around my arm. "These spirits aren't going to wait all night."

Charlie rolled his eyes at me, and I bit back my laugh. I stepped aside and let him pass through the doorway. We trooped downstairs to the basement, where Ransom had arranged every candle we'd found in the house in a wide circle on the rug.

"Did you bring the board?" he asked.

Charlie held up the battered box in reply. "As requested," he said. He set the box down in the middle of the circle and took in the candles—the tall tapers Leah had snatched from the dining room table, the votives from the fireplace, even the hot pink, pomegranate-scented candle from my bathroom—nestled in the inch-high orange shag rug. "This looks like a fire hazard."

Leah adjusted the fringed scarf she'd wrapped around her head, fortune-teller style. "It's a séance, Charlie. You need candles."

"Uh-huh. And there's a reason we couldn't do this on a table?"

"It'll be fine." Ransom sat on his heels and produced a beat-up silver Zippo lighter from his pocket. He flicked it to life with a practiced hand and lit the candles closest to him. Leah switched off the light, and I blinked against the sudden darkness—in the candles' soft glow, everything but Ransom, Charlie, and the Ouija board receded into shadow.

I stepped over the still-unlit candles closest to me and settled cross-legged on the rug next to Charlie. He rested his hand on my knee and leaned into me.

"Are you going to be okay with this?" he whispered, his lips brushing against my ear. "You freaked out last time. Just say the word, and we'll stop, okay?"

Another time, maybe, if we'd been alone, surrounded by candlelight, his words might have taken a different meaning. Maybe I would have blushed, or grinned up at him and brought my lips to his.

But not tonight.

Tonight was all business.

"I'll be okay," I whispered back. My fingers found the ring on my necklace, and I slid it back and forth over the chain. I would have said more, but Leah sat down on my other side.

"So, are we going to do this or what?" she asked. She opened the box and picked up the small wooden planchette. She handed it to me and pulled the board from the box. I closed my fist around it, the wood cool and smooth in my palm. Leah turned the box upside down and set the board atop it.

"Just a second." Ransom finished lighting the last candle and joined the circle. The flames danced as he stepped over them, sending flickering lights over the walls. He dropped down so he sat directly across the board from me. "Okay," he added. "Let's do this."

I set the planchette on the board. Everyone else leaned forward and placed their fingers on the wood alongside of mine—Leah's to my left, Charlie's to my right, and Ransom's opposite me. I stared down at it, half-expecting it to start moving on its own.

"Go ahead," Ransom said. His voice was low, but his eyes bored into mine. "See if anyone's here."

I closed my eyes and took a deep breath. What were the chances we'd contact anyone again? What were the chances that the Woman in White was hanging around, just waiting for us to summon her?

What were the chances that *Mark* was around, waiting for me?

I had to do this.

I opened my eyes and spoke in a clear, firm voice. "Spirits, we summon you. Will anyone communicate with us?"

The planchette twitched under our fingers. Beside me, Leah's breath hitched. I leaned forward. "Is someone here?" I asked.

Slowly, the guide crawled across the board. Yes.

"Who's doing that?" Leah asked. "You can't move it yourself."

"It's a spirit," Ransom said. "It's actually working."

Leah chewed on her lip. "I'm going to kill you if you're messing with me," she told Ransom.

"I swear I'm not," he said. He dropped his gaze back to the board. "What is your name?"

The planchette quivered. Then, slowly as before, it crawled towards M.

My breath caught. I wasn't going to fall for this again. I wasn't.

"M-Mark?" Leah's voice shook. "Mark?"

The planchette stilled, then drifted in the other direction. No.

Pain bloomed in my chest, as sharp as a knife, even though it was the answer I had expected. Maybe it wasn't as sharp as the last time we'd done this, but it was still there, my heart torn open and raw. Charlie leaned against me, his shoulder pressed to mine. He was warm and solid and real. I took a deep breath. I knew what I had to ask.

"Is this Marin?" I asked. Ransom's head snapped up, and he stared at me, his mouth agape. Something hard glinted behind his eyes. It took everything I had to leave my fingers on the guide and not reach up and grasp the ring around my neck.

Yes.

"Are you the woman in the portrait?" Charlie spoke quietly, his voice steady despite the slight tremble that ran through him.

Yes.

"Amelia," Leah hissed, "look at your necklace."

I glanced down. The stone set in the middle of the ring glowed faintly, an impossibly pale, pulsing blue. I reached up, but the moment my fingers touched the stone, they burned like I'd stuck my hand into a fire. I cried out and yanked my hand back to my chest. My eyes watered, and I blinked away tears. That *hurt*.

"Does the ring belong to you?" I asked. "Is that why you're here?"

Yes.

I glanced through the circle of candles to the pitch-blackness beyond. The darkness seemed to press in towards us. Like something was out there. Waiting.

Watching.

"What do you want?"

The planchette darted furiously around the board, stopping over each letter for only a moment before moving on to the next. I leaned closer, barely daring to breathe.

And then it was still, sitting in the middle of the board, unmoving, and all I could hear was the blood rushing through my veins and the echo of the words spelled out letter by letter on the board below us.

H.E.L.P. M.E.

I snatched my hands back away from the planchette. Leah glanced up at me, her brown eyes wide.

"How?" she asked. "How can we help you?"

The flames around us roared to life, and the planchette spun in a circle under their fingers, faster and faster. Leah's eyes rolled back into her head until only the whites showed. She gave a rattling gasp and slumped to one side.

"Leah!" I knelt over her. I felt for a pulse, but her skin was cold to the touch. Even under the warm, flickering candlelight, she'd taken on a deathly-white cast.

She looked... she looked...

I turned back to Ransom and Charlie. Charlie's mouth hung open, his eyes wide behind his glasses. Ransom sat, frozen. Unblinking.

"End it!" I shrieked. "Stop it!"

Charlie moved first. He grabbed the still-spinning planchette and slammed it down on the board, right over the letters across the bottom that spelled out GOOD BYE. The room plunged into darkness, and Leah let out a soft moan. She shuddered once under my hands. When her eyes opened again, they glowed blue, bluer than Charlie's, the only light in the still-dark room. Charlie cursed and surged to his feet.

"Where's the light switch?" he asked. A muffled thump and a curse followed. Before I could answer him, he added, "Never mind."

Light flooded the basement, chasing away the darkness. Leah lay pale and still on the bright orange carpet, eyes open and staring.

"Leah?" I grasped her shoulders and shook her, hard. She stared back at me, unblinking, like she couldn't really see me. I tightened my grip on her shoulders. "Come on, this isn't funny."

Ransom nudged me out of the way. He cupped her face in his hands and leaned into her like he was going to kiss her—if she was coherent right now, she'd be having a heart attack.

"Leah," he said firmly, "snap out of it."

She tried to writhe away from him, but he pulled her closer. "Snap out of it," he repeated.

She closed her eyes and went limp. He grabbed her quickly, wrapping his arms around her and pulling her into his lap. Her eyes fluttered open—thankfully back to their normal brown. She blinked up at him, confusion written across her face. Then her lips tilted up into a large, self-satisfied smile. "Hey, handsome," she said.

Ransom's ears turned red. He let go of her abruptly and moved to the couch, putting several feet of distance between them.

She scrambled to keep herself from falling flat on the carpet. "Did I miss something?" she asked.

"You don't remember?" I struggled to keep my voice even.

She squinted up at me. "What do you mean? We were doing the Ouija board, and we were getting answers, and..." she trailed off, frowning. "And then I woke up."

"And then you turned freaky," Ransom said from his seat on the sofa.

"Freaky in a good way?" Leah looked like she was torn between being scandalized and being proud of herself.

"Like Exorcist-level freaky," I said. "Minus the head-spinning and puking."

She chewed on her lip. "Oh."

"You're feeling okay, though?"

She nodded. "Totally fine. Just hungry." Her stomach gurgled in agreement, and she gave a tiny grin. "Starving, actually."

I raised my eyebrows. "Seriously? You ate an entire pint of ice cream."

"Apparently being possessed by a ghostly presence really works up the appetite," she said. "Who's up for a trip to Ollie's?"

Twenty-five

Help me.

I turned the words over in my head over and over again. *Help me. Help me.* HELP ME. The same words we had found carved into the tree at the ruins weeks ago.

Words I'd thought had been left by my brother.

I picked at my cheese fries while Leah worked her way through the mountain of pancakes on her plate. Ollie's Diner was the only place in Asylum that was open 24 hours. There wasn't anywhere else we could have gone to talk.

But we weren't even talking, not really. The four of us had barely said ten words to each other since we'd left my house.

I sat in the booth next to Charlie as he inhaled a plate of toast, five strips of bacon, and three eggs. And half of my cheese fries. In less than twenty minutes. Even Ransom watched him eat with a look approaching reverence.

"Do you think we should do it?" I dragged my fry through the bright orange cheese in the basket in front of me.

Leah stopped with her fork halfway to his mouth. She looked at me, then down at her plate, then back to me, and set the fork full of pancake down. "Like, with the ghost?"

I nodded, keeping my eyes on the French fries. "She asked for help."

Ransom twirled his straw in his drink, sending the ice cubes clinking against the glass. "I think we should talk about it before we do anything stupid."

"So talk," I said. I pushed the fries away from me and leaned forward, my elbows on the table. "Do you think we should do it?"

"I think we don't even know what that means yet," he said. He glanced over his shoulder, his gaze traveling over the empty booths and the lone waitress reading a magazine at the counter, and dropped his voice before continuing. "How do you even help a ghost?"

"Most ghosts have unfinished business, right?" Charlie asked. "That keeps them from passing over? Maybe we have to figure out what hers is."

"It won't be that easy, though. No one will even admit she existed," I said.

Across the table, Ransom frowned. My hand found the ring, *her* ring, hanging around my neck. I slid it back and forth on the chain, lost in thought, while Charlie filled Leah and Ransom in on our discovery of the painting and our inquiries at the Historical Society. What had happened to that beautiful girl to turn her into a ghost?

Robert.

It was another whisper from my dream. I didn't even realize I'd said anything aloud until Charlie stopped mid-sentence and asked, "Who's Robert?"

"She loved him. In the dreams," I added, glancing at Leah. "He'd come back from the war with her father to live with them. He was older than her, and they weren't supposed to be together. He was her baby-daddy, for lack of a better term." I ran my hand through my hair and let out a breath. "I sound crazy, don't I?"

Charlie reached over and captured my fingers, pulling them off the ring. "I don't think you're crazy."

Leah held up her hand. "Hold up. *What* dreams? I thought the nightmares had stopped?"

"They have. Sort of. These... well, they're not about the accident. They're... different. Like they're someone trying to tell me something, you know? They happen whenever I sleepwalk."

She leaned back against the red leather of the booth. "And you didn't think to mention this when I asked about the sleepwalking?"

I sighed. "No. The first one was only a weird dream, right? About a pretty, dark-haired girl dressed up like Marie Antoinette. It was just a dream," I said. "Or at least, that's what I thought. But then I had two more. The same girl, just a little older. She had a baby in the last one, but gave him up because her family didn't approve." I rubbed my hand over my face and looked at Charlie. "She's the girl from the portrait, Charlie. I think I've been dreaming about Marin."

Ransom drummed his fingers on the table. "You've been having dreams about the ghost? You think that she's been communicating with you?"

I shrugged. "I don't know. They could just be dreams."

"We don't have much more to go on right now," Leah said, "so let's say they mean something. Where do we start?"

Charlie adjusted his glasses. "We start with this guy. Robert. Do you think he had something to do with... whatever happened to her?"

They were serious. They believed me, and that alone meant more than I could say.

"I don't know." I ran my thumb over the back of Charlie's hand. I felt tired suddenly, so tired. I'd barely slept over the past two days, and it was catching up with me. "I think we need to find out more about her.

Who she was, why she was here? What happened to the baby? Maybe then we'll be able to help her." I turned in my seat, searching for the neon wall clock over the door. "I wonder what time the library opens."

Leah gave me a small smile. "We have time. If she's been dead for two hundred years, a few more days won't hurt her."

She was right. I *knew* she was right, but I still felt jittery, anxious.

Charlie let go of my hand when the waitress came by with our check. She glanced over the four of us, her eyes sweeping the table before her gaze settled on me. "I knew your brother," she said abruptly. "I was really sorry to hear about what happened to him. You holding up okay?"

I vaguely recognized her—I thought she'd been in my brother's class, making her a senior when I was a sophomore. Sarah? Susan? Sam? Sam. Her name was definitely Sam. She'd been one of the pretty girls, one of the ones who'd hung off Mark all through high school, though he had never brought her home. "Fine, thanks," I mumbled.

She stared at me for a moment longer before she nodded and left, her tennis shoes squeaking on the linoleum floor.

"Are you?" Charlie asked.

"Am I what?"

"Okay. You look... I don't know. Tired."

"Exactly," I said. "I'm just tired."

Charlie returned to his pancakes. He chewed for a few minutes, thinking. "You know," he said, stabbing his fork into the air towards me, "I just keep coming back to the ring. If it's hers, how did it end up in your brother's pocket?"

"The ring is hers?" Leah frowned. "How do you know that?"

"The girl in the portrait was wearing it," Charlie explained. "It's the same."

I slipped the chain over my head and set it in the middle of the table. It looked so out of place on the linoleum and chrome tabletop, like a relic from a bygone era. Which, when I thought about it, it was. But it was mine now too. It belonged here, with me. "I don't know how he got it."

Ransom stared down at the ring, his eyebrows drawn close together. He looked like he wanted to say something, but he chewed on his lip instead. When he finally did speak, he lifted his eyes to mine. "May I?"

I pushed it towards him. "Be my guest."

He picked it up and turned it over in his fingers, the blue stone blazing under the florescent light. "Have you tried opening it?"

I leaned forward, my elbows on the table. I'd tried three times this morning after I'd woken up. "It's stuck," I said.

"Opening it? What are you guys talking about?" Leah set her fork down.

"It's a poison ring. There's a tiny hinge here." He reached across the table and grabbed her hand. He pressed her fingertip to the gold that edged around the sapphire. "Feel it?"

"A poison ring? Was she murdered?" Leah asked.

Ransom shook his head. "Not necessarily. It just means there's a tiny compartment under the stone. Some people used it to hold poison, yeah, but mostly they held love notes or a lock of hair. There are a few in the museum," he added.

"That's what she did in the last dream." I frowned and pushed at the stone. "She flipped it open and put a lock of hair in here." I handed it to Charlie. "You try. I'm afraid to break it."

"No pressure," he muttered under his breath. He brought the ring up to eye level and squinted at it, his head tilting to the side. "There's no latch that I can see. So it should just flip up?" He pressed his thumb under the stone. It didn't budge.

Ransom held out his hand. "Can I take another look at it?"

Charlie passed it to him, and Ransom turned the ring over again in his hand. Leah leaned close to him, practically draping herself over his shoulder. "Maybe there's a reason why it won't open," she said.

Ransom lifted an eyebrow. "You think this is what she wants? For us to open the ring up?"

Leah shrugged. "It was hers, wasn't it?"

Ransom seemed to consider this carefully. His eyes met mine. "This might sound crazy," he said.

"Yeah, because nothing else has been remotely strange this evening." I waved my hand at him. "What is it?"

"Remember those books we found in that room at your house, Charlie?"

Charlie nodded, looking unsure.

"I did some poking around. One of them looked familiar, like I'd seen it before. So I did an Internet search and..." he trailed off.

"... and?" Leah prompted.

"They're spell books," Ransom said. "Grimoires, actually. They were used for magic—I saw one at the British Museum the last time I was in London. It was almost identical to the one you picked up, Amelia. The one with the hands."

The image of the severed hands dripping blood down the page swam before my eyes, and I set down the fry I'd picked up, suddenly feeling queasy. "What are you saying?"

Ransom slid the ring to me, a gold and blue flash across the speckled gray tabletop. "I'm saying maybe you're having those dreams for a reason. Maybe we found *that room* for a reason. Maybe the only way to open that ring up is with magic."

Twenty-six

I hovered on the landing, one hand wrapped around my necklace, while Charlie and Ransom went through the books in the hidden room in Charlie's attic. Sunlight streamed through the tiny window that faced the woods. It sparkled over the dusty, broken glass that littered the floor, glass I hadn't noticed the last time we'd been up here. An ancient lamp lay smashed on the ground beside the bed, its oil long since soaked into the floorboards. The papers tacked to the wall rustled with every step the boys took, making it sound like the room was alive. Like it was breathing.

I shivered. Part of me wished that Leah was here, just because she'd make me look brave by comparison. But she had to work a double shift today, leaving me alone with the boys.

"Are you just going to stand there all day?" Ransom called from inside the room. "We could use your help."

Charlie turned to look at me, his blue eyes serious behind his glasses. "You can stay out there if you want to," he said. "We'll manage."

"We'll manage faster if she's in here," Ransom said. He stared at the books strewn over the floor, his arms crossed over his chest. "Three sets of eyes are better than two."

Charlie rolled his eyes. "It's up to you, Amelia."

"It's fine," I said. I pasted on a smile and tried to hide the deep breath I took as I stepped over the threshold. The ring stayed cool against my chest, thankfully.

I pushed aside an open book with my toe. Its pages swelled with humidity, the ink smeared. Shards of glass from the lamp hit the floor with a tiny clink. "What are we looking for?" I asked.

"Anything we can actually read," Ransom said. He paged through one of the books on the desk. "One of these books has to have some sort of useful information in it."

I picked up another book and flipped it open. The paper was thick and cloth-like under my fingers, and page after page was covered in the same carefully slanted script. I picked a page near the middle at random.

To ensuyre the dezire of a suitor, it read. I snapped the book shut and blushed. At least I didn't need *that*.

"Something called 'Magic for Beginners' might be useful," Charlie said. "Think that's tucked away in here?"

Ransom held up his hands, palms out. "Dude, I'm just trying to help you out here. There's no need for that."

Charlie snorted. He tossed another book onto the pile he'd started on the bed. "I don't know how this is going to help. Magic isn't real."

"Ghosts aren't either, remember? I don't see you questioning that."

Charlie shrugged. "It's just all seems a little too convenient, doesn't it? The ghost, the Ouija board, this room... I have a bad feeling about this."

I laid my hand on Charlie's arm. "We have to try," I said. "She needs our help. If it works..."

I left the rest of the sentence unsaid. If this worked, if we could help Marin find peace, then maybe, just maybe, I could find Mark.

And then he could forgive me.

In the end, we'd carried six grimoires downstairs. I settled myself cross-legged on Charlie's bed, and Ransom took the desk chair. Charlie closed the door for a moment before he sat on the bed beside me, resting his hand on my knee. "Okay, Mr. Historian," I said to Ransom, "what now?"

Ransom picked up the book on the top of the pile and tossed it to me. I caught it and coughed at the cloud of dust that rose from its pages. "Now we read."

We spent the next few hours that way, poring over the old books until our hands turned black. The sun sank lower and lower in the sky. Somehow, Charlie ended up sprawled over the bed, his head in my lap. I ran my fingers through his hair absently, and his eyes fluttered closed, the way they had right before he kissed me. For the millionth time that afternoon, I wished that Ransom would take the hint and leave us alone. Charlie and I hadn't spent any time together—*alone* time together—in the three days since we had made out in his car.

Ransom, however, stayed put in the desk chair, occasionally mumbling under his breath and scrawling notes in the notepad he'd found in the mess spread across Charlie's desk.

Focus, I reminded myself. I forced my eyes back to the page in front of me. The cramped handwriting had faded over the years to a light brown, and as hard as I tried, I couldn't keep my mind on the letters in front of me. Page after page was filled with either recipes for potions or complex instructions for spells, but there wasn't a single clue as to how any of it actually worked or how any of this would help our ghost. I was just about to throw the book in my hands across the room when Ransom stiffened at the desk.

"I think I've found something," he said. He twirled the chair around to face us. "From what I can tell, a spell needs three things to work: intent, focus, and power." He tapped the edge of his pen against the open book on his desk.

Charlie sat up and smoothed down his hair. "Explain."

"Well, intent is simple, right? You have to have a goal in mind. So, I want to levitate this pen. That's my intent," he said. He set it down on the desk, then leaned over the book. "The words act to focus my intent, and the power is the energy I put into it. I think."

"Uh-huh," I said, resting my chin in my hands. I couldn't help feeling a bit skeptical. "So you're just going to levitate that pen, just like that?"

"Not me. You're going first, Amelia." He tossed the pen at me. It bounced off my open hand and onto the quilt beside me.

"What? Why me?"

"Because I'm a gentleman." He handed me the book, and I looked down at it, then at the pen, before looking back up at him. "Just relax and say the words."

"Okay." I took a deep breath, then squinted down at the spell. It was simple, only one word, repeated three times: *Tōfliete, tōfliete, tōfliete*. They weren't in English—at least not any English that I recognized. There were too many vowels. "How do I even *pronounce* that?"

He wheeled close, leaning over the page. "It's Old English. See the accent marks? I've only taken one course that used it, but I'm pretty sure it's pronounced like to-flea-tuh."

I straightened my back and stared at the pen, feeling slightly ridiculous. "To-flea-tah," I said, my mouth struggling to form the unfamiliar word.

Ransom held up a hand. "It's to-flea-*tuh*, he said. "Not *tah*. Tuh."

"Do you like sounding like Hermione Granger?" Charlie asked, half-smiling.

Ransom's face was blank. "Who?"

"Harry Potter? Boy wizard? Seriously?" Charlie's voice rose with each question. He shot me a wide-eyed look. "Dude, how did you survive childhood?"

"I don't really read fiction," Ransom said, completely serious. "There are enough fascinating stories that actually happened. I don't need to bother with made-up ones."

"They're movies too," I said. "I know you watch movies."

Ransom pressed his lips into a firm line and gestured to the pen and book in my hands. "Can we just get on with this, please?"

"Fine." I straightened my shoulders, trying to get serious. "To-flea-*tuh. Tðfliete, tðfliete.*"

Nothing. Not so much as a twitch. I sighed, surprising myself by feeling disappointed. I held the book out to Charlie. "Your turn."

"It's not going to work," he said.

"Just try it." Ransom leaned forward in his chair, his elbows on his knees, eyes bright. "Just one try."

"Fine." Charlie stood up, set the book down on the bed next to the pen, and stretched his hand out, like a priest performing a benediction. He breathed in. Out. He closed his eyes and frowned, concentration settling over his face.

I drew my knees to my chest and watched, hardly daring to breathe.

It wasn't going to work. It didn't work for me.

It couldn't work. Why would he be any different?

I wanted it to work.

Charlie took a deep breath. His eyes snapped open, and he said, "Tðfliete. Tðfliete. Tðfliete." The tone in his voice changed, deepened, grew more commanding with every repetition.

The pen didn't move.

But the book twitched once, so quickly that I thought I'd imagined it. "Again," I whispered, barely able to find my voice. "Charlie, do it again."

He stretched his other hand out over the book. He looked fiercer in that moment than I'd ever seen him, his brows furrowed, his stare intent on the book, like he could force it to move through sheer force of will. "Tðfliete. Tðfliete. Tðfliete," he repeated.

The book flew all right.

It lifted right off the bed and crashed through Charlie's window, shattering it, before soaring out into the yard. I shrieked and covered my head to protect myself from the glass flying in every direction. Ransom leapt from his chair with a shout, his fist pumping in the air.

Charlie sank down to the floor, staring at the broken window. I lifted my head, sending shards of glass tinkling to the bed. I stood up gingerly, trying to avoid slicing myself. If I hadn't seen it, hadn't heard it, hadn't felt it, I didn't think I would have believed what had just happened.

Charlie had done *magic*. It had worked.

I crouched down next to him. "Charlie," I said, putting my hand on his arm. "Are you okay?" His skin was cold to the touch, and he looked like he was ready to faint. He glanced up at me, then back to the window, and burst out laughing.

He laughed until tears spilled down his face. He wiped them away, his shoulders shaking. "It worked," he said, and the awe in his voice echoed the feelings rushing through me. I threw my arms around him, and he hugged me tightly. I burrowed my face along the curve of his neck, breathing in his scent. "How did that work?" he asked, his voice muffled against my hair.

"Now we just have to figure out how to explain *that*," Ransom said. He sounded amused. "Shall we blame it on the idiots at the party who tried to get you arrested for murder?"

Charlie hesitated for a moment. "That's a little extreme, isn't it?"

Ransom shrugged. "They already keyed your car. It's a logical escalation."

"It sounds like something Ben would do," I added.

Charlie looked down at me. His fingers came away red, and he winced. "You're bleeding."

I hadn't even noticed. I lifted my own hand to my forehead, which hadn't hurt until I'd known that I was cut. Now, though, it stung under my touch. "Shit," I said, looking at Charlie. Blood, *my* blood, was smeared down Charlie's neck too, where my face had been. "It's all over you too."

"How did it feel?" Ransom asked. He leaned forward on his toes, bouncing, like he couldn't contain himself. "Do you feel different?"

"I don't know." Charlie didn't take his eyes off my face. "Does that hurt?" he asked me. He climbed to his feet and held out his hand. I took it and let him pull me to my feet.

"What do you mean, you don't know?" Ransom asked. I stiffened at his tone—it wasn't triumphant anymore, or celebratory. It was cold and impatient.

Anger flashed in Charlie's eyes, letting me know that I wasn't the only one who had noticed the change in Ransom's voice. He tugged me toward the door. "What I mean is, my girlfriend is bleeding, so let me help her. I'll figure out how I *feel* later."

Ransom opened his mouth to reply, but his phone chirped, interrupting whatever he was going to say.

He pulled it from his pocket and scowled down at the screen. After a long moment, he pushed past us and headed for the stairs. "I'll get going, then," he said, his voice even chillier than before. "I'll let you two have some alone time."

And then he was gone, the front door slamming behind him.

Beside me, Charlie let out his breath. "What the hell is his problem?" he asked. He led me down the hall to the tiny bathroom. "Are you okay?"

I nodded. "I'll live," I said.

I hopped up on the vanity, letting my feet swing, while Charlie dug in the linen closet for a first aid kit. He set it on the counter next to me and pulled out a bandage, antibacterial cream, and a packet containing a small alcohol wipe. Behind his glasses, his blue eyes were serious as he tore open the packet and stepped close to me.

Gently, he cupped my chin with one hand and tilted my face up to his. My heart pounded in my chest as his gaze dropped to my mouth, and it was all I could do not to lean up and kiss him. He pressed his lips firmly together before bringing his eyes back to mine. "This is going to sting," he said.

He was right. The minute the wipe touched my forehead, tears sprung into my eyes, and I jerked back involuntarily.

"I'm sorry, I'm sorry," he said, his voice soft with worry. His hands moved surely, cleaning out the cut. "There doesn't seem to be any glass in it, at least."

"It's okay, I'm tough," I joked, trying to ignore the pain and break the tension between us. "I mean, you should see the other girl."

He laughed. "That's why I like you. You're so badass."

He tossed the wipe into the trash can and gently dabbed the antibacterial cream over my forehead with his fingers. With one hand, he cradled the back of my head, holding me still while he smoothed the bandage against my skin with the other. His fingertips trailed down the side of my face, sending fire shooting under my skin.

"Is that the only reason?"

The corners of his eyes crinkled, and instead of answering, he bent down and pressed his lips to mine. I wound my arms around his neck and pulled him closer.

Downstairs, the front door slammed, and we broke apart slowly.

He rested his forehead against mine, his eyes still closed. Our noses brushed together, and I couldn't help smiling. I didn't think I'd ever get tired of kissing Charlie.

I leaned back in to kiss him again, but suddenly Minion was wiggling between us, trying to lick at my face, his paws on the counter. I threw my hands up and laughed.

"Minion!" Charlie grabbed him by his collar and hauled him off me. The dog flopped to his back at Charlie's feet, showing his belly. I hopped off the counter and knelt down, happy to oblige.

"Charlie? Is that you up there?" The stairs creaked as Ms. MacAllister made her way upstairs.

She found us all in the bathroom. "Should I even ask?" Her eyes roamed over us. Minion's tongue lolled out of his mouth. He let out a happy sigh as I rubbed his belly, and Charlie looked down at us with one hand in his hair, all smiles. Then she noticed the blood from my cut that was still smeared down the side of his neck, and she narrowed her eyes. "What happened to you?"

My free hand flew to the bandage, but before I could answer, Charlie had grabbed her elbow and led her out into the hall. "We had a bit of a problem. I think someone threw a rock through my bedroom window."

The lie spilled effortlessly from his lips. "There's glass everywhere."

"And Amelia was in your room when that happened?" she asked, glancing back at me. Her blue eyes, so much like Charlie's, met mine, and I felt the blood rush to my face. "Are you all right?"

"Yes, ma'am," I answered.

"Mmhmm." She rubbed her hand across her own forehead. "There are some boxes and tape in the basement, Charlie. Run on down and grab them so we can at least get the window covered."

Once he was out of earshot, she turned to me. She kept her voice low, but urgent. "Your uncle stopped by my shop today and warned me that something like this might happen. People in town are angry about those girls that drowned. They're looking for someone to blame."

I caught my bottom lip between my teeth. "And he makes an easy target," I said. "It's not fair. He didn't do anything."

"He's a MacAllister," she said simply. "It's our curse."

"It isn't fair," I repeated.

Her expression softened into something like sympathy. "You're a good girl, Amelia. He's lucky to have you on his side."

I didn't know what to say to that, so I just shrugged and looked down at the toes of my scuffed-up sneakers. Of course I was on his side. There wasn't anywhere else I could imagine being.

But it wasn't like I could say that to her.

She cleared her throat, breaking the silence that stretched between us. "I need some help down at the shop," she said suddenly. "Nothing major, just a few hours a week. Would you be interested?"

I blinked at her. "What?"

"You did such a nice job with the attic," she said. "Your mother said you didn't have a summer job, so I thought..." she trailed off and spread her hands wide. "What do you say?"

"I..." She'd rendered me speechless twice in the course of two minutes. A *job*. And more than that, it would be a public show of my support for the MacAllisters. For Charlie.

"Just think about it," she said. "And let me know what you decide."

Twenty-seven

"Two words," Leah said. Her voice sounded tinny and far-away over the phone. "Surprise double date."

I stared up at my bedroom ceiling, at the glow-in-the-dark stars I'd begged my dad to put up when I was ten. "That's three words," I pointed out. "And how do you have a surprise double date?"

"Well, we don't *tell* Ransom it's a double date. We just invite him to go to the movie on the Green tonight with you and me and Charlie, but Ransom and I have to drive separately."

I rolled over onto my stomach. "And we have to drive separately because...?"

"Because you guys are going out to dinner beforehand. Keep up, Dupree."

I giggled. "You really like him, don't you?"

Leah sighed into the phone. "I really do," she said, her voice suddenly serious. "He's the first guy I've really liked since... since Mark."

I closed my eyes. "Okay," I agreed. I couldn't say no to her, not when she put it like that.

Charlie was way more into the dinner and movie idea than I thought he'd be. He texted me back immediately, saying he'd pick me up at seven. And he did—he knocked on my door a few minutes before seven with a bouquet of daisies in his hand. He'd dressed nicely again, the way he had for the party. I was glad I'd taken the time to curl my hair and put on makeup. Luckily, the cut on my forehead had been shallow, and I was able to ditch the bandage.

"Hey," he said. He pressed a kiss to my cheek and handed the bouquet to me. His eyes lingered on the hem of my short sailor-style shorts. His ears reddened, and he cleared his throat. "You're beautiful."

I brought the flowers to my face to hide my blush. "Daisies are my favorite."

"I know," he said, grinning. "Leah told me."

I couldn't help myself. I kissed him again. Mom took the flowers from me the minute I walked back inside and promised to find a vase and bring them up to my room. "Go have fun," she said. "I expect a full report."

I rolled my eyes at her.

She blew me a kiss and closed the door.

Charlie caught my fingers in his on the way across his yard. He swung our hands between us and smiled down at me. "How does a picnic dinner sound?"

I raised my eyebrows. "You made dinner?"

"Grams helped a little," he admitted. "But I'm actually a pretty good cook. I thought we could get to the Green early and stake out a spot."

Charlie wasn't kidding. He'd stashed an old-fashioned wicker picnic basket and red-checked blanket in the back seat of the Mustang. He started the engine and pulled out of his driveway.

"So I went through some of those books today," he said.

"Did you find anything interesting?"

"They're kind of hard to read," he said. "But I think..." he trailed off. He seemed to reconsider what he was saying, and drummed his fingers on the top of the steering wheel. "I think Ransom's right, as much as I hate to say it. I think it could work."

Excitement bubbled in my chest. "You think we can help her pass over?"

"Yeah," he said. "I do."

"I can't believe it actually worked," I said after a moment. "You did magic yesterday, Charlie. *Magic*."

His grin mirrored my own. "It's pretty incredible, isn't it?"

"Incredible isn't really the right word," I said. "It doesn't seem big enough."

He was quiet for a moment. "It makes me wonder about my family," he said. "Do you remember what Mrs. Ovet said to me the day we asked your mom about Marin?"

I bit my lip. "She said you were cursed," I said. "You don't really believe her, do you?"

Charlie shrugged. "I didn't believe in magic until yesterday," he pointed out. "But maybe it's something that runs in families."

"Like diabetes?" I wrinkled my nose. "Mrs. Ovet is a busybody, Charlie. There's no curse."

"She's not the only one who thinks that," he said. "Leah told me what your brother used to say about Grams. How you all thought that she was a witch."

I stiffened in my seat, my mouth dry. "Charlie—"

"You were kids," he said, brushing off my discomfort. "It doesn't bother me. But what if you were right about her?"

"Do you think she knows about the magic?" I dropped my voice, even though there was no one around to hear.

He rubbed his hand over the back of his neck, his eyes fixed on the road. "I think she knows something.

But it almost feels she's trying to keep it a secret from me. Like I'm not supposed to know that she knows, or something like that."

"Why would she do that?"

He shifted gears. "I don't know," he said. "But my mom left here for a reason. It makes me wonder what that reason was."

"You could ask."

His laugh was short and bitter. "You don't know my mom."

I thought of the picture in the yearbook we'd found, of the girl who had been my mom's best friend. "I don't," I agreed. "But I know my mom. And we might be able to ask her about it."

He reached over and grabbed my hand. He lifted it and pressed his lips to the back of it, his breath warm against my skin. "You're right," he said. "We'll figure this out."

We parked in one of the spots in front of the Historical Society. Charlie snagged the basket from the back and carried it down to the Green, the blanket tucked under his arm. People had already started to gather in front of the giant screen near the river—mostly families with small kids who chased each other over the grass, shrieking. He spread the blanket on the ground under one of the big oak trees, a spot that was far enough away from everyone else to talk, but that still gave us a great view of the screen. I settled to my knees on the blanket and watched as he unpacked the basket in the late afternoon sun.

"Turkey and brie sandwiches," he said. He handed me a bundle wrapped in white paper, then pulled out two glass bottles of root beer, a bag filled with strawberries, and a yellow container. "Homemade chips," he explained, popping off the lid.

Warmth, almost to the point of pain, filled my chest. I set the sandwich in my lap and stared at him, unable to form words. Ridiculously, tears prickled at the corner of my eyes, and I swallowed.

Get it together.

He looked up at me and froze. His gaze swept my face, his worried eyes searching mine. "Hey." He rose to his knees and grasped my hand. "Amelia? What's wrong?"

I shook my head. "Nothing. This..." I trailed off and motioned to the basket, the food, him.

His cheeks tinged pink. He looked down at our hands and shrugged. "I wanted this to be special," he said. "Is it too much?"

"No." I leaned forward and pressed a kiss to his cheek. "It's perfect. It's the sweetest thing that anyone has ever done for me."

Charlie and I spent nearly two hours eating and talking and kissing on the blanket, until all of the food was gone and the sky was painted in broad strokes of blues and purples and pinks. We steered clear of anything related to the ghost or magic or my brother—instead, we learned about each other. I told him about the time I'd skipped school to spend a day reading fanfiction; he told me about his plans for college, how he wanted to help people, like his parents.

"I don't want to go to seminary or anything," he explained, looking down at me. I lay sprawled across the blanket, my head in his lap. He ran his hand through my hair absently. "I'm nowhere near as religious as a preacher's son should be, you know? And I don't want to be a doctor like my mom. I just want to help."

I caught his hand and pressed a kiss to his palm. "You will," I said.

"What about you?" he asked. "What are your plans for college?"

I opened my mouth and closed it again. "I don't know," I admitted. "I used to know." I had thought that I'd go to college on a swimming scholarship or something, and find something I liked to do. Maybe history, like my mom. "I kind of lost my way after Mark died. I don't know what I want anymore."

He studied me carefully. There wasn't pity in his gaze, or judgment. Just understanding. "You'll figure it out," he said. "Not everyone has a plan right away."

Leah chose that moment to arrive, cutting off my reply. She dropped her bag at my feet and flopped to the blanket beside me.

"You guys need to get a room," she said. "Gross."

I sat up and pushed my hair behind my ear. "Hello to you too," I said.

"I have popcorn and lemonade from the cafe," Leah added. "How was dinner?"

"Perfect," I said. "Where's Ransom?"

She waved her hand loosely. "He had to stop and pick something up from his desk at the Historical Society," she said. "He'll be here in a minute."

He took more than a minute. He didn't arrive until it was fully dark and the giant screen was lit.

"Sorry," he said. "I ran into Mrs. Edy. That woman can *talk*."

I grinned, remembering the time Charlie and I had run into her, the day we'd found the portrait. It felt like a lifetime ago. "Charlie knows all about that, don't you?"

He blushed. "Old ladies like me," he said. "I can't help that."

"Everyone likes you," Leah said. She tossed a piece of popcorn at him that he caught with his open mouth.

"I never took you for a liar, Leah."

I whipped around at the sound of Ben's voice. He stood behind us, arms crossed over his chest. "I don't like him."

Charlie tensed beside me. I laid a hand on his arm and squinted up at my ex-boyfriend.

Leah was already on her feet, poking her finger into Ben's chest. "What's wrong with you, Ben?"

"What's wrong with me?" He shook his head like he couldn't believe what he was seeing. "What's the matter with *her*?"

"Go away," I said. Heat crept up my neck. Around us, people were starting to stare.

"No, Amelia," he said. "Listen, I don't know what sort of thing you have going on here, but it has to end now. Do you have any idea who this guy is? What he's done?"

I was on my feet now. "He hasn't cheated on me!" My voice was shrill. "He hasn't broken my heart. And he definitely hasn't proven to be the world's biggest asshole."

Charlie stepped between us. "Do you have something to say to me?" he asked, his voice deadly quiet.

"Yeah, *man*," Ben said. "I do." He stepped closer, until his toes nearly touched Charlie's. "I don't know what kind of shit you got away with where you came from, but it ends now. I know what you did to my cousin. To Yvette. And I know everything else."

Charlie's hands curled into fists at his side. "You don't know anything."

Ben was practically leering. "I Googled you, man. Charles MacAllister Blue from Dillion, Montana. Did you tell Amelia what you're really doing here? Did you tell her what happened to your last girlfriend? The one who ended up dead? Becca, right?"

Charlie hit him.

He moved so quickly that I couldn't stop him. I couldn't do anything but stand there and watch as Charlie's fist connected with Ben's jaw with a sharp crack. Ben staggered back, his hand to his face.

For a split second, I thought that maybe that would be that. That maybe Ben would let it go.

But then Ben launched himself at Charlie, tackling him to the ground. Behind us, someone screamed. They hit the grass with a thud and a grunt, and then they were rolling, each landing punches, cursing at the other.

"Stop it!" I shouted. Leah wrapped her hands around me, keeping me from running at them. Ransom jumped into the middle of the fight and grabbed Ben, pulling him off Charlie.

Ransom shoved Ben hard. "Get lost," he said, pointing his finger in the other boy's face.

Behind Ransom, Charlie climbed to his feet. Blood spilled down his face from a cut on the bridge of his nose, right where his glasses should have been.

Ben shook free of Ransom's grasp, wiping the blood from his mouth. I tensed, sure he was going to attack Charlie again. He looked right at me, his eyes wild.

"I warned you," he said. "You can't say I didn't warn you." He spat at Charlie's feet.

And then he was gone.

Charlie sank against the trunk of the big oak tree, cradling his head in his hands. I stepped beside him and put my hand on his shoulder. He shrugged it off.

"Are you okay?"

He shook his head. He kept his face buried in his hands, his voice muffled when he spoke. "I'm so sorry, Amelia," he said.

"There's nothing to be sorry for," I said.

Leah appeared beside me. Charlie's glasses were in her hands, broken at the bridge, the left lens shattered. She held them out like an offering, cupped in her palms.

He looked at them, and I held my breath, unsure of what he was going to do.

Charlie threw back his head and laughed. He laughed and laughed until he was doubled over, until he was gasping for air, until tears rolled down his face and I wasn't sure if he was laughing or crying.

Ransom had shoved the blanket and trash into the picnic basket. "Let's get out of here," he said. "I think you need a first aid kit."

"There's one at the Society," I said. I took Charlie's hand gently, careful to avoid the cuts on his rapidly swelling knuckles. We walked back across the Green in silence, despite the questions burning their way through me. What had Ben meant? Why hadn't Charlie said anything about what had happened to that girl?

Leah fished my keys out of my purse and unlocked the door. Ransom punched in the alarm code and led the way upstairs, not even bothering to turn on the lights in the gallery. I directed Charlie into one of the plastic chairs in the kitchenette and located the first aid kit under the counter while Ransom flipped on the fluorescent lamp overhead.

"Check the freezer for ice," Ransom told Leah.

I flipped open the white plastic box and pulled out an alcohol swab, gauze, and medical tape. I tore open the little foil packet. "This might hurt," I said, acutely aware of the fact that just yesterday he'd said those words to me.

"Why are you doing this?" Charlie's voice was barely above a whisper.

I frowned down at him. "You're hurt," I whispered back. "I want to help you."

"You heard what Ben said," he said. He sounded close to tears. "You hardly know me."

"I know you well enough."

"Aren't you going to ask me what happened to her?"

"You'll tell me when you're ready to," I said. "Now let me help you."

Charlie swallowed and kept his eyes on the ground. His breath hissed out, and he flinched away when I cleaned out the cut on his nose. Before the accident, blood had made me feel faint. But not now—now I stood firm, my hands steady and sure as I taped gauze over the cut. Ransom handed Charlie a wad of wet paper towels, which he used to clean the blood and dirt from his hands.

"I don't think you're going to need stitches," I said when I was done. "I think it was your glasses that cut you, not Ben."

"Still hurts," he mumbled. He pressed the plastic bag full of ice cubes that Leah had given him against his jaw.

"It's going to hurt," Ransom said. He leaned back against the counter, his legs crossed at the ankles and his arms crossed over his chest. "Maybe you should have thought of that before you hit him."

"Screw you," Charlie said. "You'd have hit him too."

Ransom shook his head. "I wouldn't have given him the satisfaction. He was goading you, man. He wanted you to hit him."

I scowled at Ransom. "Do you mind?" I asked.

"I'm just saying what everyone's thinking," Ransom said. "Why don't you tell us what Ben was talking about?"

Charlie stared at the ground, stone-faced.

"You don't have to tell us anything," I told him.

"I think he does." Ransom pushed off from the counter. "We're his friends."

"Which is why he doesn't have to say anything. Leah?" I turned to her, my gaze beseeching.

She shook her head and held up her hands in surrender. "I'm not involved in this," she said, voice soft. "I just want you to know that I'm on your side, Charlie."

"We're all on his side," Ransom said.

"Really?" I asked. "It sure doesn't feel like it."

Ransom rolled his eyes and raked his hand through his hair.

"Her name was Becca."

My attention snapped to Charlie. He didn't look up, didn't raise his head. He kept his gaze fixed on the ground, and he spoke. "Her locker was right next to mine freshman year. That's how we met," he said. "We were inseparable."

My heart grew heavy. "Charlie, you don't have to—"

"I want to." He lifted his eyes and stared at me. "You told me about Mark, Amelia. You deserve to know about Becca."

I nodded stiffly.

"I loved her," he continued. "There was never any doubt in my mind that she was the one, that we'd be together forever." A tear rolled down his face, and I stepped close to him, ready to wipe it away. He leaned into my touch, and my heart plunged even further. I wrapped my arms around him, holding him tight.

"She killed herself," he said simply. "She jumped into the river right after Christmas and drowned. Just like the girls here."

"Oh, Charlie," Leah breathed. "I'm so sorry."

Ransom didn't say anything. And for a long second, silence stretched between the four of us.

"Son of a bitch," Ransom said finally. "Ben thinks you killed all three of them."

Twenty-eight

Charlie looked awful.

I found him lying on the floor in his bedroom, wearing a pair of dark green basketball shorts and nothing else. Bruises stretched across his ribs, streaks of red and purple and brown mottling his smooth white skin. "Go away, Grams."

I dropped my purse on his desk and closed the door behind me. "It's me," I said. I tried to keep my voice light.

In the three days since his fight with Ben, the skin around his eye had purpled, his lip swollen. His glasses were on his desk, still broken in half, leaving his face looking naked.

He cracked open the eye that wasn't bruised. "You're here," he said. He sounded surprised. And he had every right to be—he hadn't responded to a single text since Leah had dropped him off the other night, or answered the phone when I'd called.

"I'm here," I repeated. I stepped over him and perched myself on the edge of his bed. "Your Grams called me and asked if I could come talk to you. She's worried about you."

He closed his eye again and threw his arm over his face. "She worries too much."

I nudged him with my toe. "I'm worried about you."

"I'm fine."

"Don't lie to me." My voice wobbled, betraying the way my stomach twisted. "You've spent the last three days ignoring me. Which is fine, whatever. You needed your space. I can forgive that. Just don't lie to me."

"Amelia—"

"Why haven't you called me?"

He sat up with a wince. "And say what? Sorry I ruined our first date? Sorry I punched your ex-boyfriend in the face? Sorry I didn't tell you about my dead girlfriend, even though you told me all about your brother? Sorry I disappeared for three days? What was I supposed to say?"

"Any of those would have been acceptable," I said, my jaw clenched.

"I *am* sorry," he said. As he reached for the shirt thrown across the end of his bed, his arm brushed against my bare leg, sending sparks shooting through my bloodstream. He froze, shirt in hand, his blue eyes fixed on mine. "I am."

I don't know who moved first, but the next thing I knew, Charlie's lips were on mine, and I was lying back against his pillows, my heart slamming against my ribs. I wound my arms around his neck and pulled him closer. His hands slipped up the back of my shirt, his palms flat and hot against my skin. I jumped under his touch, arching my back until we were chest to chest. I had to close the space between us, I had to get as close to him as possible. Need pulsed through me, unlike anything I'd ever known. The bed creaked beneath us, and I froze.

"Amelia?" Charlie pulled back just enough to talk. He rested on his elbows, one on either side of my head.

I reached up and cupped his jaw with my hand. "I missed you," I said, keeping my voice soft. I ran my thumb along his cheekbone, and he closed his eyes.

"I'm sorry," he repeated. He dropped his forehead until it rested on mine. "I should have talked to you."

"It's okay," I said. And it was. I brushed my mouth against his. He sighed and rolled off me, onto his side. He wrapped me in his arms and pulled me close, until my head rested on his chest and the steady *thump thump* of his heart echoed through me.

"Were you ever going to tell me about her?" I asked a little later.

His Adam's apple bobbed in his throat. "I wanted to," he said. "Especially after you told me about Mark. But I didn't know how to bring it up without making you feel like I was comparing my loss to yours."

I let my eyes fall closed. "I wouldn't have felt like that," I said.

"I know." His arms tightened around me. "I'm sorry."

"Stop apologizing," I said. I traced my fingers over his bare skin. "What have you been doing over the last few days?"

He sighed. "Feeling sorry for myself, mostly," he said. "Though Ransom stopped by and convinced me to do a bit more digging through those books." He motioned vaguely towards his desk, where the grimoires were spread over the surface.

"And?" I asked. I pushed down the sting of jealousy over the news that he'd seen Ransom but not me. "Did the two of you figure anything out?"

He smiled at me then, the first real smile I'd seen in days. "Give me a few hours and I'll be able to show you."

"So," Mom said the moment I walked into the kitchen, "what's on the agenda for today?"

I grabbed myself a mug and a teabag and poured the remains of the kettle into the cup. I slid into the chair across from her. "I think I'll ride into town and see when Ms. MacAllister wants me to start, and then I have plans with Charlie."

She raised her eyebrows. "I take it that you two figured things out?"

My mind flashed to this morning in Charlie's bed, his lips on my neck, his hands on the bare skin of my back. He'd sent me on my way with a kiss and a promise that he'd have something to show me later this afternoon. I made a noncommittal sound and pretended to be very, very interested in my tea.

Mom threw back her head and laughed. "I see," she said. "That good?"

Oh my God. I sank down in my seat, trying to figure out how quickly I could get out of the kitchen. My face flushed, and I stared at her. "Mom."

She waved her hand at me. "Just make sure you're being careful, okay? I'm not raising any grandbabies."

"Oh my God, *Mom.*" That was it, I was going to die. Why couldn't my mother be normal, like Leah's mom, and just ignore everything that I did? "I'm not... we're not... We're not having this conversation right now."

"We have to have it sometime," she replied, completely unfazed. She stood, rinsed her mug out in the sink, and grabbed her purse off the counter. "It may as well be now."

"There's nothing to talk about." I gulped down my tea and pushed away from the table. "I should get going."

"I can drop you off at the Tea Exchange, at least," she said. "It'll save you the bike ride."

I grumbled, but I grabbed my purse and followed her out to the car. Thankfully, she stopped the questions about Charlie, and we'd moved onto tamer topics by the time she dropped me off.

The bell over the door jingled softly as I stepped into the Tea Exchange. Even though I'd lived in Asylum for my entire life, I'd never actually gone into Ms. MacAllister's shop before.

It was smaller than I'd thought it would be, lined from floor to ceiling with fat round jars, each filled with varying amounts of tea or spices. It smelled a bit like the MacAllister's house, actually—black tea, cinnamon, and a pinch of something else I couldn't quite place that reminded me of Christmas. She didn't have the overhead lights turned on—the only light came through the large plate glass window in the front of the store. The natural light, coupled with the wide, rough-hewn beams in the ceiling and the smooth plaster walls, made me feel like I'd stepped back in time. The only concession to the twenty-first century was the air conditioning.

I stepped up to the row of jars closest to me, letting my fingers trail over the handwritten labels.

"I was wondering when you'd stop by."

I turned quickly and let my hand drop to my side. Ms. MacAllister stood just in front of a doorway separated from the main room of the shop by a beaded curtain. Her hand rested on a long, curving counter topped with a large brass scale and an ancient cash register, and she wasn't smiling, not really, but she wasn't scowling, either, and I figured that meant I should go on.

"I'd like to take the job," I said.

She nodded once. "Excellent. Do you know anything about herbal medicine, Amelia?"

"Ma'am?"

She waved her hand at the various jars lining the walls. "Natural remedies, holistic treatments. Things of that nature."

"I—I don't. Sorry."

"There's more to this shop than tea and spices. If you're going to be working here with me, you'll have to learn fast."

"I can do that."

She turned and walked through the curtain, the beads clacking together. I hesitated for only a moment, rocking on the balls of my feet, before I plunged through the doorway after her. The back room was as neatly organized as the front, the only differences being the light spilling from a Tiffany lamp set on a round table and the contents of the jars looking a little... weirder. I couldn't place any of the names, and there were a few that seemed to be filled with... blood?

But no. That couldn't be right.

A steaming tea pot and two delicate cups were set beneath the lamp, almost like she'd been waiting for me.

I tore my gaze away from the table and took in the rest of the room. An overstuffed leather armchair sat in the corner in front of a bookshelf packed from floor to ceiling with leather-bound books, chunks of crystal, and strange figurines. Some of the books looked familiar, and I leaned closer, trying to peek at their titles.

Ms. MacAllister took a seat at the small table and motioned at the other chair. "Sit."

So I did. The woven straw seat creaked under me in protest, and I had a vision of myself ending up spread-eagled on the floor with the chair in bits beneath me. But she was watching me closely, and I willed myself to relax.

The chair held.

I set my purse on the floor by my feet and folded my hands in my lap, waiting. She picked up the pot of tea and poured it expertly into the two china cups. She pushed one towards me.

"Uh, thanks," I said. I gripped the saucer and pulled it the rest of the way.

She stirred a spoonful of sugar into her own cup with a small spoon. It didn't clink once against the china, not even when she set it down on her saucer. "I like you, Amelia," she said. "I've known you since you were born, you know. When you were just a baby, your mother would come over to visit with me and bring you with her. I like to think it was more than kindness on her part—you see, when my daughter went away, she left a void in both our lives. You were the quietest baby I'd ever seen. So alert. So curious about everything. Not like your brother, rest his soul."

I frowned. "I don't remember that."

She tittered like one of the old women in church, something that seemed as out of character as Erin West in a convent. "Oh, you wouldn't. Your father never liked me much, and by the time you were a toddler, your mother would come by herself. I just..." She trailed off, her eyes focusing on something beyond me. She shook her head slightly and returned her attention to me. "Charlie's had a rough time of it, and you've made him happy. I can't thank you enough for that."

I took a sip of tea. Flavors exploded in my mouth—mint, citrus, and something sweet and floral that I couldn't place. "I needed a friend too," I said.

She nodded, seemingly satisfied, and sat back, her manner suddenly all business, her voice brusque. "You can start tomorrow. I'm expecting a shipment in the morning, so we'll start with that. We can figure out the rest of your schedule then."

Her attention turned to the front of the shop, and a moment later, the bell jingled. I jumped, but Ms. MacAllister slid to her feet as gracefully as a ballerina and disappeared through the beaded curtain, leaving me alone.

I sipped at the rest of my tea and took another look around the room. It seemed rude to leave without saying goodbye or finishing our conversation. It wouldn't hurt to stick around for a few minutes longer.

The chair creaked under me when I stood and made my way back to the bookshelf. The figurine closest to me caught my eye, and I shifted my teacup to my left hand.

The moment my free hand touched the figurine, my ring, tucked under my shirt, warmed instantly against my skin.

"What are you?" I murmured to the small carved woman. She was carved from smooth wood and stark naked, her hands twined over her faceless head, revealing the kind of curves that you saw on a pin-up girl: broad hips, tiny waist, and full, round breasts. A small blue stone winked in her navel.

The longer I held onto her, the hotter the ring burned, until it seared my skin and I yelped in pain. The figurine and the teacup both fell from my hands. The china shattered on the floor, while the woman rolled under the table.

"Shit," I gasped, pulling the ring out from under my shirt and running my hand over the skin where it had rested right under my breastbone, which was still warm to the touch. The ring sat in my hand, as cool and lifeless as it had been before I had picked up the figurine.

Almost like I'd imagined the entire thing.

I tucked the ring back under my shirt and knelt in a puddle of tea, picking up bits of the shattered china. Not even technically on the job, and I was already screwing things up.

The beaded curtain rustled. "Everything all right, Amelia?" Ms. MacAllister asked.

I turned halfway, grimacing, and held up the bits of teacup. "I'm so sorry, I tripped." My cheeks burned, and I scrambled to my feet.

If she knew I was lying, she didn't show it. She just ducked back through the doorway and returned with a small broom and dustpan. She handed it to me and waved off my other apologies. "Clean this up, and I'll see you tomorrow," she said. "Be here at ten."

Twenty-nine

"It *burned* you?" Charlie's voice rose almost an octave. "Are you okay?" He stopped so suddenly that I walked a few steps past him before realizing he wasn't next to me. I turned back to him and grabbed his hand.

"I'm fine, I promise," I said, pushing my bangs out of my face. The forest around us was hot and sticky with typical early-August humidity. I pushed down the neck of my tank top, exposing the skin where the ring had rested. "Not even a mark, see?"

Charlie's whole face turned pink, and too late, I realized just how much chest I was showing off. "Nope," he said, his voice sounding oddly strangled as I pushed my shirt back up. "Looks perfect to me."

The awkwardness hung in the air between us for a few seconds. I forced a laugh and kept walking, trying to return to normalcy.

"I can't believe you stole it."

It was my turn to blush. "I didn't *steal* it. I borrowed it." The figurine felt heavy in my bag, almost like it was alive. I didn't know what had possessed me to take it when I'd left the Tea Exchange, but I'd slipped off the ring and placed them both into my purse. "Anyway, I'll put it back tomorrow. I wanted to see what you thought of it, but that's silly. You've probably seen it a million times."

"Actually, I haven't."

My brow creased, and I looked up at him. "But how? It was right there on the shelf, in plain view."

He clambered over a fallen log, turning back and holding out his hand to me. I took it, and he helped me over. "I've never actually been to Grams' shop."

"What? Why?"

Charlie shrugged, keeping his hand closed around mine. "She's never offered to bring me down there, and I didn't want to pry. Grams can be weird about her privacy."

I frowned.

We walked through the blighted trees in silence. Just like the last time, the living trees began suddenly, surrounding the ruins. The sight of the roofless, crumbling walls took my breath away, and the sounds of the forest melted away. Sunbeams danced through the treetops, making the stones sparkle in the light, making it almost look alive. Still, my skin crawled with the same feeling of wrongness. I hadn't even realized that I'd stopped walking until Charlie tugged me forward gently.

We stepped through the doorway. Charlie slung his backpack around to his front and unzipped it. He pulled out a blanket and spread it out at the base of the oak tree before settling down onto it. I dropped down beside him. He held out his hand, and I pulled the figurine from my purse, holding her gently in my fingers. "Here," I said.

I passed her to him. He took the figurine reverently, like she was made from glass instead of carved from wood. Once she was safely in his hands, he let out a low, soft sigh.

Around us, the entire forest seemed to sigh too. From behind me, a cold wind rose, ruffling the hair on the back of my neck with icy fingers. I shivered and drew my legs closer to me. Dark clouds gathered above us, covering the summer sun and pitching the tall stone walls into shadow.

Charlie didn't notice.

He closed his eyes and took in a deep breath. The small stone in the figurine's belly began to glow with the same blue light that had shone through my ring in Charlie's attic. The same blue as Charlie's eyes. Below us, the ground began to tremble, and a low, keening hum filled the ruins. I scrambled backwards, pressing myself against the oak tree until the bark scraped at my skin.

Charlie didn't move.

The ground shook again, throwing me to my hands and knees. Stones from the wall to my left began to hit the ground dangerously close to where I'd been sitting a moment before. Dangerously close to Charlie.

I needed to think. We needed to get out of here before...

The wall split with a tremendous crack. The top half toppled backwards into the woods. I tried to climb to my feet, but the ground pitched sharply, like the deck of a ship in a storm, and I hadn't taken two steps before I was thrown to the ground again. My chin hit one of the tree roots, and I cried out, the coppery taste of blood filling my mouth.

"Charlie!" I screamed. I crawled towards him, staying low to the ground. I grabbed his shoulder and shook him, hard. Under my hand, he felt like he was carved from ice. Even through the thin fabric of his t-shirt, I could feel an unnatural cold seeping off him. I shook him again, my throat thick with tears. "We have to go," I said, pulling at him. The blue light from the figurine pulsed even brighter, bright enough that I had to squint my eyes against the glare.

I had to get the figurine out of his hands. Whatever was happening, she was the cause of it.

"Let go of it," I begged. My fingers found his, and I tried to pry them away from the carved wooden woman, but his grip was too tight. He didn't respond to anything: not my pleas or cries or the sound of the walls crumbling around us. He sat, figurine in hand, like he was in some kind of trance, while the entire forest trembled around us in the middle of centuries-old ruins. "Charlie!" I yelled again. I rose to my knees in front of him and did the only thing I could think of.

My open palm met his cheek with a sharp slap, and he jolted like I'd electrocuted him.

"Amelia?" He looked up at me, blinking the clouds away from his eyes, and the figurine slipped from his fingers onto the blanket. The light in her belly winked out, and around us, the earth quieted and the clouds slipped away, letting the sun back in. He grabbed me and pulled me hard against him, wrapping his body around mine and letting out deep, shuddering breaths, and I pressed against his warmth.

"You're shaking," he whispered, his lips grazing my ear. "Why are you shaking?"

I sat back on my heels and stared up at him, trying to find words. *We almost died. You caused an earthquake. You were still as a statue, cold as ice.* Any of those things would have been fine, but my mouth moved soundlessly as my eyes searched his face.

"Amelia?" His eyes creased at the corners with concern. "What happened?"

"What happened?" I repeated, then cast my gaze around the ruined house. Three walls still stood—the fourth lay in a heap, its stones scattered across the ground. "You scared me," I whispered.

He followed my gaze and swallowed hard, his Adam's apple bobbing in his throat. "What happened?"

he asked again, only this time, there was a tremor in his voice. "What did I do?"

"It wasn't all you," I said. I pushed the little woman away from us with my toe. "What do you remember?"

He shuddered. "The minute I took that thing from you, it was like I stepped into the eye of a hurricane. All around me, I could feel this horrible power whirling, trying to grab me, trying to pull me under. And I was trying to stay in control, but it kept coming closer, until suddenly I was back here with you and it didn't matter anymore."

Nothing made sense. How could a carved figurine, barely larger than my hand, affect him that way? But it had, and the earth itself had responded to the battle that had been raging inside of Charlie.

I slid my hand down his arm and squeezed his hand. "I'm just happy you're okay."

"I could have hurt you." His voice was hollow. "Amelia, what if I'd hurt you?"

He almost had. But I could see the pain reflected in his eyes, and I knew that if I told him that, he'd never forgive himself. So I stood and brushed the dirt from my shorts. "You didn't, so we're not going to worry about it."

He followed me across the overgrown floor. The remains of the wall towered over me. I didn't trust it to stay standing; it leaned like a football player at a house party, ready to collapse at the slightest touch. It wasn't safe here, not any more.

"What's that?" Charlie moved away from me, closer to the wall, kicking stones out of his way. A crack had opened in the ground near the middle of the wall, and a grimy, rusted handle was visible in the dirt.

Keeping one eye on the wall, I helped him clear away the debris until the sharp angles of a trapdoor took shape beneath our hands. The wood was rotted and held together with rusted iron bands. One of the boards gave way the moment my fingers touched it, crumbling into the black abyss below.

Charlie lifted the rest of the door carefully, sending a cascade of dirt pouring into the hole. The hinges groaned in protest, but they held, and we were left looking at a set of narrow stone steps curving down into darkness. He rested the door against the ground and wiped his hands on his jeans. He rocked back and forth on the balls of his feet and looked over at me, the beginnings of a smile stretching across his mouth. "Want to take a look?" he asked.

I peered down into the darkness. It was probably full of spiders and snakes, and who knew how sturdy it was—Charlie had, after all, just caused what had felt a lot like an earthquake. But he looked so hopeful, standing there with his hand stretched toward me, that I couldn't say no. I took his hand and said a quick little prayer that we wouldn't be buried alive.

With the tiny ray of light from Charlie's phone's screen illuminating our path, we crept down the stone steps. I kept one hand on the wall to my right and tried to ignore the soft, sticky cobwebs that coated the stones as we turned in a tight spiral. In front of me, Charlie stayed hunched over, his curly hair brushing the ceiling, until the stairs ended and we stood not in a cellar, but in a space so narrow that I couldn't even stretch out my arms fully before I touched both walls. At least the ceiling was higher—Charlie straightened to his full height in front of me. I crowded close to him, squinting into darkness so black it was like the entire world had been swallowed up.

The light blinked out, plunging us into utter darkness.

I shrieked and grabbed for Charlie, but my fingers met only stone and air, and I could feel the walls pressing in on me, surrounding me. I sucked in a breath, the air heavy with the smell of dirt and rot and mildew and something else, something that I couldn't identify but that set my teeth on edge. *This is what it must feel like to be buried alive*, I thought.

"Amelia?" Charlie's voice bounced through the blackness around me, and I spun in a circle, reaching for him.

"I'm okay," I managed to say. "What happened to the light?"

"I don't know." I could hear him banging his hand against the plastic phone, trying to get it to turn on. "It just went dead."

Something scurried across my foot, and I screamed again, kicking out into the air. My bare shoulders touched something wet and slick, and I jerked forward. I had to get out of here. Light. I needed light. Of course, I'd left my purse up in the clearing. "Let's go back outside," I said.

"Just hold on one second." His voice sounded further away, and I forced down the panic bubbling in my chest. This was not how today was supposed to happen. None of it was supposed to happen like this.

"Charlie, please," I begged. "I don't like this."

He didn't answer me.

"Charlie?"

My skin prickled, and a rush of hot air blew past me. The section of the tunnel closest to me erupted into light so brilliant that I had to throw my arm over my eyes.

"It's okay, Amelia."

I lowered my arm and blinked until my eyes adjusted to the light. Torches lined the tunnel at regular intervals, each one burning with blue flame. Charlie stood a few feet away, his hands shoved in his pockets, looking bashful. "I didn't think it would be that bright," he said.

I stepped to the torch closest to me and waved my hand near the flame. It gave off no heat that I could feel, but the light flickered and moved like fire. It was incredible, pure and simple, and I'm sure my amazement was written plainly on my face when I spun back to face him. "You did this?"

"Ransom and I have been practicing," he said, the corner of his mouth turning up into half of a smile. He turned on his heel and started down the tunnel. "Come on. I don't know how long I can keep this up."

I hurried along, sticking close to him. The torches behind us sputtered and died almost as soon as we'd moved past, allowing more torches ahead of us to spring to life, which meant that every step of the way, we were bathed in a bluc glow that seemed to leech the life from everything—my hair, my clothes, and even my skin, turning me corpse-like and pale. I looked like Marin, I realized with a jolt. The same blue-white light had surrounded her.

We walked for close to ten minutes like that, with nothing behind or ahead of us but darkness, like we'd been swallowed up by the earth itself. At any moment, the ground above us could fall and crush us like bugs. Not exactly a pleasant thought. Ahead, in the distance, I could hear the faint but unmistakable roar of water. It grew louder with every step.

Gradually, the tunnel sloped downwards, and the walls grew further apart, until we were standing in a large, round chamber. Light, real light, daylight, filtered into the room through round windows spaced in the ceiling. Charlie extinguished the torches on either side of us. His shoulders sagged, and he wiped at his forehead with the back of his hand. He leaned for a moment against the wall, resting his hands on his knees and taking deep breaths, like he'd just run several miles.

I rubbed my hand over his shoulder. "Are you all right?"

He knew what I was asking and nodded. "I'm fine," he added, practically shouting over the roar of the water that had to be close by. "That just took more out of me than I thought it would."

The chamber was plain, the walls smooth but undecorated, broken only by a curved archway on the opposite side, and nearly empty. Except for what looked like a large altar in the middle of the floor, carved from a solid chunk of glistening blue stone.

Susquehanna Bluestone.

I tried to picture the map in my head, the way the river curved along the edge of the forest.

Of course.

I let my fingers trail over the rough surface of the stone as I crossed the chamber, making my way towards the arch. "I think I know where we are," I yelled.

"Where?"

I beckoned him closer and stepped through the archway into another chamber. This one was more like a cave than a room; it was damp and smelled of mildew, and the walls were rough, natural stone. The ceiling sloped downwards, and it all was illuminated by a sliver of light pouring through a narrow opening to my left.

Sunlight.

I squeezed my way through the opening sideways, and even then, just barely. Rough edges scraped against my shoulders and hips, drawing a line of fire across my skin, but then I was free. I pushed the branches aside and stepped out into the sunshine waiting for me along the riverbank. I breathed in the summer air, letting the warmth slide over my skin like a blanket as I made my way down to the rocky shore, down to where the Standing Stone stood, tall and proud, glistening in the afternoon light.

Down to where a girl lay face-down in the water, her long brown hair tangled around the rocky shore.

Thirty

Uncle Frank's radio crackled to life as he finished taking my statement. He tucked his pen into the pocket of his shirt and turned away from me, answering whatever the dispatcher had asked him. I leaned back against the brown SUV and scrubbed my hands over my face.

The last three hours had faded into a blur. Charlie and I had pulled the girl out of the water. She'd been pale and bloated, but I'd recognized the maroon apron.

Erin West.

I didn't remember calling Uncle Frank, and I didn't remember how we'd ended up back at the place where the trail down to the Standing Stone began, surrounded by the memorials for Brit and Yvette. Charlie was still talking to Dave across the clearing. Sometime between when we'd found Erin and now, heavy rainclouds had gathered overhead, threatening to spill down on us. I shivered despite the sticky heat.

Erin West was dead.

Once upon a time, she'd been my friend. Back before she'd become popular, and before she'd hooked up with Ben, Erin had camped out with Leah and me on my bedroom floor. She'd played Barbies with us and helped Mark spy on Ms. MacAllister.

And now she was dead.

I rubbed my hands over my face. I didn't know what to do or how to feel. Normal people cried when someone they knew was dead. They wailed, they wept, they got angry. I'd certainly done that after Mark had died. And I'd cried for Brit too.

But now? Now I was hollow. Numb.

Frank reappeared at my side. He touched my elbow, his green eyes searching my face. "You okay, sweetheart?"

I shrugged. He wrapped me in a hug, his touch warm and reassuring. "You're safe. That's what matters."

I stepped back and wiped my eyes with the back of my hand. "Did someone do that to her?" I asked.

Frank sighed, suddenly looking much older than his thirty-nine years. He didn't answer me, and I knew, deep in the pit of my stomach, what the answer was. "They're going to blame Charlie," I whispered. "Ben Liancourt has it out for him because of me, Uncle Frank. He'll want to see him burn for this."

The first raindrops began to fall, catching like tiny, glittering diamonds on the brim of his uniform hat. "You leave the police work to me," he said, his voice soft. "Deal?"

Frank drove Charlie and me home. He could have sent us off with Dave hours earlier, but he'd wanted to keep me close. Wanted to keep an eye on me, I guess. It was a short drive, and neither Frank nor Charlie said much. I didn't talk, either—I just sat in the passenger seat of the big brown SUV and stared down at my hands.

Erin was dead.

And I couldn't shake the feeling that someone had killed her.

Mom bustled us inside and sat the three of us down on the sofa. She handed Frank and Charlie each a cup of coffee, black, and set a mug of tea onto the table in front of me. Charlie rested his hand on my knee as I leaned forward to pick it up. The ceramic was almost too hot to hold, but I wrapped my hands around it anyway, glad for the heat searing my palms.

It meant I could still feel something.

"She's holding up all right, Issy," Uncle Frank said like I wasn't even there. "She's bound to be in some sort of shock. It's a lot to take in."

Mom's voice was soft. "It's a lot to take in for all of us. I can't help thinking…"

He put his mug on the coffee table and leaned forward, his elbows on his knees. "It brings a lot back, doesn't it?"

"It's like Rose and the others all over again," Mom said. Pain flashed across her face, and she closed her eyes. "God, that was the worst summer of my life."

I lifted my head, suddenly interested. "What happened?" I asked.

Mom and Frank exchanged a glance. "It's not important," she said after a moment. "It was a long time ago."

"Who's Rose?" Charlie asked.

"She was a friend," Frank said. He drained his coffee in one long gulp. "Like your mom said, it was a long time ago."

"What happened to her?" Anything to get my mind off Erin's blue lips, her bulging eyes, the grayish tinge of her skin.

They exchanged another glance. Then my mom lifted her shoulder as if to say, *What's the harm?* "She died the summer I turned eighteen," she said. "That was what, Frank? The summer of 1990?"

"I was just going into freshman year of high school," Frank agreed, nodding his head. "Jesus, that was a mess."

"What happened?" I repeated.

Frank cleared his throat and stretched his long legs out in front of him. "Have you ever heard of something called a suicide cluster?"

I shook my head.

"It's a sort of psychological phenomenon. Sometimes one suicide can trigger others. Like a wave. One after another, often in a similar manner," he explained.

"That's what happened that summer," Mom added. "There were five in total, all girls who went to school with us."

My mouth went dry, and dread took hold in my middle, wrapping thorny tendrils around my stomach. "They drowned," I said, more statement than question.

"At the Standing Stone," Frank said. He let out his breath. "The last one was Rose MacAllister."

Charlie made a strangled noise beside me and tightened his grip on my knee. "MacAllister?"

Mom's eyes went wide. "You don't know, honey?" She exchanged another glance with Frank. "Rose MacAllister was your mother's twin sister, Charlie. She was your aunt."

Charlie's phone rang the minute we pulled into the parking lot. "It's my mom," he said, staring down at the screen. His voice sounded hollow.

"Are you going to answer it?"

"What do I say? Hey, how come you never told me about your twin sister? Even after Becca?" He gripped the steering wheel so hard his knuckles turned white.

"Charlie..." I let my voice trail off. I didn't know what to say—it wasn't like I could tell him what to do, one way or another. He had to make that decision for himself.

The phone rang again, and he sighed. "I'll be right in," he told me. "We have to talk."

He swiped his thumb across the screen as I slid out the door and sprinted for the coffee shop. I made it up the steps and under the porch roof before I was totally soaked, and pushed the door open. The bell jingled overhead, and every head turned to look at me.

The coffee shop was packed. People I'd known for my entire life huddled around the tables, cups of coffee left untouched. I smiled at Mr. Yardley. He *harumphed* and turned to the woman sitting next to him. Mrs. Ovet. She pursed her lips like she'd tasted something sour.

I hurried to the counter, which Leah was wiping down. The mural loomed overhead, its artist's signature almost at eye level.

R. MacAllister.

Rose. Charlie's aunt.

A girl who had drowned in the river here almost twenty-five years ago.

I tore my eyes from the mural and propped my elbows up on the counter. "Hey," I said.

She jumped and dropped the rag. "Amelia," she hissed. She glanced over her shoulder, toward the back office where her parents worked. "What are you doing here? Didn't you get my texts? I texted you like a million times."

I pulled my phone from my pocket. Sure enough, there was a missed call and six texts from Leah. I scrolled through them quickly.

Don't u answer ur phone?
Must talk 2 u asap.
Where ru?

Amelia I'm not kidding call me.

Mom is on warpath, don't come to the shop today. And keep Charlie at home. Every1 is talking.

CALL ME.

"What's going on?" I asked.

"Not here," she said. She pulled the apron over her head. "Upstairs."

"Charlie's in the car."

"Text him and tell him to stay out there."

"What's going on?" My skin crawled like every person in the cafe was staring at me. I refused to turn around.

"Shhh," Leah said. "Listen."

And then I could hear it.

"*—heard there was trouble out west, that's why he's here...*"

"*—got in a fight with the mayor's son the other night... dangerous...*"

"*What do you expect, living with her? There's something off about all of those MacAllisters...*"

"*—happening again...*"

I gripped the counter so hard my knuckles turned white. "They're talking about Charlie," I said. My stomach lurched, and I closed my eyes. "Do they think...?" I couldn't even say it. I couldn't think it. "But he was with me," I said.

"We have to get out of here," Leah said. "Now. Before he comes in here."

"He was with me." My voice rose. "He didn't do anything!"

I turned around slowly. Mrs. Ovet still stared at me, her eyes glittering like two black diamonds. I had the sudden urge to wrap my hands around her wrinkly neck. Against my skin, the ring grew warmer. Leah grabbed my arm, but I shook free of her grasp.

The low murmur of voices stopped.

"Did you hear me?" My voice climbed even higher. "Charlie had nothing to do with what happened. You all need to leave him alone."

The bells over the door danced. Charlie stood in the vestibule, phone in hand. His face was pale. "Amelia?"

Leah didn't give me time to respond. She yanked me towards him and pulled us both outside into the rain.

"Get in the car," Leah said. "We're leaving right now."

Charlie started the engine. "What's going on in there?"

Leah slid in next to me, pushing me to the middle of the bench seat. Her face was paler than usual, and she kept her eyes on the window as we pulled out of the parking lot. "Everyone's talking about Brit, Yvette, and Erin. They're looking for someone to blame."

Charlie's breath left him in a *whoosh*. "Me."

Leah's look was sympathetic. "You're a stranger, Charlie. It's easy to blame someone you don't know."

"And Ben's been spreading stories about what happened to Becca." Charlie slammed his hands down on the steering wheel. "Damn him."

"They were accidents," Leah said. "Anyone with any sense knows that you had nothing to do with it."

"Sense is one thing this town doesn't seem to have," Charlie muttered.

"Uncle Frank is looking into it, Charlie. He'll get to the bottom of it and show everyone you're innocent. I know he will."

I just hoped he'd be able to figure it out before anyone else ended up dead.

Thirty-one

The next week passed in a blur. I worked six days straight at the Tea Exchange alongside of Ms. MacAllister. Despite her earlier questions about holistic treatments and herbal medicines, my job was pretty straightforward: work the register, keep an eye on the door, and measure out tea leaves by the ounce. The shop wasn't that busy—Ms. MacAllister had been managing for years by herself—so I spent most of my shifts making work for myself. I organized the little area behind the cash register, arranged the spices alphabetically, and even spent a few hours flipping through various books on herbs that Ms. MacAllister kept in a stack on the counter. I'd managed to slip the little figurine onto the shelf in the back room on my first day; hopefully she hadn't even noticed that it was missing.

Charlie and Ransom spent their days out at the ruins, searching for a spell to open the ring. Ransom had suggested that they take the ring with them, just in case they found something that would work, but I'd been hesitant to let it out of my sight. It might have been hers at one point, but it was mine now, and I was going to be there when they opened it.

On Monday afternoon, Ms. MacAllister poked her head through the beaded curtain that separated the main room from the back area and swept an assessing gaze around the shop, over the dusted shelves and rearranged jars holding teas and spices. "You've done a lovely job in here, Amelia," she said. "It looks brand new."

I smiled at her. "I liked doing it," I said, and I was surprised to realize that I meant it. Being in the shop had given me something to focus on besides Marin.

"Good." She pulled a key ring with a set of keys and a bright blue fob from her pocket and set it on the counter between us. "I wanted you to have this, just in case you ever have to open or close when I'm not here." She flipped the little fob over. "The alarm codes are written on the back of this."

"I..." I didn't know what to say. "Are you sure?"

She lifted her eyebrow. It was amazing how many of Charlie's mannerisms I'd seen in his grandmother over the last few days. She looked so much like him at that moment that I relaxed. "I mean, thank you," I said.

The ghost of a smile flickered across her face, gone almost as soon as it had appeared. "Are you going to the vigil tonight?"

The mayor and his family had organized a town-wide candlelight vigil in memory of Yvette, Brit, and Erin to be held on the Green at dusk. My mom and uncle were going, but I wasn't so sure about myself. On the one hand, I'd known all three girls, especially Erin. But I wasn't sure how Charlie would feel if I went, or if Ben would cause another scene. I shrugged. "I'm not sure yet."

"Charlie and I will be there, if you and your mother would like to ride with us," Ms. MacAllister said.

"Is that the best idea?" The words left my mouth before I could stop them. Charlie had mostly kept to himself since the night of the fight.

"You know that my grandson has nothing to hide," she said, each word launched like a missile through the air. "And neither do I. We're going to pay our respects to those poor girls."

"It's not about what I think," I said. "It's about what *they* think."

She sighed. "If I gave one fig about what some of those people thought about me and my family, I'd never leave my house. Our friends know the truth. The rest of the town doesn't matter."

"But–"

"I know you want what's best for Charlie, Amelia. Believe me, I do. But I've been alive a lot longer than you have, and I've seen them in a frenzy like this before. They'll talk about us if we're there, but they'll talk louder if we aren't." She crossed her arms and stared out of the shop window, watching people stroll along the waterfront. "He's been so happy with you, honey. Even with all this other business happening around him, he's been happy."

My cheeks warmed, and once again, I was at a loss for words. I tucked the new keys into my pocket and stood up from the stool. "I'll be there tonight," I said, finally. "If he needs me, I'll be there."

Dusk settled over Asylum, deep grays and purples and blues wrapping around its corners, filling the empty alleyways and assuming some of the somberness that had filled our tiny town over the last few weeks. By the time Mom parked her Camry in front of the Historical Society, it seemed like half the town was already there, a mass of black-clad people filling the Green, clutching thin white candles in their hands.

Charlie had been silent for the entire drive into town, his forehead pressed against the window, his hand wrapped around mine. Mom flipped down the mirrored visor in front of her seat and checked her lipstick—a dark red, like blood. Her eyes met mine in the mirror, and she gave me a quick smile. I thought she meant for it to be encouraging, but it didn't quite reach her eyes. The last time there had been a vigil on the Green, it had been for my brother. I had still been in the hospital, and she'd gone alone.

I wondered if she was thinking about that too.

"Ready?" she asked.

Beside me, Charlie sighed and pushed up his new pair of glasses, almost identical to his old ones. The bruises across his face from his fight with Ben had faded from vivid purple to a dull yellow, but dark circles stretched under his eyes, making him look tired and wan. I wanted to give him a hug and promise him that everything would be okay, that we weren't walking into a disaster. But every fiber of my being was telling me otherwise.

Ms. MacAllister was already climbing out of the passenger door. She adjusted her wide-brimmed hat and threw her black-tasseled scarf over her shoulder. "It won't get any easier if you wait," she called back to us.

"Come on," I whispered. "I'll be right beside you."

He squeezed my fingers. "It's not me I'm worried about," he said. "I don't care what they think about me."

"I don't care either," I told him.

He nodded once. "Then let's do this."

Late-August humidity wrapped around me like a blanket the moment I stepped out of the car. I started sweating immediately—I could feel my hair already starting to escape from my braid in little wisps that curled around my forehead.

"You're going to overheat in that sweater." My mother tugged at the thin sleeve of my black cardigan. "Leave it in the car."

"I'll be fine," I said. The black linen sundress I wore was strapless and would put my scar on full display. The sweater was my only armor against people's stares. "It's staying on."

"Suit yourself," Mom said. She looked cool and effortless in her black sleeveless shift dress, her blond hair curling around her chin. She turned to Ms. MacAllister. "I have something I'd like to show you quickly at the Society, Lilian. It'll just take a minute."

Ms. MacAllister nodded, keeping one hand on her hat. "We'll find you two later, all right? We'll meet back here when it's over."

"Yes, ma'am," Charlie said. I would have killed to know what he was thinking right then. I was a jumbled mess inside, full of dread and anxiety, waiting for something bad to happen. He stepped up beside me and grabbed my hand.

"We're in this together," he said. "They can't hurt us."

I took a deep breath and wrapped my fingers around my necklace.

We'd see about that.

Leah was waiting for us on the edge of the crowd. She caught sight of us and waved her hand in the air. "Charlie! Amelia! Over here!"

Several people turned to look at her—at *us*—with disapproval written all over their faces. A low murmur swept through those closest to us. I thought about giving them all the finger, but Charlie didn't seem to notice.

Or care.

"Hey," she said when we joined her. "Ben and his gang of Neanderthals are handing out all of the candles, so I sent Ransom to grab them for us."

"Good call," I said. "We don't want to give him a reason to cause a scene."

"Exactly." She tossed her long black hair over her shoulder and turned to Charlie. "How are you holding up?"

"Fine," he said. He stuffed his hands in his pockets and rocked back and forth on his heels. "I don't like these sorts of things, but Grams thought it'd be best if we came."

"Your Grams is right," Ransom said, appearing behind Leah. He held four white candles in his hand, each shoved through the center of a thin cardboard disc. "The sheriff ruled them all suicides. Everyone with a brain knows you didn't do this."

I took the candle Ransom offered, the wax cool and smooth against my hand. "I hope you're right," I said.

Leah shook her head. "I don't think it's personal, Charlie. It's just that–"

"I'm a MacAllister," Charlie interrupted. "Yeah. I got that loud and clear."

Leah opened her mouth and closed it again without speaking, crimson spilling across her cheeks.

Ransom slid his gaze between them, his eyebrows quirked with amusement. "Amelia," he said, his voice low, "did lover-boy here tell you that we figured out a spell today?"

My hand flew to my necklace. "Don't tease me, Ransom."

"He's not," Charlie said. "It takes a lot out of me, but I think I can manage to do it."

"He's being modest," Ransom said. "Your boy split a tree in half."

A Magic Dark & Bright

Leah let out a low whistle. "Is that why you look so rough, Blue?" she asked. "You're turning into a human chainsaw?"

Before he could respond, a muffled thump came through the speakers set up near the gazebo, where Mayor Liancourt stood beside his wife. Three portraits, blown up to poster size, were set on easels behind him.

He tapped the microphone again, and cleared his throat. "Can everyone hear me?" he asked.

"First, I want to thank all of you for coming tonight. We gather as a community to remember the three beautiful young women that we lost this summer, to grieve, to mourn, and ultimately, to celebrate their lives, cut short too soon. My niece Britney D'Autrement, Yvette Montrose, and Erin West will be missed, not just by their families, but by all of us here in Asylum." He paused and shuffled the notecards in his hands. Beside him, Mrs. Liancourt dabbed at her eyes with a tissue. "We also gather tonight to raise awareness for suicide prevention. I've partnered with the Sheriff's Department and with the health officials in Bradford County to launch an awareness campaign. For those of you out there struggling, especially our young people: you are not alone. Together, we can fill this darkness with light."

He lit his candle with the match his wife held out for him and stepped off the gazebo steps to light the candle of the woman standing before him—his sister. Brit's mother. Tears threatened the corners of my eyes, but I blinked them away before they could fall.

Charlie slipped his arm around my shoulder. Was he thinking about Becca, his ex-girlfriend? Her death, so similar to theirs, had happened over a thousand miles away from here. I leaned into him despite the sticky heat and pressed my face against his chest.

We lit the candles wordlessly, one flame passed to another as full dark settled over the Green. Charlie tipped his candle towards mine, the two wicks meeting as the flame flickered between them. Leah waited on my other side and gave me a small, sad smile as I tilted my candle to hers.

I couldn't help but wonder who would be next.

Thirty-two

"Who are your friends, Dupree?" Alicia LaPorte stood over us, tapping her pen against the chipped laminate tabletop. "Have you been hiding these fine boys away from me all summer?"

I grinned up at her. Alicia had been my co-captain on swim team, a tall, lanky blonde with the foulest mouth I've ever heard. While we hadn't ever been close, she'd been one of the only girls to stay friendly with me after I'd quit. "Hey Alicia," I said. "This is Ransom, my mom's intern. And Charlie, my boyfriend."

"What a shame." She winked at him. "He's too cute to keep to yourself."

Heat crept up my neck, and beside me, Charlie squirmed in his seat.

Leah snaked her hand across the table, catching Ransom's fingers in her own. Claiming him. Ransom looked down at their hands, joined together, something like amusement flashing over his face. "Alas, gorgeous," he said to Alicia, "it appears we're both spoken for."

"I guess I'll just have to wait until college," Alicia said with a sigh. "All right. I know you aren't in here just to flaunt your beautiful boys in my face. What can I get you?"

She scribbled down our orders and left, her hips swaying with every step. The minute she was out of earshot, Leah leaned forward and rested her elbows on the table. "So tell us more about this spell," she said, looking at Charlie. "Do you really think it'll open Amelia's ring?"

Charlie, strangely enough, slid his gaze to Ransom. "Go ahead," he said to the other boy. "You're the one who found it."

Ransom straightened in his seat. "I found a sheet of paper tucked into one of the grimoires," he said. "It looked like it was torn out of an older manuscript. Late thirteenth, maybe early fourteenth century, by the handwriting, if I had to guess."

"And it worked?" I asked Charlie.

"It's not really an opening spell, per se," Ransom said before Charlie could answer me. "It's a severing spell. I think he can use it to break apart whatever's holding the clasp together."

"I have to work on my precision," Charlie said. He slipped his glasses off and pinched the bridge of his nose. "It's an intense spell."

"I told you to stop being modest. The spell isn't intense—you are," Ransom said. "Charlie has some insanely powerful juju going on."

Charlie's smile was brief. "Yeah, well. We'll see how long that lasts." He sat back as Alicia set a steaming cup of black coffee in front of him. "Thanks," he said.

"No problem, hot stuff," she said. "You guys good here?"

I picked up my fork and dug into my pie. "We're great, Alicia. Thanks."

She saluted me and turned on her heel. "Holler if you need anything."

"What do you mean, Charlie?" Leah asked. "Will you run out of... of..." she dropped her voice, "... *magic* before we can open the ring?"

"He'll be fine," Ransom said. "He'll get plenty of rest once we open the ring."

I frowned at him across the table. "Maybe we can wait a few days," I said. "After a few hundred years, how much will a few days matter?"

"We have to do it now." Ransom gritted the words through his teeth. "I don't have much time left. Just a few weeks before I go back to school."

The bell over the door danced. I glanced over and locked eyes with Ben as he stepped into the diner. He faltered, the smile falling off his face at the sight of me. Ransom lifted his hand in a wave, smirking.

Ben scowled and took a seat at the counter with his back to us.

I tore my gaze away from him and turned back to Charlie, resting my hand on his knee. "We do this when you're ready. Not before."

He raised his gaze to mine. His eyes, normally brilliant blue, were muddy and tired in his face. "Maybe Ransom's right," he said. "Maybe it's better just to get it over with."

I shook my head. "If you're sure," I said.

I thought he meant for his smile to be reassuring, but instead it just made the shadows under his eyes look deeper. I didn't know how much more of himself he had left to give.

I hoped that whatever Ransom was asking wouldn't be too much.

I am twenty-one years old, and I hate the place I have been exiled to.

Saint Domingue is hot and humid and sticky, especially now, at the end of August, and my new husband, the Viscount de Laval, is old and fat and boring. Twice now, I have had to stop myself from stopping his heart in his sleep. His children from his first marriage, all older than me by a decade or more, do not trust me, and killing him would only see me turned out onto the street. Since I have given him a son and a daughter less than a year apart, he has taken to traveling the island for weeks at a time to survey his various smaller plantations and make business deals in Port au Prince, leaving me in the big house on his largest sugar plantation with the children. There have been rumblings of discontent among the slaves in the cities, but here, on the northern end of the island, we are removed from the troubles.

We are safe.

For that, at least, I am thankful.

I run my fingers over my daughter's curls, black as a raven's wing. She rolls over, thumb tucked in her mouth. I pull it out gently and turn to my son. He sleeps like a starfish, limbs spread wide. It is hard to look at him and not think of the babe I abandoned.

The babe Robert tricked me into giving away.

The babe he stole from me.

As always, the anger comes hot and fast. A blue glow envelopes my hands, and I stop myself before I set the bed aflame. These children—my children—are innocents. They shall not suffer for my sins.

"Madame?" Nori, the slave who nurses the children, stands in the doorway, a lit candle in her hand. Her eyes are wide in the dim light, and at first, I think she has caught me at my magic. The slaves have whispered once or twice about me, rumors that I have had to find and snuff out at the source.

I rise, taking care to hide my still-effervescent hands behind my back. "Did you need something, Nori?"

She licks her lips. "Madame, you have a visitor. It is the Comte d'Edys' man. He says it is very important."

The Comte d'Edys owns the plantation closest to ours, a hard three-mile ride in the daylight. That he is here in the dark hour before dawn is troubling. I follow the girl down the stairs to find a travel-stained and dark-skinned young man—little more than a boy—clutching his hat in the parlor. He tries to bow the moment he sees me, but staggers forward instead. The front of his shirt is slick with blood.

"Madame," he breathes. "Treachery. The Comte is lost. Come. To warn you."

And then the madness descends upon us.

The window to my left shatters, sending a glittering cascade of glass into the room. Nori screams and runs for the stairs, but I am frozen, my feet stuck fast to the ground.

"Madame!" The Comte's man grabs me and pulls me from the room as the other window explodes. Someone tosses a torch inside, and the linen curtain catches fire immediately.

This time, I do not push the anger away. I shrug out of the boy's hands and open myself up to the power swirling within me. It responds eagerly, tugging at my edges, threatening to drown me in its depths. This time, I do not try to hide the glow that envelopes me.

This time, I embrace it.

"Get the children to safety," I tell the boy. He scrambles backwards, up the stairs. If I can only buy time for him, and for Nori and the children...

I turn to face the door. One flick of my wrist and it flies free, crashing against the wall.

Outside, there is chaos.

I step out onto to the veranda, barefooted and wearing my dressing robe. Smoke rises from the sugar fields, and already, I can hear screams. Somewhere in the distance, a gun is fired. But my attention does not linger in the distance. I focus on what is in front of me.

I focus on the mob, already bloodied, hungry for more.

I focus on the men, armed with machetes and pitchforks and battered old swords and a hunting rifle here and a pistol there.

I focus on these men who have come to burn my house with my children sleeping inside, who have come to kill my family.

I focus on the men I will destroy.

The power surges from me as the sun begins to rise, bright blue streaks against a deep purple sky. At first, they do not pay attention to me—they are too busy looting and raping and burning and murdering. Smoke pours from the house as the first of the men stumbles to the ground, a gaping hole in his chest. His heart, torn free, falls to the dirt beside him.

It is still beating.

Thirty-three

Something was wrong.

I sat up, gasping for air. The ring burned hot in my hand, and I dropped it in the dew-dampened grass beside me. I felt stiff and sore, like someone had jumbled all of my bones around under my skin before setting them back where they belonged.

Something was very, very wrong.

I shook my head, trying to remember something, anything. But the last thing I could remember was curling up on the sofa in my basement, clutching one of the worn pillows to my stomach before drifting off to sleep. And then I'd started dreaming so vividly...

Around me, the trees rose like dark sentinels, stretching into an endless sky, keeping me trapped. The forest was unnaturally silent around me—not a cricket chirped, and no branches creaked in the light breeze. I shivered. My knit shorts and tank top didn't offer me much protection from the cool night air.

I was alone.

I drew my legs up to my chest and buried my face in my knees, forcing myself to think. Panicking wouldn't help.

Think.

Somehow, I had ended up in the woods, alone and in my pajamas. Barefoot.

Think.

It was still the middle of the night, meaning no one would be looking for me for hours yet.

Think.

I had no idea where I was, what direction home was from here. If I started walking, not only would I probably end up deeper in the forest, I might fall in a hole and break my leg and be left unable to move. No one would know where I was, so I'd probably end up starving to death, unless a bear came along and ate me first. Either way, I was going to die out here. Alone.

My heart skittered in my chest. Alone, like Brit and Yvette and Erin.

So much for not panicking.

I forced a breath in and out. All I had to do was wait here until it was light enough to walk home.

In my bare feet.

I wiggled my toes against the grass, wondering *how*. I must have walked—barefoot—all the way out here in my sleep, which was so unsettling I couldn't even follow that train of thought, considering I didn't even know where *here* was.

"*Amelia...*" It was as soft as a whisper.

The hair on the back of my neck stood at attention.

Maybe I wasn't alone.

No. No. I was just imagining things.

I thought of Erin, face down in the water.

"*Amelia...*"

It came from behind me. I jumped to my feet and whipped around, not knowing what to expect.

I didn't expect to see her.

She floated a few feet away from me, her bare feet hovering inches above the grass. She didn't flicker, didn't flit from place to place. She didn't even glow as brightly as she had before—she was just bright enough for me to see her clearly in the dark forest. A pale pearly sheen seemed to come from under her skin.

Marin stood before me, almost as real and solid as myself. She was still as young and beautiful as she'd been in my dreams, with black hair hanging nearly to her waist and bright red lips curved into a small smile. Her long white dress still twisted around her, like she was standing in a wind that only she could feel. Her blue eyes glittered in the darkness, like two frozen sapphires staring back at me.

Impossible.

"Amelia," she said again. Her voice sounded like it was coming from far away. She lifted her arm, and I had a sudden flash of the dream, of a beating heart on the ground and hot blood on my face.

Fear spiked in my chest. I stepped back, away from her, right onto something hard and sharp. *The ring.* I picked it up, clutching it until the edges dug into my palm. If need be, I could throw it at her. It wasn't much in the way of protection, but it was all I had.

Her face twisted, and she drew her hand back like I'd slapped her. "Amelia," she said again, her words dripping with pain. "Help me. Please."

"What happened to you? Why are you different?"

"Help me," she repeated.

"This was yours," I said, holding the ring out on my palm. I took a step closer to her. "Wasn't it?"

Her smile turned cold, and she turned her palms to face me.

"What happened to you?" I asked again.

Bright blue-white light erupted from within her, filling the clearing and blinding me. I threw my arm up over my eyes, and then I was the one screaming, screaming until I dropped to my knees and realized that she was gone.

And I was alone.

"Amelia!"

I jerked my head up. This voice was deep and desperate and familiar. *Charlie.*

Off in the distance, a single beam of light bobbed through the trees, moving quickly toward me. I scrambled to my feet and waved my arms, even though it was so dark that I doubted he could see me. Relief flooded me as he crashed closer. The light grew brighter as he moved, bright blue against the inky black forest. It wasn't a flashlight after all, I realized, but the same blue-white light he'd used in the tunnel under the ruins, a brilliant sphere floating just ahead of him. The same blue-white light that had erupted from Marin.

His magic.

I moved towards him, and before I knew it, he had his arms wrapped around me, his face buried in my hair. I pressed my face against his chest, and his heartbeat echoed through me as he struggled to catch his breath. I let the sobs burst lose from my chest. "She was here," I cried. "She was here."

"Who was?" he asked against my hair. "Who was here?"

"The ghost. Marin. Whoever she is," I said through my tears. "I think—I think—"

He kissed me, stopping the words at my lips. When we parted, I stepped back and stared up at him. "I'm so happy to see you," I said.

"You're okay?" he asked. He moved his hands from my waist to my chin, tilting my face up to his. He looked even worse than he had earlier at the vigil, the blue-white of his witch light leeching all of the color from his face.

I nodded. "I'm fine," I said. "How did you know where to find me?"

"Your mom called me panicking. She couldn't find you. I've been looking for you for an hour. Your uncle has half the town out looking for you." His voice was hoarse, like he'd been shouting for me that entire time. He leaned closer. "What are you doing out here?"

"I don't know," I said, and I didn't. The last thing I remembered was falling asleep on the couch. "I just woke up, and I was out here."

"You're still sleepwalking?" His fingers traced my jaw, and I leaned closer to him. I was so tired. So, so tired.

"No. Yes. I don't know," I replied, my voice barely a whisper. "I've been having the strangest dreams." I pressed the ring into his hand. "I think the ring is doing something to me."

He frowned at me. "What do you mean?"

"I don't know," I said. "But just—take it. Please."

He nodded and closed his fingers around it. He tucked it into his pocket and pulled out his phone. "I have to call your mom," he said. "She's been worried sick." He redialed his most recent call and pressed the phone to his ear. "I found her. We're about a half-mile from the house. We'll be back in about twenty minutes." He gave me a faint smile and said, "Yeah. I will." He hung up the phone and wrapped his arms around me, like he couldn't quite believe I was there.

"You're shaking," he said. He shrugged out of his sweatshirt and handed it to me. I tugged it over my head and let myself be wrapped in the soft fabric, still warm from his skin. It smelled like spice and pine and Charlie. "You're okay," he said. "You're going to be okay."

It was too dark to see his face, to see what he was thinking. Did he think I was crazy?

Was I crazy?

"You're okay," he said again, capturing my lips with his own. The light around us burned even brighter as he crushed me to him, his hands slipping under the sweatshirt and resting on the skin of my back. "You scared the crap out of me."

"I'm sorry."

"Don't be. It's not your fault," he said. He pushed my hair back from my face. "I just realized how easily I could lose you. And I don't know if I could survive that."

"Charlie—"

"Just let me finish," he said. "I think—I think I'm falling in love with you, Amelia."

I think I'm falling in love with you.

I tugged his head down to me and kissed him with everything I had.

I didn't think. I knew.

I was in love with Charlie Blue too.

Thirty-four

Uncle Frank sat, stone-faced, and stared at me across the kitchen table. He waited to speak until I stopped shaking, at least.

He leaned forward, resting his big arms on the table, his gaze fixed on the mug of tea in my hands. "How long has this been going on?"

I sipped the tea. It was too hot, and it scalded my tongue, but I didn't care. I was still cold, frozen inside.

"Millie?"

"All summer." I couldn't look at him. I didn't want to see the glance that he and my mother exchanged over my head.

"You said it stopped." Mom's voice was reedy and thin. The spoon in her hand clattered against the ceramic mug. "If I'd know, I'd have made you go see Dr. Gibson. You lied to me, Amelia, you lied and—"

"Issy." Uncle Frank reached out and gripped her hand. "She's safe."

"But what if she hadn't been? That other girl—"

"That other girl isn't Amelia. She's safe, Isabelle."

I shook my head. I still felt fuzzy around the edges, like I was lagging behind while everyone around me moved in hyper-speed. "Wait," I said. "What are you talking about? What other girl?"

My uncle's face was grim. "We found another girl in the river while we were out looking for you. Looks like a suicide, just like the others."

My mother pressed her hands to her mouth, and I felt sick. After everything, I could only imagine what must be going through her head. Four. This was the fourth.

What was going on?

"Who?" I demanded.

Mom and Frank exchanged glances. "Millie," he said. "This is official Sheriff's—"

"Who?"

"Alicia LaPorte."

My heart sputtered, and my mouth went dry. "No. I just saw her."

Alicia, our waitress from Ollie's. All I could see was Ransom laughing as my pretty blond teammate served him pie last night. Alicia, always quick with a dirty joke or a snappy comeback.

Alicia, facedown and blue in the Susquehanna. Just like Brit. Just like Yvette. Just like Erin.

Four.

I didn't realize I was on my feet until Mom's arms came around me, warm and reassuring. "When the news came in over the radio, I thought it was you," she whispered against my hair. "And when Dave said it wasn't, said it was the LaPorte girl, I was actually relieved. Can you believe that? Of all the horrible, selfish things, a girl is dead, and all I can feel is relief that I won't be burying you beside your brother. I'm a monster."

"Isabelle, it's okay." Frank was on his feet now too, pulling my mother away from me and into his arms. She sobbed into his chest, sagged against him, and he held her gently, tenderly. Not like a friend or a brother-in-law, but like something else.

Like my dad should have held her all those months ago.

His eyes, gold-speckled green, so much like my own, so much like my father's, met mine over her head, and everything snapped into place.

Mom's overnight visits with her 'friends' in Scranton, the long lunches. The fact that he'd been with her each and every time they'd found a girl in the river.

Uncle Frank was in love with my mother.

I watched, open-mouthed, as he persuaded her out of the kitchen and upstairs, and I waited, arms crossed, leaning against the counter, until he returned, his hands stuffed in his pockets.

"How long?"

"Millie, honey, you have to understand—"

"How long?"

He sighed. "How long have I loved her? Or how long have we been together?"

"Is there a difference?" My words came out harder than I'd wanted them to, but all I could think was that this, *this*, was why Dad had left after Mark's funeral, why he'd left me. Mom had been having an affair with his brother.

Frank, who had taught me how to ride a bicycle while my dad was away on business.

Frank, who dressed up as Santa every Christmas Eve and delivered exactly one present during dinner, promising the rest would come in the morning.

Frank, who had been the first one on the scene the night of the accident, the one who'd put his jacket over me and held my hand while I lay still, bleeding scarlet against the bright white snow.

Frank, the one who'd watched as they'd pulled my brother's broken body from the car.

Frank, who'd stayed.

"Did he know? Is that why...?"

"What?" For the first time, Frank looked shocked. "Sweetheart, no. Your mom and I—it's complicated. I've loved her for my entire life. But she loved your dad, and when he left, he nearly destroyed her." He gripped the edge of the doorframe, his knuckles white under his skin. "I tried to stay away from her. What kind of man wants his brother's wife? But I couldn't."

I wanted to move towards him, but I couldn't. My feet stayed still, rooted to the linoleum floor.

He shook his head. "I help people. It's what I do. And she needed me, Mils. I don't know if it was right, but I love her, and I'm not going to let her down the way he did. I'm not going anywhere." This time, when his eyes met mine, they blazed.

"You love her?"

"Since I was six years old." His grin was crooked and watery. "And for whatever reason, she loves me back."

"But why didn't you tell me?"

"We weren't sure how you'd react. You'd just lost Mark, and then your dad, and the last thing you needed was another change. After a while…" he shrugged. "I'm sorry, sweetheart. You deserved to know."

I let my head thunk back against the cabinets and closed my eyes. "This is beyond fucked up. You realize that, right?"

"I know it must be a lot to take in right now."

"You have no idea."

"I'm surprised you haven't taken a swing at me."

"That's still a possibility."

He threw back his head and laughed, and before too long, my own laughter bubbled up inside of me, bursting out from my chest, and I let my uncle take me by the arm. I didn't fight him as he pushed me gently towards the stairs. "Rest, Mils," he said. "We'll talk more when you wake up."

Thirty-five

I woke to my cellphone buzzing next to my head, loud and insistent. I didn't recognize the number on the screen. "Hello?"

"Is this Amelia Dupree?" The woman's voice on the other end of the line was clipped and tense.

I sat up and dragged my hand across my face. The clock on the table next to me blinked 4:35.

Less than two hours ago, I'd been in the woods. *So much for sleeping.*

"Yes, that's me." I said.

"Miss Dupree, I'm with the Safe-Tech Alarm Company. It looks like there's been a disturbance at the–" there was a rustle of papers, "–the Asylum Tea Exchange. We have you down as a secondary contact."

That didn't make any sense. Ms. MacAllister had only given me the keys–and the codes–yesterday. I rubbed the sleep from my eyes. "What about Ms. MacAllister?" I asked.

"There was no answer, ma'am."

"So what do you want me to do?"

The woman on the other end paused. "Normally you either instruct us to call the local police department, or you have someone go to the store to shut the alarm off. It's your choice."

I looked at the clock again. Uncle Frank had been out all night trying to find me. It'd be cruel of me to wake him now. "Don't worry about the police," I said. I climbed out of bed and slipped into my flip flops. I grabbed Charlie's dark green hoodie off the back of my desk chair. "I'll handle it."

Mom kept the key to the Jeep hanging on the key hook next to the front door. It took about two seconds to grab it, shut the front door behind me, and start the car. I clutched the steering wheel and took a deep breath.

It was just a car.

I could do this.

I put the Jeep in reverse and slowly backed out of the driveway. I kept the headlights off until I made the turn onto the main road. Thankfully, the pre-dawn roads were dark and empty. Deserted. I wasn't too worried about being caught driving without my license, considering a solid half of Asylum's police force was sound asleep in my mother's bed.

Ick.

Mom and Frank.

Frank and Mom.

That idea was definitely going to take some getting used to.

I drove slowly, my fingers white-knuckled against the wheel. I parked the Jeep in the tiny alley that ran along the side of the shop. All I had to do was go in, punch in the alarm code, and go home.

Easy enough.

I fished my key ring from my purse and headed to the front of the store. The streetlights along the riverfront were out, the sidewalk wrapped in darkness. I wished I'd thought to bring a flashlight—instead, I was stuck with the little blue rectangle of light my phone cast on the ground.

The ground that was sparkling.

Shards of broken glass littered the sidewalk in front of Ms. MacAllister's shop, covering the concrete like wickedly sharp icicles. I tilted my phone up, shining the light over the space where the large plate glass window had been. Now it was broken, a jagged hole in the center, like someone had thrown a rock through it.

Shit.

I dialed Ms. MacAllister's house, then Charlie. Both phones rang and rang, but no one answered. I bit my lip, considering my options.

Mom and Frank would be pissed if they knew I was out here alone, especially considering that there'd been two girls found dead in as many days. They would have been mad even if I'd just left without telling them and gotten a ride down here—but sneaking out *and* taking the Jeep?

Not so smart, Amelia.

No. My only option was to switch off the alarm and tell Ms. MacAllister about it in the morning. And hope that she'd cover for me. It was a thin plan, as far as plans went. But at least it was a plan.

I unlocked the door and stepped inside. More broken glass crunched under my flip-flops, and I crept my fingers along the wall, feeling for the light switch. I flipped it up, but the shop stayed dark. The hair at the back of my neck prickled, and I took a deep breath and flipped the switch again, just to make myself feel better.

Spoiler: it didn't help.

The beaded curtain in the back of the shop rustled, the beads clicking together softly, like someone had drawn a hand across it. I froze. I gripped my keys one hand and shined the light from my phone toward the doorway.

"Hello?" I called out. "Is anyone there? I'm calling the police."

Silence.

I picked my way carefully across the floor. The weak blue light danced over the glass jars, knocked off their shelves and smashed, their contents strewn over the floor. With every step, my heart felt heavier. This was more than just a rock thrown through a window. Someone had been in here.

Get in the back, punch in the code, leave.

The room behind the beaded curtain seemed impossibly far away as I picked my way across the glass-strewn floor.

"I'm calling the police," I repeated, even though I kept my phone out in front of me, its tiny beam of light my only protection from the encroaching darkness. I hoped whoever was back there wouldn't call me on my bluff. "So you should probably just leave now."

I pushed the curtain out of the way and stepped into the back room. My shins hit something hard; I yelped and nearly stumbled. The light from my phone revealed one of the chairs turned on its side, the upholstery ripped from its frame.

Only a few more steps, and I would be able to leave. I moved around the chair and kept walking, one step at a time. *Just a little further...*

I tripped again, this time falling to my knees. My phone flew from my hand and skittered across the floor. It bounced a few times before coming to rest several feet away, right at the door to the stock room. I crawled towards it as fast as I could, but before I could get there, a pale hand reached down and closed around the phone.

Don't scream. He can't see you, I reminded myself. I covered my mouth with my hands and froze, unwilling to move even another inch.

The light winked out, leaving me in the oppressive blackness that surrounded me. My own heartbeat seemed to echo through the dark, sending fear racing down my spine and putting every nerve on high alert, like I was a child tucked into bed, seeing monsters in the shadows.

Only this time, the monster was real. I could feel his presence a few feet away, hear the gentle rhythm of his breaths, biding his time until I revealed where I was.

"I can hear you, Amelia," he called out, his voice rough and sing-song. Familiar. Goosebumps marched over my skin. I knew that voice. *Who?*

Something hard and plastic clattered to the ground beside me. This time I couldn't stop my scream, and I didn't care. I had to get out of there. *Now.*

I jumped to my feet and ran in the direction I thought the door was, only to collide with something hard and warm.

Not something.

Some*one*.

A rough hand gripped my upper arm, and a ball of blue light bloomed in the darkness, so bright that I had to blink against the harsh glare.

Ransom held his free hand aloft, his face impassive under the glow of the witch light.

"Boo," he said, his lips twisting upwards into a facsimile of a smile.

I yanked my arm back, trying to break free of his grip. But his fingers stayed clamped around me. "What are you doing?" I asked. "Why are you here?"

I should have felt relieved. Instead, dread filled my middle, like I'd swallowed a handful of thorns.

His not-quite smile grew. "Haven't you figured it out yet?"

"Did you come here to look for me? Charlie found me, you know. I was sleepwalking again. Right into the woods this time."

"I'm almost disappointed in you, Amelia. You're supposed to be a smart girl."

I took a deep, shuddering breath. "Did you do this?" I waved my free arm toward the darkness, where the rest of the shop lay in disarray.

He let out a short, barking laugh and let go of me. "I had to get you down here somehow. I don't care about this pathetic little shop, or the sorry excuse for a MacAllister who runs it," he sneered. "You know what I want, Amelia. Give it to me."

"I don't know—"

"The ring. Give me the ring."

My hands went automatically to my collarbone, where my necklace usually rested. My fingers met bare skin. "I don't have it."

"Don't lie to me, sweetheart." He waved his hand, and something frigid and rock-hard, like bands of ice, slammed into place around my upper arms, locking them against my sides.

"What are you doing?" I cried, struggling against the bonds as the sick feeling in my stomach grew. "How did you...?"

"Do you really think your boyfriend could have figured out all that magic on his own?" Ransom raised his eyebrows. "He needed someone to teach him. Someone who knew what he was doing."

"You," I said. He'd been the one to find the books, the one who had helped Charlie with the spell. The one who had suggested we try magic in the first place.

The one who had shown up unannounced and inserted himself into every facet of our lives.

"Who are you?" I asked.

"A very bad man," he said, his smile falling away. "Give me the ring."

"I told you, I don't have it."

He flicked his wrist, and I flew upward with such force that I couldn't stop the scream that tore from my lungs. He waved his hand again, and I jerked to a stop, my hair just brushing the wooden ceiling beams.

"I will hurt you." He leaned back against the wall and crossed his arms over his chest. "You have no clue about the things I've done for no reason at all."

I closed my eyes, willing away the tears that threatened to spill onto my cheeks. I wasn't going to give him the satisfaction of letting him see me cry.

"Ransom, please."

He let me fall. The ground rushed up to meet me, and I screamed again, bracing myself for the crunch of my bones hitting the concrete floor.

It didn't come.

He let me hover a few inches off the ground. "You're lying," he said. "You haven't let it out of your sight all summer."

I sagged against my invisible bonds. "I swear, I don't have it."

He stepped close to me, his gray eyes flashing. "Then tell me where it is, or I swear I'll rip your heart out right here and now."

Ransom looked crazed under the witch light, his normally coiffed hair standing on end, his shirt untucked. Maybe he really would. Maybe he was what he said.

A *very bad man.*

"I don't know," I whispered.

I didn't scream this time, not even as I flew upwards so hard I bit my tongue. My mouth filled with the coppery tang of blood, and I winced.

"What do you mean?" His voice quavered ever so slightly. "I'll let you fall, Amelia. I will."

I stared down at him, at the sad, pretty boy who had kissed my best friend under the moonlight and put hot sauce on his popcorn and who had been working with my mother all summer. The boy who'd moved into my dead brother's room and had helped me make pancakes just yesterday, and another piece of the puzzle clicked into place.

"You're working for her, aren't you?" I asked. "You know something about her that we don't."

His head snapped up. "I know lots of things," he said.

"Then you know there's something wrong with her," I said quickly. "She's bad, Ransom. I can feel it. I don't know what she wants, but I know it isn't good. What could she possibly have over you to make you serve her?"

"Bad?" He laughed again, and I dropped a few inches. "You don't know what you're talking about, Amelia. I don't *serve* her. I'm helping her because I love her."

I couldn't help it—I gaped at him. "She's dead, Ransom."

His face twisted. "You don't understand," he said. "Now tell me where the ring is."

The bands around my arms tightened, squeezing so tight I could barely breathe. "Ransom…"

"Where?" he shouted.

"I gave it to Charlie," I managed to gasp out. "He was going to put it somewhere safe."

Ransom let the witch light wink out, but left me suspended in the air, feet kicking far above the concrete floor.

"If you're lying to me, I'll kill everyone you love. Starting with him."

Thirty-six

My age no longer matters.

An ancient woman, dark-skinned and stooped and wrinkled, leans over me. I struggle to blink, to sit up, but she pushes me back down against the mat with firm hands.

"You've come too far, child. You must rest now."

The images come in a flash: the curtains of the parlor, engulfed in flames. The men, dead at my feet, the mud tinged red. My power, coursing through my veins, electric blue against the black night sky.

And the blood. Mon Dieu, the blood.

The woman mutters under her breath in the slave tongue and shakes a bundle of bones tied together with a blue ribbon over my chest.

"You're a witch," I say. My voice feels strange in my mouth when I speak, gravelly and rough. My skin too is wrong—my face feels tight, like someone has exchanged it for another's.

"Some even call me a queen," she says. Her eyes, bright blue, glimmer like sapphires. "You may call me Madame."

I bite back the words on my tongue, that I am the daughter of a count, the wife of a prominent landowner, a peer of the realm, and I will call no lowly slave woman Madame. Instead, I struggle to sit. "My children," I say.

"You do not remember?"

I close my eyes.

I remember.

I do.

I remember tucking them into bed, pressing kisses against their perfect, smooth brows.

I remember their screams, high and piercing, the kind of screams that ripped my heart in half, over the smoke and chaos that covered the house.

I remember falling to the ground beside their still forms, their eyes already staring deep into forever, while I sucked in air through the gaping wound in my chest.

I remember closing my eyes and surrendering myself to death's dark embrace.

My hands fly to my chest, and I tear at the thin linen shift until the fabric gives way and my breasts lie bare, but the skin is smooth, untouched, unscarred.

Perfect.

"What did you do?"

The woman raises her eyebrows. "Death is not through with you yet, cherie. He chewed you up good and spat you out, right back here with me, but he did not want you." When she smiles, her teeth are black and rotting, and I close my eyes and turn my head towards the wall. My home is destroyed. My children, dead.

And yet, I live.

Over the next few weeks, the old woman nurses me back to health. She prays over me, chanting and sprinkling me with bits of ash and sand and herbs, and forces foul-tasting potions down my throat. Despite myself, I grow stronger, and in the third week, when I can finally stand without my knees knocking together like a newborn colt's, she takes me with her down a long, deserted stretch of beach.

"The power is strong within you," she says. "And so is the darkness. The anger. And that is good, yeah? The anger and the darkness is what he bring you to me for."

"I don't understand," I protest. "Who is he?"

She clicks her tongue against the roof of her mouth and grins, exposing her rotted teeth. "That don't matter right now. What matters is that darkness. Someone has wronged you, yeah? Someone has taken what is yours. Stolen from you."

His face swims before my eyes, unbidden. His golden hair curls around his shoulders, his brown eyes crinkle at the corners, and his mouth crashes down on mine.

And then another face, this one small and dark-haired, clutching at my breast.

The pain comes swiftly, so sharp that I stumble and sink to my hands and knees in the sand.

Something stolen.

My son.

"How do I even know that he lives?" I choke out. "My parents and sisters are dead. How do I know that he did not perish with them?" Even as the words spill from my lips, I know that I am wrong. Somewhere, my son, my Henri, is alive. A pulsing fills my chest, tugging me in a direction toward the sea.

Toward him.

"You know, cherie," Madame says. Her eyes blaze bright blue against her dark skin, and she taps one thin finger against my chest, over the spot where the rebel's knife had pierced it. "And I will teach you how to take back what is yours."

And she does.

The first time is the hardest. The girl is young, maybe eleven or twelve. She stares up at me with tears in her eyes, even after Madame has given her the potion to paralyze her limbs. I hesitate, unsure that I can continue, but Madame nudges my hand, causing the knife to draw a brilliant bead of scarlet blood. I close my eyes as I draw the sharp blade across her throat. I hum loudly, trying to drown out the wet gurgles of her dying breaths. I lean close and press my mouth to hers, taste the blood on her lips.

A soft blue glow surrounds me as the girl's soul fills me. Fire shoots down my limbs and wraps around my heart. I gasp and wrench away from her. The power that courses through me is unlike anything I have ever felt before. It's too much to control—I turn and open my hands toward the fireplace. Bright blue flames erupt from my palms and race up the chimney.

Madame's hand falls on my shoulder.

My smile matches hers.

By the time I board the ship heading for Philadelphia, I am no longer a simple woman with natural talents. I am a weapon, forged by fire, shaped by darkness, and destined for one purpose:

Revenge.

Thirty-seven

"Hello?" Ms. MacAllister's voice came from the front room. She crunched over the broken glass on the floor, her footsteps quick and sure. "Is anyone here?"

"Help," I croaked out. My voice had gone hoarse sometime after the sun had risen, sending mist-wrapped light through the broken windows. "I'm back here."

Ransom had been gone for hours. He had left me floating in the back room, my feet dangling almost seven feet above the floor. Never again would I think a twelve-foot ceiling was impressive, I promised myself. Why couldn't the shop have an eight foot ceiling? Then there'd be a much smaller drop.

Ms. MacAllister's footsteps came closer. She pushed her way through the beaded curtain and gasped when she saw the damage Ransom had done to the room.

"Help," I said again.

Her head snapped up, and her eyes went wide with shock. "Amelia? What on earth?"

"Please," I said. "You have to call Charlie. He's in danger."

She set her mouth in a grim line. "First things first," she said. "Let's get you down from there."

"I don't—"

She waved her hand, just like Ransom had done. The bands of ice around my arms softened and warmed, and I lowered to the ground slowly. The minute my feet hit the floor, I crumpled into a heap, my legs jelly.

The older woman caught me before I completely collapsed. "Now you tell me who did this."

"Ransom," I rasped. "He's after Charlie. We have to help him."

Horror dawned on her face. "Ransom," she said slowly. "Your mother's intern?" She let go of me and produced a key from her pocket. She knelt in front of one of the cabinets and opened the door.

"He's not who we thought." I didn't have time to make her understand. "We have to stop him."

She pulled a faded brown photo album from the cabinet and flipped it open. "Amelia," she said, "I need you to be calm right now and think clearly. Is this the boy you're talking about?"

She pushed the album into my hands and pointed a manicured finger at a photo on the left side of the page. There were two boys standing next to each other dressed in somber black suits, one at least a foot taller than the other. The younger boy stared up at the taller one, an adoring look on his face. I'd seen a photo of him before; he'd been one of the boys in the picture in the hidden room—the one with his head still intact.

I turned my attention to the older boy. He scowled at the camera, his hands tucked into his pockets.

Ransom.

I tore the photo from the page and flipped it over. In a spidery hand on the back, someone had written *Ransom and Francis, June 1913. Ages 17 & 11.* I turned it right side up again, the bile rising in my throat.

"How is this possible?"

"Is it him?" she asked.

When I nodded, she climbed to her feet. "Get in the car, Amelia. I'll explain everything to you back at the house."

We left the Jeep parked in the alley. Mom was going to kill me when she found out, but as long as she killed me *after* we saved Charlie from Ransom, I didn't care.

Ms. MacAllister sped through town, knuckles white against the dark brown leather of her steering wheel, mouth pressed into a thin, grim line. "I'm sure you have a lot of questions," she finally said, darting a glance over to me. "I don't even know where to begin."

I bounced my knee on the seat, one hand gripping the handle over the passenger-side door as the trees outside whipped by. "It's true what they say about you," I said. "You're a witch."

She nodded.

"And you haven't told Charlie."

"Not yet. It's complicated. His mother and I... well. We wanted to keep him safe."

"He isn't safe now," I pointed out, my voice quiet. "He deserved to know."

"I know," she said. "I just hope..." She let her voice trail off, but it wasn't like she had to finish her sentence. I knew what she was going to say.

I hoped it wouldn't be too late too.

"He knows about the magic," I said after a moment. "It was Ransom. He's the one he told us, and Charlie really took to it. He's been practicing."

She swore under her breath. "Of course he has," she said. She pressed her foot down on the gas and turned onto Laurel Street, tires screeching against the asphalt. "He's his mother's son, after all."

I didn't get a chance to ask her what she meant, because she jerked the car to a stop in her driveway. By the time she turned off the engine, I was already halfway across the lawn, my flip-flops smacking against the soles of my feet. Minion's barks carried across the grass in long, mournful howls. I took the steps two at a time and launched myself at the door. I closed my hand around the knob just in time to register the smell of burning metal seconds before heat seared across my palm. I yelped and yanked my hand back.

"Stand back," Ms. MacAllister said. She strode up the porch stairs, her long black skirt swirling around her ankles, and I wondered how I'd ever convinced myself that she *wasn't* a witch. She swiped her hand across the air in front of the door. The locked clicked, and the door swung open into the dark foyer. It slammed shut behind us, loud enough that I jumped. "The house has some ways of protecting itself," she explained as I trailed her across the checked tile floor. "It should have been enough to keep Ransom out. Charlie!" she called. "Charlie, honey, are you home?"

Minion gave another bark as he rounded the corner from the kitchen. His eyes were wide and wild, his droopy ears swinging as he ran down the hall.

I cradled my burned hand against my chest. "But he's been in the house," I said quickly. "More than once."

Minion whined, and Ms. MacAllister froze, her spine ramrod straight. "Ransom MacAllister has been in this house?" Her voice raised to a near-shriek. "Charlie invited him inside?"

I nodded stiffly. "We didn't—"

"Know," she finished for me. "Damn that daughter of mine. Charlie!" she yelled again.

Charlie appeared at the top of the stairs, a towel slung around his bare waist, his wet hair pushed back from his forehead. Relief, sweet and pure, cascaded over me.

Ransom hadn't gotten to him yet.

"Thank God you're home," he said. "Your dog has been howling for the last twenty minutes." He slipped his glasses on and blinked down at me. "Hey, Amelia. I, uh, didn't know you were coming over?"

"Get dressed and get down here," his grandmother said. "We have to talk."

"Okay," he said. He didn't move. "Is something—"

"Get dressed first, questions later."

He ducked into his bedroom, and she turned to me and pointed through the double doors that led off the foyer. "Parlor. Now. I'll be right back."

I did as she asked. Minion paced in the doorway, his gaze intent on the front door, fur bristling. I tried sitting on the sofa, but like the dog, I was too on edge to stay still. I fiddled with the photos on the table closest to me. I looked up as Charlie bounded down the stairs, pulling a shirt over his head.

"What's going on?" he asked as soon as he reached me, and folded me into his arms. "You're shaking. Is this about last night?"

"It's Ransom," I said. "I—"

"He's not missing anymore, if that's what you're worried about. He was here just a few minutes ago. I guess no one told him you'd turned up. He'd been out all night looking for you."

I stiffened in his embrace. "He was here?" *No. No no no no.*

"Yeah, like five minutes ago. He..." Charlie trailed off, his eyes searching my face. "What's wrong?"

I gripped the front of his shirt. "The ring. Charlie, did he ask for the ring?"

His face paled. "How did you know that?"

"Did you give it to him?"

"I—"

Ms. MacAllister appeared in the doorway, a small iron box in her hands. "Sit down, both of you. We have a lot to talk about."

"What's going on?" Charlie asked again. He dropped down onto the sofa and looked up at his grandmother, his brows dipping beneath his glasses. "Is everything okay?"

Ms. MacAllister gripped the metal box in front of her. "No, honey. It isn't."

He frowned. "Grams?"

She set the box on the coffee table and settled herself into the overstuffed armchair beside the couch. I sat beside Charlie and grabbed his hand. He squeezed back without looking at me.

Ms. MacAllister took a deep breath. "I know you know about the magic, Charlie."

His mouth dropped open. "Grams—"

She held up her hand, silencing him. "I'm not angry with you. It's my fault, really. I've been keeping something from you, Charlie. And I'm very sorry about that."

He sucked in his breath, but didn't speak.

"Our family has what some might call a special talent. Magic. Witchcraft. I have it, your mom has it. And I know that you have it too."

"And my aunt? The one who killed herself? What about her?"

Pink tinged her cheeks. "It wasn't my choice to keep these things from you, Charlie. Your mother made me promise—"

"My *mother* is the one who sent me here to live with you!" He pulled his hand from my grasp and ran it through his still-damp hair. "You both lied to me."

"She wanted to protect you," Ms. MacAllister said. "Your mother has spent twenty years trying to escape her blood. After your girlfriend died, she realized she couldn't stop what was going to happen, but she didn't want to be a part of it. That's why you're here, Charlie. So I can help you."

"Lying to me isn't helping me," he said.

"I know that." She sighed, suddenly looking older than I'd ever seen her look before. "Your mother asked me to let you have this summer. She wanted you to have one last happy summer before you learned the truth. Against my better judgment, I agreed to honor her wishes."

"So why are you telling me this now?"

Ms. MacAllister looked at me. "Amelia was attacked this morning in my shop, and I think it was intended as a message for me. And for you."

Some of the anger seemed to drain from Charlie as he turned to me and his hands found mine again. "Why didn't you tell me?" he asked. "Are you okay?"

I nodded. "It was Ransom, Charlie. He's after my ring. Did you give it to him?"

He went ghostly white. "Amelia—"

Ms. MacAllister was on her feet, speaking over him before he could finish his sentence. "What ring?" she demanded. "What does it look like?"

"I... It's a ring. It has a sapphire set in the middle of it." I stared up at her. "Mark had it when he died. I don't know where he found it. I gave it to Charlie last night."

"And I gave it to Ransom about twenty minutes ago," Charlie whispered. "He said he wanted to take it down to the Historical Society to photograph before we tried the spell—" he glanced up at his grandmother, "—just in case anything happened to it."

The room spun around me. Ms. MacAllister let out a low moan and crumpled back in her chair. "This is all my fault," she said, her hand against her forehead.

"I don't understand what's going on." Charlie said. "Why would Ransom do that?"

I pulled the photo from my pocket and handed it to him. "Look."

Charlie took off his glasses and squinted down at it. "What is this?"

"Turn it over," Ms. MacAllister said.

Charlie flipped the photo over and read the back. He shook his head. "What does this mean? Who is he?"

Ms. MacAllister pursed her lips together and took the lid off the metal box. She lifted a small brown book, an enamel brooch, and a scrap of cloth from inside and arranged them in a row on the table.

"Give me your hands, and I'll show you. Both of you," she said when Charlie took her hand in his. She stretched her arm towards me. "You should see this too, Amelia."

Her palm was cool and dry as I slipped my fingers through hers. "Hold on tight," she said. "And keep your eyes closed until I tell you otherwise."

Thirty-eight

We were weightless, like the moment when a roller coaster reaches its peak, when you hang suspended in midair, right before you're sent plunging down through the atmosphere.

I clutched at Charlie and Ms. MacAllister's hands as my stomach lurched back down to earth. Wind screamed around my ears and tugged my hair from its ponytail, causing it to whip against my face.

And then, as suddenly as we had started, we stopped falling, and the ground slammed into my feet. I stumbled forward, and would have fallen, if not for Ms. MacAllister's firm grip on my hand. Beside me, Charlie swore, his voice hardly rising above the howling wind.

"Keep your eyes closed," Ms. MacAllister yelled. "We're almost there."

"Almost *where*?" Charlie shouted back.

If she answered, her reply was swallowed by the wind. The howl had decreased to a low roar, but it still drowned out everything else within earshot. I kept my eyes closed tight as the wind battered us in place, like ships in a storm. Finally, after what could have been hours or seconds, the wind quieted, an eerie stillness descending in its place.

"The question isn't where, Charlie," Ms. MacAllister said. "It's *when*. Open your eyes. You're both in one piece?"

"I think so." I opened my eyes. We still stood in Ms. MacAllister's living room, but it wasn't the room we'd left behind us. Heavy velvet draperies shrouded the windows, and dark patterned paper lined the walls. Ms. MacAllister's photos were replaced by two of the stern-faced portraits that hung in the hallway during our time. Her furniture was missing as well, replaced by a tiny camelback sofa upholstered in forest green, where a small, dark-haired girl sat, twisting her hands in her lap. A Basset Hound that looked remarkably like Minion lounged at her feet.

My breath caught in my throat. Ms. MacAllister smoothed her skirt over her hips and followed my gaze. "Don't worry, she can't hear or see us."

"How?" Charlie kept his hand wrapped around mine. "We're invisible?"

"Not quite. All of this—" she waved her hand around the room, "—is the past. It's a memory. We can't alter it or interact with it. We can only watch. And listen."

"Who is she?" Charlie asked.

"My aunt," Ms. MacAllister said. "Pretty, isn't she?"

The girl was more than pretty. She was strikingly beautiful, her heart-shaped face pale, her bowed lips pink, her eyes ringed with thick black lashes. She wore a light blue dress, short-sleeved, that tied around her waist in a bow, and a cameo at her throat—the same cameo that Ms. MacAllister had pulled out of the metal box. The girl stared at the door behind us, tapping her foot against the oriental rug that covered the wooden floor.

"This memory that we're in…" Charlie trailed off, rubbing his hand along his chin, like he was searching for the right words. "Is it hers?"

"Partially," Ms. MacAllister replied. "It's been stitched together from several sources other than Winnifred's—my father and grandfather both worked to create this."

My head snapped up at the name. "That's Winnifred MacAllister?" I asked before I could stop myself, my mind's eye flashing to the statue in the cemetery, the girl wrapped in the angel's arms. "Were you the one leaving the flowers?"

Ms. MacAllister nodded. Her eyes were sad. "It's a beautiful statue, isn't it? Her parents loved her very much."

Somewhere behind me, a door slammed. I swallowed over the lump in my throat as Winnifred stood, very much alive. I thought of the dates carved into the granite slab, fifteen years apart.

"What year is it?" I asked, even though I knew deep in my heart what the answer would be. This girl looked to be just about fifteen.

"Just listen," Ms. MacAllister said, ignoring my question.

"Freddie!"

The girl and I whirled around at the same time. She let out a little cry and launched herself at Ransom, who stood in the doorway. The dog leapt to his feet and growled, his fur bristling, inserting himself between Winnifred and her brother.

"Back, old boy," Freddie said, stepping out into the hallway and closing the door in the dog's face. He whined and scratched at the door, but we were moving again, the room whirling and melting around us as the heavy wallpaper gave way to the dark wood paneling in the foyer, where Winnifred and Ransom stood staring at each other.

Ransom looked nearly identical to the boy who'd lived in my house all summer, almost impossibly so. But the Ransom I'd known had been poised, polished—

nothing like the half-crazed boy in front of us. His hair stood on end, his coat torn, his face smudged with dirt. He wrapped his trembling arms around the girl and hugged her close, then pushed her back to look into her face.

"Son of a bitch," Charlie swore beside me. "This can't be real."

"Where have you been?" Winnifred demanded. "Father has been looking for you all night. He's really angry, Ransom. He says that you're the one who killed those girls."

"And you believe him?" Ransom asked. He glanced over his shoulder. "I need your help, Freddie."

"I can't," she said. "If he sees you..." She followed his gaze. "You have to leave."

Ransom seemed to crumple. "He's wrong about me, and about her. I'm your brother, Freddie. You have to trust me."

"Ransom, please," she said, her voice pleading. "You have to leave. He's going to kill you."

"Just get me the ring, and I'll go," he said. "You know I'm right about her. She needs me."

Freddie closed her eyes. "I—"

"I've never lied to you," Ransom whispered, his voice fierce. He gripped her shoulders and shook her, none too gently. "I need you to do this for me."

He released her, and she stumbled backwards. "You swear to me that you're doing the right thing?" she asked him. "You swear that if we do this, we'll be done with her? Done with this curse?"

"I swear on my life," Ransom said. "Everyone has been wrong about her."

Freddie closed her eyes and let out a soft sigh. "I trust you," she whispered as the room dissolved around us again and we began to fall. "I'll meet you in the woods at sunset."

Almost immediately, a new scene began to form around us, even before my feet hit solid ground. Orange-tinged sky peeked through the trees as Winnifred hurried through the forest. We seemed to race alongside of her, even though our feet stayed planted on the ground. The entire world whipped past us, like we were a camera zooming through a movie scene. Winnifred moved surely over the path that Mark and I had taken over and over again, though now it was wide and well-tended, unlike the overgrown trail it was in my own time.

She was heading to the ruins.

Charlie gripped my hand tightly, like he was afraid of what would happen if he were to let go. I didn't blame him—I was afraid of the same thing.

Ransom sat on the remains of a low stone hill, his leg bouncing wildly, passing a small, shiny object from hand to hand. He leapt to his feet the moment his sister entered the clearing, and shoved whatever it was into his pocket. "It's about time," he snarled. "Were you followed?"

His sister shook her head. "No one suspected a thing."

"Good." He held out his hand, palm up. "The ring?"

A sick feeling took hold in my middle and spread throughout my veins. "Don't do it," I said, even though she couldn't hear me. Ms. MacAllister sent me a sympathetic glance.

Freddie hesitated. "Ransom," she said, her voice wavering as she lifted her hand and pointed across the clearing. "Is that... is that *her*?"

Beside me, Charlie's breath caught in his throat as the clearing spun around us until we could clearly see what Winnifred was pointing at.

Who Winnifred was pointing at.

Marin waited beneath the thick branches of the gnarled oak tree, her feet hovering a few inches above the ground. She looked the same as she had last night in the clearing—almost solid, almost human, almost *alive*—except last night was technically a century removed from Winnifred's memories.

Ransom slid his arm around his sister's shoulders and pulled her closer to the tree. "Beautiful, isn't she?"

"She looks different." Winnifred struggled against his grip.

"She's almost ready to transition," Ransom said. Marin's glow reflected in his eyes, which were wide and wild. "I've—*we've*—worked so hard to get to this point. You have no idea the things I've had to do."

Terror flashed across Winnifred's features, and she froze. "Ransom," she said. "You didn't…"

"I did what I had to." He tilted his head to look down at his sister. "You understand that, don't you? If it wasn't for Father's stupid rules…"

"The rules exist to keep us safe," Freddie said.

"They exist to keep us weak. Don't you see that? We could have anything we wanted, Freddie. Do anything we wanted. We're the powerful ones." He spread his arms wide. "*They* should be cowering before us. *They* should be serving us. Not the other way around. Why should we weaken ourselves by using our own magic, feeding off our own souls, when there's a whole world out there of people who could help us?"

Freddie didn't flinch. She lifted her head, the wobble of her chin the only sign of her fear. "He was right. You murdered those girls."

"It's not murder, little sister. It's survival. They are the antelope, and I am the lion."

"Even Rachel?" Her reply was choked. "You were supposed to love her."

"How could I love one of *them*?" His voice was bitter.

"She trusted you."

"Until the very end."

Freddie's gaze slipped to the ghost behind Ransom. She reached up, touching a tiny bump under the bodice of her dress in a familiar gesture. My fingers drifted to my own chest, where the ring usually hung.

"She's turned you into a monster," Freddie whispered, "and I'll have no part of it."

Ransom's gray eyes turned to flinty steel. He too looked at Marin, who only stared back at him.

Slowly, the ghost nodded, and Ransom sighed.

"She warned me about this." He sounded resigned. "She said Father was going to turn you against me."

Freddie lifted her hands and held them, palm out, towards him. "Don't come any closer," she said. "Father didn't turn me against you, Ransom. You did that the second you murdered my best friend and betrayed everything our family has worked for."

He raised his eyebrows and motioned towards her upraised hands. "You can't stop me. You're too weak."

"Like hell I can't," she spat at him. "I can't let you do this."

He sighed again. "Freddie, sweetheart. Just give me the ring. Please."

She swiped her hand toward him in response. Blue sparks leapt from her fingertips and arced toward him, but he didn't even flinch. The sparks fizzled a few inches from his face.

"Freddie." He stepped across the clearing towards her. "Don't make this harder than it has to be."

And then she was in the air, her hands trapped at her sides, the same way I'd been only a few hours ago. Her feet kicked frantically against the air, but she didn't scream or beg or plead. She just stared down at him with a look of disgust scrawled across her face, even as he put his hand in his pocket and pulled out the object he'd been fiddling with earlier. The low evening light bounced off the knife's wickedly sharp blade. "Stay still," he said. "I don't want to hurt you."

And my heart sank—I knew what was coming. I turned and buried my face in Charlie's shoulder, unwilling to watch. But Ms. MacAllister tugged at my other hand. "Eyes open, Amelia," she said, her tone leaving no room for argument.

When I dared to look again, Ransom stood in front of his sister, knife tucked in his belt, while Marin floated a few inches behind him. He reached up and wrapped his fingers around the chain hanging from Winnifred's neck, and with a sharp tug, he tore the necklace free.

"You won't get away with this," Freddie whispered. "It's not going to work."

"Shut up," he said. He let the chain drop to the forest floor and held the ring out towards Marin, chanting words low under his breath. The Latin was unmistakable—I was nothing if not my mother's daughter. "*Aliquid est latet. Absconditis tuis sciri, Aperi pro me. Ego dimittam te. Ego dimittam te. Ego dimittam te.*"

I release you.

The ghost extended her hand and let Ransom slip the ring over her third finger, the place where a wedding band would sit. The moment the metal touched her skin, the blue-white glow around her dissipated, and she drifted to the ground.

She took in a deep breath and smiled at Ransom. He bent low over her hand and pressed a kiss to her knuckles. "My love," he breathed. "It worked."

"Not quite." Marin's voice was musical and light. "There's one more thing you must do for me."

He raised his head, his question written in his eyes. "My love?"

With her free hand, Marin pulled the knife from Ransom's belt. "The spell isn't complete," she practically sang. "There's one last thing I need."

"No!" I cried.

"Eyes open," Ms. MacAllister commanded again. It was unnecessary. I couldn't have looked away.

He took the knife from her and turned it over so the hilt rested against his palm. "I don't understand," he said.

"I think you do," Marin replied. "Blood of my blood."

Now Freddie started to struggle. She kicked her legs harder, and the scream that tore from her lungs was so loud and sharp that it startled a flock of birds from a nearby branch. "Ransom," she begged. "Please, no."

Her brother turned toward her, seemingly in a trance. "Blood of your blood," he repeated. "And then you'll be free?"

Marin nodded, eyes bright.

Beside me, Charlie took a deep, shuddering breath.

Ransom drew closer to his sister, his footsteps crunching over the forest floor, knife gripped in his fingers.

"Ransom," Freddie said again, looking even younger than her fifteen years. "Don't do this."

"I need you to do this," Marin called out. "For me, *mon coeur*."

Ransom lifted the knife and looked his sister right in the eyes. "I'm sorry," he whispered.

Freddie closed her eyes, tears rolling down her face. "Please," she said again. "Ransom."

He didn't hesitate. He plunged the knife into her chest. Her eyes flew open, and she screamed again, the sharp sound mixing with my own. He pulled the knife out, her blood thick on his hands, and plunged it in again. And again. And again. He hacked at her until he was drenched in her blood, until it mixed with the tears running down his face, until she hung limp and pale in the grip of his magic.

Finally, he dropped the knife to the ground at his feet and turned to face Marin.

But she was already gone.

Thirty-nine

Ms. MacAllister's living room slammed into place around us. I crumpled to the floor the minute my feet touched solid ground. Charlie knelt beside me and wrapped me in his arms. I pressed my face against his chest and cried, my sobs mixing with the frantic echo of his heartbeat. He glared up at his grandmother. "What was that, Grams?" he shouted, even though his voice was hoarse.

"You had to see what he was capable of," she replied. She handed us each a tissue before lowering herself into the arm chair and replacing the brooch, the cloth, and the journal in the metal box with trembling hands. "You had to see how dangerous he is."

Charlie shook his head. "He was here all summer, Grams, and you did nothing."

"I didn't know!" She slumped back in the chair. "Believe me, Charlie, if I had known…"

"But the girls," I said, struggling to sit up. "Those girls he killed in 1918. He did the same thing this time, didn't he?"

She nodded curtly. "I think so."

"And the last time too. In 1990?" I rubbed my forehead, trying to figure out the pattern.

"It wasn't him that time," Ms. MacAllister answered. "For that, at least, Ransom wasn't to blame. That was all Rose."

Charlie inhaled sharply. "I don't understand," he said. "But she..."

"Died," Ms. MacAllister finished when his voice trailed off. "Yes. She did. But not before she nearly destroyed this town, and *did* destroy her family." She shifted in her chair and sighed, looking older than I'd ever seen her. "Charlie, honey, my daughter—your aunt—she wasn't a bad girl. She was manipulated by evil, the same way Ransom was."

"By Marin," Charlie said. "I don't get it. If he managed to bring her back from the dead all those years ago, why is she still a ghost? What happened?"

Ms. MacAllister started at him for half a heartbeat, like she was weighing her words. When she finally spoke, she sounded tired. "For whatever reason, it didn't work. By the time my father and grandfather found Winnifred's body, Ransom was already gone. They didn't know what had happened to him until later that fall, when they received a telegram informing them that he'd gone missing in action in Europe. It seems he'd run away and joined the army, and that was the last anyone heard of him. Until now."

"Why would he do that?"

I gripped my hair. All of the answers had been in the dreams I'd been having—dreams I'd ignored. "Their souls," I whispered. "He needed their souls."

"You're exactly right, Amelia," Ms. MacAllister said. "There are two kinds of magic, Charlie. White and black. White magic, pure magic—the kind we're blessed with—comes from an internal source." She tapped her finger over her breast. "For lack of a better term, our magic comes from deep in our souls. We're limited only by our own strength. As for black magic..." she trailed off and shuddered before beginning again.

"Black magic, for lack of a better explanation, feeds off the souls of others. So for someone like Ransom—someone using black magic—a war would be the ideal place to gather souls. To gather power."

Charlie scrubbed his hands over his face. "The girls in the river?" he asked. "He's been stealing their souls?"

She shook her head. "I don't think so. I know for a fact that Rose never crossed that line for herself. She wasn't the one using their souls."

"Marin was," I said. "That's how she's gotten the power to become more..." I struggled to find the words. "Less ghostly? Isn't it? All of the girls have died at the Standing Stone. I saw how you reacted to it, Charlie—it has some sort of power, doesn't it?"

"Bluestone doesn't have any sort of power on its own," Ms. MacAllister said, "but it reacts strongly when magic occurs *around* it. It helps to concentrate that power, to make it stronger."

"Strong enough to sever someone's soul from her body?" Charlie's voice shook slightly as he asked the question.

"Just enough to allow the girls' souls to transfer over to Marin, it appears." she replied. "She needs five to complete the transition. It's always five."

"Not this time," I said. "There have only been four."

"Then we have time to stop him," Charlie said. He leaned forward, like he was ready to jump to his feet and attack Ransom, like the other boy was lurking in the doorway. I put my hand on his knee, stilling him.

"I don't understand," I said. "He had the chance to use me to complete the ritual. But he didn't."

"Maybe he wasn't ready yet," Ms. MacAllister said. "He'd needed the ring, which had belonged to her. And then he'd need Charlie, of course. Blood of her blood and all."

"So we're descended from her," Charlie said, his voice matter-of-fact. "Aren't we?"

"It's a long story," Ms. MacAllister said. "I don't have time to tell you everything now. Just know that her son was our ancestor, Charlie. His name was Henri MacAllister."

The puzzle pieces clicked together in my head. "The baby she gave away," I whispered, remembering my dreams. "She blamed Robert for taking him from her."

If Ms. MacAllister was surprised that I had made that connection, she gave no indication of it. "Exactly so," she said. "She came here in 1793, intent on retrieving her son. But he wasn't a babe in arms any longer; he was already eleven years old. He didn't want to part from his father. She couldn't accept that, and began exacting her retribution on the settlers here. Robert MacAllister, himself descended from hedge witches and a practitioner of white magic, realized what she was doing and decided to stop her. He managed to kill himself in the process, and Marin..." she trailed off. "Well, with Marin, he didn't quite succeed. A piece of her remained trapped in the woods. Henri, realizing the danger that even the ghost of his mother posed to this town, took it upon himself to make sure she stayed dead. And now our family is bound to this land by Henri's choice. As long as there are MacAllisters alive, at least one must live in this house and protect this town from her."

"The curse," I breathed. "Mrs. Ovet wasn't making things up."

Ms. MacAllister rolled her eyes. "That woman is a menace, a busybody, and a gossip," she said. "But she's halfway right about that. Some of us have felt that our responsibility, our power, was more curse than blessing. The ring—Marin's ring, the one you had, Amelia—is what she uses to try to manipulate her descendants into doing her bidding. And some of us—like Ransom and my Rose—are weaker than others. Marin's very powerful, even as she is. And her power is seductive." She gave us a sad smile. "I think she was using you to get to Charlie, Amelia. She was using the ring to manipulate both of your emotions."

Charlie stiffened beside me, while I stared at his grandmother, open-mouthed.

"What are you saying?" he asked her, gripping my hand harder. "You're saying that I don't lo—" he caught himself, swallowing hard. "That what I feel for Amelia isn't real?"

I looked over at him, warmth spreading through my chest. I remembered his words from last night. *I think I'm falling in love with you.*

But then the reality of what Ms. MacAllister was trying to tell us washed over me, and the warmth was replaced with a chill that spread through my bones.

"I'm sorry," she whispered. "Marin will stop at nothing to get what she wants. And it seems that she has set her sights on you, Charlie, and used Amelia to do that."

"You're wrong," Charlie whispered, even as I pulled my hand from his. He turned to me, his eyes pleading. "Amelia."

I shook my head and tucked my hands under my arms, fighting back tears. I didn't know what to say to him.

Of course our relationship, our attraction to each other, was too good to be true. I didn't deserve this, didn't deserve happiness, not after what had happened to Mark. That it wasn't real—that Marin had used whatever powers she had on us to make us fall in love, that she had manipulated us, manipulated our feelings for each other—that made sense.

Too much sense.

Charlie kept staring at me, waiting for me to say something. To agree with him, to tell Grams that she was wrong, that what we felt for each other was real and true and good. His eyes held so much hope that I couldn't keep looking at him. I couldn't open my mouth and lie to him just to spare his heart, even as my own was shattering into a million little pieces.

I turned away from him, knowing my silence would be all the answer he needed. I straightened my shoulders and looked at Ms. MacAllister, then took in a deep, shuddering breath. "I still don't understand why Ransom left me there," I said. "He could have used me as bait for Charlie."

"Maybe he would have, but didn't get the chance. He didn't have the ring yet," Charlie said stiffly. "Not until I gave it to him."

"And I showed up before he could come back for you," Ms. MacAllister said. She watched us carefully, tapping her fingers on the edge of her chair. "You were gone, so he panicked. He had to choose someone else."

"He could have picked anyone," Charlie said,

"He could be taking someone right now." I leapt to my feet. "We have to tell Frank. Before it's too late."

Ms. MacAllister held up her hand, stopping me. "One of the girls he murdered in 1918 was his fiancée, Rachel Liancourt. Does Ransom have a romantic attachment to anyone?"

My heart dropped to my stomach. I dug for my phone and dialed her number as Charlie whispered, "Leah."

Straight to voicemail.

I swiped through my contacts until I found her home number. "Come on," I pleaded.

"Hello?" Mrs. Howards answered on the first ring.

"Is Leah there?" I didn't even introduce myself, just spoke, my words tumbling over each other.

"Amelia? Honey, is everything okay?"

"I need to speak with Leah," I said. "It's really, really important."

She paused. "I'm sorry, hon, you just missed her. She just left with your friend Ransom. Try calling her cell?"

I hung up and dropped the phone on the coffee table. "He has her," I said, trying to suppress the panic clawing through my middle, ripping me to shreds from the inside out. "He has Leah."

Forty

Ms. MacAllister leapt to her feet. "There isn't any time to waste," she said. "We have to get to the Standing Stone. That's where he'll try it this time, I'm sure of it."

Minion hefted himself to his feet beside her and gave a low, rumbling growl. "Of course you can come," she told the dog. "I'll need you, old friend."

He pressed his head against her palm, and she ruffled his ears.

Normally, this type of exchange would cause me to send Charlie a wide-eyed stare. But I kept my eyes fixed on my toes, on the purple polish already chipping off my nails. I couldn't look at him right now. I couldn't think about what Ms. MacAllister had just told us. I had to concentrate on stopping Ransom.

I had to concentrate on rescuing Leah.

Ms. MacAllister was already climbing the stairs with Minion at her heels. "Run home, Amelia, and change your shoes," she called back over her shoulder. "You can't expect to beat a hundred-year-old madman and the ghost of an evil witch while wearing flip-flops. My grandson and I will meet you outside in a few minutes."

Her tone left no room for arguing, and the last thing I wanted to do was to be left alone with

Charlie. He didn't appear to have such reservations, however—he grabbed my hand as I turned to leave and pulled me to him, his fingers tangling with mine, desperation shining in his eyes. He didn't even give me time to protest before he slid his other hand into my hair and captured my lips in a searing, white-hot kiss. Any resistance I'd had melted away as my mouth parted for him, and I kissed him back. He guided me backwards until I was pressed against the wall, pinned between smooth plaster and his warm body. My free hand curled into a fist against his chest—I couldn't tell whether I was holding him close or pushing him away.

As abruptly as he'd started, Charlie stepped back, his breath ragged, and dropped his forehead to mine. "I don't care what she says," he growled. "I don't believe for a second that what I feel for you is anything but real. This is real," he said, motioning between us, his blue eyes burning bright. "*That* was real. I love you, Amelia. She can't take that away from us."

I pressed my hands to my mouth, holding back tears. "I'm sorry," I whispered back. "I... I..."

I didn't finish my sentence. I ducked under his arm and ran for home as quickly as I could, leaving him standing in his grandmother's parlor.

Alone.

I sprinted down the steps and across my driveway. I tore through the house until I found a pair of my sneakers sitting by the back door. I pulled them on hurriedly, blinking away tears.

Leah. We have to find Leah. There'd be enough time to worry about my love life—or lack of one—once she was home safe and sound.

"Honey?" Mom hovered in the doorway leading to kitchen, worry creasing her face. "Is everything okay?"

I wiped at my eyes and climbed to my feet. "Fine," I lied.

"You'd tell me if there was something wrong, wouldn't you?"

I paused, my hand on the knob. "Of course." Another lie.

She sighed. "Going out with Charlie?"

I nodded. What was one more lie, at this point?

She smiled. "He makes you happy. I like him."

I couldn't help it. I flung myself at her and wrapped her in a hug. "I love you, Mommy."

She stiffened in surprise, but relaxed almost immediately, holding me tight. She pressed a kiss to my forehead. "I love you too, sweetheart. You're sure everything's all right?"

"I'll tell you later," I promised, and raised myself onto my tiptoes to press a kiss to her cheek before I pulled myself away and opened the back door. "I promise, I'll tell you everything later."

She smiled, the worry never quite leaving her eyes. "Have fun!" she called after me.

I stepped out onto the porch, straightened my shoulders, and hoped more than anything else that I'd be able to keep that promise to my mother.

Ms. MacAllister and Charlie waited at the edge of the woods with Minion pacing back and forth at their feet. Ms. MacAllister's face was pale and drawn, her arms crossed over her chest. Charlie had his back turned toward me, his posture stiff. My stomach twisted at the sight, but I took a deep breath.

Leah. I had to focus on Leah.

The dog regarded me with worried eyes as I approached; once he deemed I was near enough, he *woofed* softly and took off toward the path. Charlie followed, never once glancing back in my direction. I fell in behind Ms. MacAllister, who strode swiftly, black skirts swirling around her ankles. We walked in silence until we reached the first fringe of blighted trees. Ms. MacAllister's breath caught. "I hadn't realized it was so bad," she said.

Neither had I. Last night, it had been too dark for me to see anything, but the last time we'd been out here in daylight, we'd walked for another five minutes or more before we'd reached the blighted section of the forest. It had spread quickly.

Too quickly.

"Listen, you two," she said. "When we reach the clearing, I need the two of you to stand back and let me take charge of things. Ransom is little better than a madman. He's been killing people for a century to stay the way he is. There's no telling what he'll do."

"Grams, no," Charlie said. "I can't let you do that."

She clapped her hand on his shoulder and spun him around to face her without breaking her stride. "You listen to me," she said, her voice stern. "I swore to your mother that I would protect you. Allowing you to think that you're any match for Ransom is doing the opposite of that. It's my fault you're untrained. I'm the MacAllister, and while I still draw breath, I will not let you throw your life away. Do you understand me?"

His eyes met mine, and he flinched, jerking out of her grasp. "You're wrong, Grams. *He* trained me. I know better than anyone the way he thinks."

"You know only what he *wants* you to know!" she cried. "Charlie, if you do nothing else, please listen to me."

He stared at her, his face a mask of stone. "I can do this."

"I believe in you," she said, her voice pleading. She stepped toward him and laid her hand on his cheek, her touch tender. "But I'm asking you to let me do what I promised myself I'd do the day you were born. Let me protect you, my darling boy."

"I can't just stand there and do nothing," he whispered.

"I'm not asking you to." She inclined her head toward me. "I need you and Amelia to do whatever it takes to get Leah to safety. Do you hear me?"

"What about you?"

"I'll be fine," she said softly, like her tone could mask the lie that hung in the air between them. "I'll meet you back at the house. Don't wait for me. Don't look back. Just take Leah, and then you run as far and as fast as you can."

Charlie swallowed. "Grams, I–"

Pain etched over his face, and I ached to step to him, to wrap him in my arms and hold him tight. But I was part of the reason that pain was there in the first place, and I was afraid that touching him would only make it worse for both of us in the end. I clenched my hands into fists at my sides.

She did this to him. To me, I reminded myself. Marin had treated us both like puppets, had tangled our feelings together until there seemed to be no escape.

I vowed right then that she'd pay for that.

Ms. MacAllister dropped her hand from Charlie's face. "I'll meet you back at the house," she repeated. Minion nudged her leg, and she ruffled his ears. She took a deep breath and closed her eyes. When she opened them again, they glowed a brilliant blue in the shadow of the trees around us.

"Let's go."

Forty-one

Ransom sat on the remains of the low stone wall, his leg bouncing wildly, head bowed. He lifted his head as we approached, his face catching in the sunlight. His skin was pale and gray, the shadows under his eyes deep. He looked haunted.

And after what he'd done to all of those girls—to Brit, Yvette, Erin, and Alicia, and to his sister, and every other person he'd murdered in cold blood—he deserved it.

"I know you're there, dear niece," he called, his voice a cheerful sing-song that didn't match the pallor of his face. "Have you come to play with me?"

"You could say that," Ms. MacAllister said. She stepped into the clearing with Minion at her side. "I have to tell you, Uncle, I don't much care for games."

Minion growled his agreement beside her. Ransom dropped his gaze to the dog, his eyebrows arching. "You're still around, old boy? I thought you'd have given up the ghost by now for sure."

Minion growled again.

Ransom laughed. He rose to his feet with liquid grace, allowing himself a languid stretch. "Hello there, Charlie," he called. "Amelia, dear. You're looking surprisingly well."

This time, Charlie was the one who growled, his hands curling into fists at his sides. But Ms. MacAllister held up her hand, stopping him in his tracks. "Where is she, Ransom?"

He feigned a look of surprise, his mouth rounding into an 'o'. "To whom are you referring?"

I wanted to punch that smug look off his face, and I wasn't the only one, from the way Charlie stayed tense beside me. "If you've hurt Leah, I swear..."

"You'll what, Amelia? I think I showed you earlier just how useless it is to fight against me. Your friend learned the same lesson, I'm afraid."

I couldn't help it. The scream ripped from my throat, and I lunged for him, my hands reaching for his neck. Only Charlie's hand on my arm stopped me.

Ransom had produced a knife out of nowhere, and he twirled it in his fingers. "Good thinking, man," he said to Charlie. "I'm not a fan of filleted girlfriend, either."

"She's not my girlfriend," Charlie growled.

Pain sliced through me, hot and sharp, and I almost thought I'd prefer it if Ransom had stabbed me with his knife.

Almost.

I stepped away from Charlie, out of his grasp.

Ransom threw his head back and laughed. "Figured it out, have you? Good. You two were very nearly disgusting." He tucked the knife in his pocket and pulled out something else, something that glinted blue and gold in the sunlight. My heart lurched as my hand flew to the spot where the ring usually rested against my collarbone. "In any case," he continued, "I must thank you all for coming. It's been too long since I've had any sort of audience for my tricks. Leah, sweetheart," he called over his shoulder. "That's your cue."

Leah stepped out from behind the massive oak. She moved stiffly, her limbs jerking unnaturally as she walked to Ransom's side. Confusion danced over her face when she saw us all standing there. "Millie? What's going on?" she asked. Something about her voice sounded wrong. It was too high-pitched, too light.

"What have you done to her?" I screeched. I moved to go to her, but Ransom dropped his hand to the knife in his pocket, and I froze.

"Let the girl go," Ms. MacAllister said.

"Sweet Lillian," Ransom said, "you know why I can't do that, don't you? That brother of mine must have taught you *something*, even as he filled your head with nonsense."

"He taught me all about you," she replied. "And how mad you are."

Ransom's laugh was a sharp bark. "Mad? Tell me what's mad, niece–spending your life as a slave to the whim of our ancestor, the man who betrayed his own mother, or simply wanting to be free?"

Ms. MacAllister struck so quickly I almost missed the bolt of blue that flashed across the clearing. Ransom's head snapped back with such force that I thought for a split second, as he crumpled to the ground, that Ms. MacAllister had surely killed him. But he shook himself off and straightened his spine, baring his teeth in something that didn't quite resemble a smile.

"Come now. Surely you've got something better than *that*."

"Let the girl go," Ms. MacAllister repeated.

"Gladly," Ransom said. He shoved Leah hard; she stumbled forward, her feet tripping over the tree roots. Her head struck the low rock wall, and she went limp, her body folding to the ground.

"No!" I rushed to her, frantically placing my fingers against her pulse. Her heartbeat fluttered weakly under my fingertips, but at least he hadn't killed her. Charlie dropped to the ground beside me.

"Is she...?" His question was so low I almost thought I'd imagined it, but the tremor of fear in his voice convinced me it was real.

I shook my head, and he let out his breath, the slump of his shoulders echoing my thoughts. *Thank God.*

"Now," Ransom said, tapping his finger to his mouth. "Where was I? Right! Marin, my sweet. You have some visitors."

My ghost materialized out of thin air just a few feet ahead of me, closer than she'd been last night. She was just as solid as she'd looked in the moonlight, only the soft glow of her skin and the few inches between her feet and the ground betraying the fact that she wasn't quite human.

Yet.

Minion's growls turned into snarls, and he leapt forward, jaws snapping. But before he could reach Marin, he thumped against a barrier of some kind and fell to the ground with a yelp. He lay still.

Ms. MacAllister raised her hands in front of her again. "I'm not afraid of either of you," she said, her voice strong. Her eyes fell on Charlie and me, hovering together on the ground over Leah.

"Then you're a fool," Ransom sneered. "But don't worry. There's time enough for that. First, though..."

He waved his hand, and Charlie was ripped from the ground beside me. He flew through the air until he floated between Ransom and Ms. MacAllister, every muscle in his body locked tight. His eyes were wild in his face as he struggled against Ransom's bonds to no avail.

"Blood of my blood," Ransom said with a smirk. "Will he do, my sweet?"

Marin nodded slowly.

Ransom's grin spread. He pulled the knife back out of his pocket and stepped closer to Charlie, dragging the wicked blade along his chin.

Charlie didn't flinch. His eyes found mine and held them. All I could do was stare, my heart stuck fast in my throat.

Blood of my blood. Charlie.

Whether or not the feelings I had for Charlie were a byproduct of Marin's manipulations, the fear that tore through my veins at the thought of that knife cutting into Charlie's skin was real.

"Wait!" Ms. MacAllister's cry echoed through the clearing. "Before you do anything rash, there's something you should know."

Ransom froze, the blade still pressed to Charlie's throat. "I'm all ears," he said. He moved the knife until it rested under Charlie's ear. "Would you like one?"

"No!" I found my voice, this time a rasping sob. "Ransom, please. Don't do this."

"Ransom, please," he mimicked. "Begging doesn't become you, Amelia."

"It won't work," Ms. MacAllister said. "For the same reason it didn't work with your sister, and it didn't work with Rose. You've been doing it wrong. The blood—her blood," she added, pointing to Marin, "has to be given *willingly*."

Ransom stepped away from Charlie, his fingers limp around the blade. "What are you saying?" he asked.

"Let Charlie go, and you can have me."

No. My hands flew to my mouth.

Charlie's eyes bugged, and he shook his head wildly. Ms. MacAllister stared at him, her blue eyes wide. "Let them all go," she amended. "Let them all go, and you'll have me willingly."

Ransom slid his eyes to Marin. She lifted one shoulder, as if to say, *What the hell?*

Charlie dropped to the ground with an *oomph*. "Grams, no," he said, standing. "You can't."

"Come here, darling," she said. She held her arms open to him, and he rushed towards her, wrapping her in his arms. Her lips moved against his hair, and he gave a barely perceptible nod.

When he stepped back, his eyes were wet. He turned and looked at me like he was trying to tell me something. But then Ransom was in between them, pushing Charlie out of the way. "You're not as foolish as you look, niece. My apologies."

Ms. MacAllister raised her chin. "I'm not doing this for you."

Ransom's eyes blazed. "That really doesn't matter."

He turned to Marin, her ring held in one of his outstretched hands, the knife in the other. "My sweet?"

She floated closer to him. My stomach clenched. Charlie stepped beside me, ducking to press his lips to my ear. "We're going to stop this," Charlie whispered. "You get the ring. I'll take care of Ransom."

I nodded, my eyes fixed on Marin.

"Ready?" He breathed into my ear. "One, two..."

He didn't have to say three. We moved as one, right as Ransom brought the knife down into Ms. MacAllister's chest. She gave a little gasp, and then Charlie was on top of both of them, wrestling Ransom to the ground. The ring dropped into the grass at their feet.

I slammed into Marin, right into a wall of ice-cold pain, like I'd fallen into freezing water. A scream ripped from my lungs. She crumpled beneath me in her not-quite-solid state. She rolled, and I grabbed onto her hair, which slipped through my hands like gel. She wriggled away from me, reaching for the ring. She slipped it over her finger as I brought my elbow down on her back with a grunt. As the blood pooled under Ms. MacAllister's still body, Marin rolled beneath me and shoved, throwing me off of her. I slid to the ground beside Leah, every bone in my body thudding from the impact.

Marin swiped her hand across the front of her body, and Charlie and Ransom were pulled apart, each thrown into the air on opposite ends of the clearing. She made the same motion toward Leah and myself, and I was airborne, trapped against bonds I couldn't see or break. Leah hung limp in the air beside me, her head lolling on her chest. I swallowed hard and forced my gaze off my best friend.

Marin approached Charlie first, her feet gliding over the forest floor. She ran her hand along his chin, studying his face.

He didn't flinch. He stared down at her, tears running down his face. "Just get it over with," he said. "Just do whatever it is you're going to do."

But she just patted his cheek gently. "You're a good boy," she said, her words drifting through the clearing.

She stepped away from him and turned to Ransom.

His nose bled, and his eye was already swelling shut. At least Charlie had managed to slow him down, I thought. Even if...

"My sweet," Ransom said, struggling against his bonds. "What are you doing? Put me down."

"My Ransom," she said, her low voice almost a purr. "You've failed me."

His face drained of color. "I—I don't..."

"You let her soul go to waste." Marin reached up and tapped his chest with one pale finger. "You've very nearly ruined everything."

"I—I..."

He didn't have time to explain himself. Marin pressed her lips to his and let her finger drift up to his chin. In one swift movement, she drew her fingernail firmly along his throat, his skin opening under her touch. Blood gushed madly from the wound, and she let him fall, crumpling to the ground at her feet. Blue light rose from the stone in the center of the ring and wrapped around her, so bright my eyes watered, forcing me to look away. When the light dimmed, she turned back to face us, her hand slick with blood.

Marin raised her finger to her mouth and slowly licked the blood off, her gaze drifting back and forth between Charlie and me, her blue eyes shining brightly. The glow around her had disappeared, and she lowered to the ground, fully human.

Fully alive.

As one, Charlie, Leah, and I dropped to the ground. I struggled to my feet as Marin clapped her hands together and smiled wide, her teeth brilliant white against the blood on her lips.

"My darlings," she said, her voice breathless and girlish. "We have so much work to do."

Author's Note

One of the best parts about writing fiction is the ability to twist history to suit your own needs. Asylum, Pennsylvania is—or at least, was—a real place. French aristocrats really did settle along a horseshoe bend on the Susquehanna River in the late 18th century. The settlement was called French Azilum, and legend has it that the refugees there really were preparing a safe haven for Marie Antoinette. Unfortunately, she was executed before their dreams could be realized, and life on the frontier proved to be far harsher than they anticipated. By the turn of the 19th century, most of the original settlers had migrated to other French communities across North America. Others returned to France after Napoleon's rise to power. Only a few of the original refugees remained in the Pennsylvania wilderness, and helped establish other local communities.

Today, a small historic site marks the original settlement. To learn more about the settlement of French Azilum, please visit the website of the French Azilum Historic Site at www.frenchazilum.com.

Acknowledgements

Publishing A *Magic Dark & Bright* is, in many ways, a dream come true. And it wouldn't have come true without the support, encouragement, and love I received from so many amazing people in my life. Indie publishing can be a long and lonely road—I'm so grateful to the people around me who have helped me on every stage of this journey, from the very first word to the last.

To Shannon Montgomery, for reading every single version of this (multiple times!), brainstorming plot points with me over cupcakes on our lunch breaks, and masterminding the rejection letter drinking game. And for the entire character of Ransom—that was all you.

To L.S. Mooney, for your tireless cheerleading and your ability to read my mind the way you could in college, despite the years and miles between us. And for loving these characters as much as I do—not many people would send me a 2,000 word email begging for a character's life (I'm sorry).

To Sarah Kettles, best friend, editor, and critique partner extraordinaire. Thank you for not giving up on our friendship in fifth grade—I can't imagine doing this with anyone but you! You whipped my words into shape (I swear, I CAN spell judgment. Sometimes.).

You've been my rock through this entire process and I love you to pieces.

To Serena Lawless, who championed this book from the beginning and who teamed up with me to design this cover. Thank you for your faith, your friendship, and our epic gchats.

To Danielle Ellison, who talked me through countless plot problems, kept me (sort of) on task with regular writing dates, and gave me the push I needed to make the decision to publish this book myself. I'm so lucky to have you as a friend!

Rachel O'Laughlin, Faith McKay, and Leigh Ann Kopans, thank you from the bottom of my heart for your sharing your wisdom with me, for guiding me along this journey, and most of all, for your patience. I wouldn't have been brave enough to do this without you leading the way.

The fabulous ladies of The Great Noveling Adventure: Serena Lawless, Sarah Kettles, Kit Klaber, E.M. Castellan, Valerie Lawson, Megan Orsini, Alyssa Hollingsworth, L.S. Mooney, and Lauren Garafalo: you guys rock. I'm so happy we get to go on this crazy adventure together.

To the amazing friends who read this at any (and every) stage imaginable—thank you your gentle criticism, kind words, and outright enthusiasm. Katie Biggs, Tory Cwyk, Tricia Kubrin, Amanda Reynolds, Alice Mackey, Rachel O'Laughlin, Lauren Garafalo, Alyssa Hatmaker, Amanda Alwyn, Caroline Richmond, Sarah Brand, Marieke Nijkamp, Alex Yuschik, Mark Carson, Erin Steele, Cindy Thomas, Susan High, and Emily Simoni: you all have mattered more to this book than you can ever know.

To my classmates and faculty at the Johns Hopkins University Writing Program, especially Mark Farrington, Rae Bryant, Julia Rocchi, Emmy Nicklin, Lily Brodine, Erin Slater, and Jennifer Ryan: I can't begin to thank you all enough. You're the reason *A Magic Dark & Bright* exists at all. I'm sorry my time with you was so short!

To my coworkers at the SAIS Library: every single one of you make it a joy to go to work every day. Thank you for encouraging me, for supporting me, and being as excited about this as I am!!

To my family: My brother Patrick, who read the first chapter and said, "Hey. This is like a real book!" and locked himself away to read the rest of it, my sister Kelly, who told me I could make it scarier, and my brother Mike, the person who has put up with me for longer than anyone else. My brother-in-law, Danny, who read this book on family vacation and compared it to Teen Wolf, which is pretty much the highest praise ever, and Ali, my sister-in-law, who texted me the second she finished reading and demanded the sequel. My mother-in-law, Carla, who has believed in this book since the beginning and helped me hammer out more than a few plot points. My Grandpa Simpson, who told me it was "pretty good, even if there was too much of that kissing stuff" (Sorry, Grandpa. I added even more!). My grandmothers—Grandma Simpson and Grammie Adams, who have always, always believed in me and who fueled my love for stories from the very beginning. Gram—I hope this is creepy enough for you.

Mom—thank you for always saying "yes" to books, even when I'd stay up all night scaring myself silly, and for telling me that "maybe there's something to this writing thing after all." Daddy—did you realize that when you handed me *The Eye of The World* that it would lead to this? Because I'm pretty sure this is all your fault.

And last but not least: to Eric, the most loving, patient person I know, for plotting with me over long car rides and countless trips for Vietnamese food, for listening to me read every single draft of every single scene out loud, for keeping me from starving to death and for never, ever letting me give up.

   This one is for you.

About the Author

Jenny Adams Perinovic has always loved books. By day, she works in a library, and by night, she writes YA fantasy, romance, and horror about brave girls, the boys who love them, and their battles against dark forces (also, kissing). She graduated from The Ohio State University in 2010, where she wrote papers about monsters in medieval literature (yes, really!). She lives in Washington, DC with her husband and small menagerie. On twitter, she's @JennyPerinovic. You can also find her at jennyperinovic.com and thegreatnovelingadventure.com. A *Magic Dark & Bright* is her first novel.

Printed in Great Britain
by Amazon.co.uk, Ltd.,
Marston Gate.